A Chor

Jose Yglesias

"Yglesias is a fine novelist."
—*The New York Times Book Review*

"A writer who has given much pleasure."
—*Publishers Weekly*

"Mr. Yglesias is a writer of considerable subtlety
and perceptiveness,
with a strong sense of narrative form."
—*The New York Review of Books*

"In so many ways, an adroit and gifted writer."
—Novelist and journalist Dan Wakefield
(*Going All the Way, Starting Over: A Spiritual Journey*)

"A fine writer."
—*Booklist*

"An accomplished novelist."
—*Kirkus Reviews*

(*please turn the page for rave reviews of* **A Wake in Ybor City**)

Fiction by

Jose Yglesias

Break-In

Double Double

The Guns in the Closet

Home Again

The Kill Price

The Old Gents

One German Dead

An Orderly Life

Tristan and the Hispanics

The Truth About Them

A Wake in Ybor City

A Wake in Ybor City

Jose Yglesias

With a New Foreword by Rafael Yglesias

Arte Público Press
Houston, Texas
1998

This volume is made possible through grants from the Rockefeller Foundation, the National Endowment for the Arts (a federal agency), the Andrew W. Mellon Foundation, and the Lila Wallace-Reader's Digest Fund.

Recovering the past, creating the future

Arte Público Press
University of Houston
Houston, Texas 77204-2174

Cover illustration and design by James F. Brisson

Yglesias, Jose.
   A wake in Ybor city / by Jose Yglesias.
   p.   cm.
   ISBN 1-55885-248-4 (alk. paper)
   1. Cuban Americans — Florida — Tampa — Fiction. 2. Ybor
City (Tampa, Fla.) — Fiction. I. Title.
PS3575.G5W3 1998
813'.54—dc21   98-28336
                                           CIP

8 9 0 1 2 3 4 5 6 7   10 9 8 7 6 5 4 3 2 1

Foreword

A Wake In Ybor City, my father's first novel, was published in 1963, when I was nine and my father forty-three years old. It feels eerie to my heart (although my head knows it's a meaningless mathematical coincidence) that on its re-publication I am the same age my father was when a career he had longed for since childhood began in earnest.

As a son who had to compete with the fulfillment of his father's life-long ambition in order to get his father to play catch with him, I am keenly aware of the struggle the writing of this novel represented for Jose Yglesias. He was not raised, as I was, by well-read parents, people who were fluent in English, who had, as my mother Helen had, edited the work of important writers, or translated, as my father had, novels by influential Latin American authors. Jose Yglesias, growing up in Tampa, Florida, during the intoxicated twenties and the depressed thirties, did not benefit from living with someone like him, a man who, in many ways, lived to read and to write, whose deepest desires were to appreciate and to contribute to what fiction does so well: express the individual's experience of a world we share, but that seems newly fashioned for each of us. In fact, Jose Yglesias did not benefit from growing up with a father, literate or not.

In 1921, when Jose was two, his father, slowly dying of paralysis from encephalitis, left Tampa, hoping to be cured by revisiting the pure mountain air of Miamán, his Spanish hometown in the province of Galicia. Instead, his condition worsened. My grandfather tried to return to his wife and two children (Jose and my aunt Dalia), but not being a U. S. citizen, and presumed infectious, he was refused entry to Florida and deported to Spain, via Cuba. My father was five years old when he saw his father for the last time, a pale man he hardly knew, too weak to rise from a hospital bed in Havana. My grandfather died two years later, suffocating in a tomb of flesh, an ocean away from his wife and children, unable to write or dictate a farewell letter.

This sad story was much better told by Jose Yglesias in *The Goodbye Land*, what publishers call his "breakthrough book," a memoir written in 1967, well before heartbreaking personal recollections of childhood became a burning literary fashion. It is the commonplace irony of writers' lives that their deepest wounds yield precious ore, and my father's novels about the Latinos of Tampa gleam with their often funny, but always sad, failures to sustain a vibrant, literate, political, and idealistic community against the creeping and ultimately fatal paralysis of a modern culture hostile to virtually every value they held dear. Jose Yglesias's novels, the first of which you hold in your hand, also shine with his affection and gratitude, because they—the cigar-makers of Ybor City— served as his moral and spiritual fathers. My father had written fourteen books by the time he died, a prodigious output considering his late start, and most of them evoke and pay tribute to the world of the cigar-makers. In a sense, *A Wake In Ybor City* is the first in a series of thank-you notes, some of them grudging, some of them gracious, all of them written with the only enduring beauty a writer can give to a subject: his loving and unsparing remembrance.

Today I am forty-three and, like my father, I am a novelist, but not a novelist who is just starting out. My first book was published when I was seventeen, an early beginning inspired by my father, a nagging muse. One of the first lessons Jose Yglesias taught me was to try to write as closely to my true feelings as I and readers (a skittish and easily offended group, editors assure me) can bear. Thus I feel compelled, as an obedient son, to write that for me this re-publication of *A Wake in Ybor City* is a mixed pleasure. So mixed that pleasure hardly seems to be an ingredient at all.

As my father's literary executor, naturally it became my job to do those things that writers do when a book is coming out. Because this readying for publication is so familiar to me, between my father's fourteen books, my mother's six, and my eight, these tasks have reminders of past triumphs and happy times. But again I would fail as a student of my father if I did not add that they contain vivid reminders of disappointments, a few crushing, and even more memories of insults, the thousand cuts that each publication seems to bring and that do not heal so much as scab over. It is a failing of mine that I do not easily let go of slights, but harbor and cherish every mean and stupid instance as a miser does his gold, recounting his store each night with grim glee. I am sorry to report that with the re-publication of *A Wake in Ybor City* my unhappy treasury has grown.

I was nine when *A Wake in Ybor City* was published, and so I did not read its reviews. I was asked to dig them up to find blurbs for the cover of this edition, and that took some effort. I should have known there wouldn't be an out-and-out rave among them. I don't remember my father ever discussing the reviews of *A Wake In Ybor City* and, as a novelist, I can assure you that out-and-out raves will certainly be mentioned by their recipient—with the utmost casualness, of course, as if the topic were an unavoidable inconvenience. So I suspected that my father's reviews couldn't have been memorable one way or the other, because reviews stick only when they are very harsh or gloriously fulsome. My father and I discussed his reviews at least half as often as we discussed mine. (He didn't play catch with me, but he did let me do the lion's share of complaining.) Thus I was shocked he had never complained about a short review by Harry Gilroy that appeared in *The New York Times* on July 12, 1963. Here it is, in its entirety:

> Part of the Batista-Castro conflict was fought in the Latin section of Tampa, Fla., by people like those in this novel. It centers on three widowed sisters, one a cigar wrapper and the others linked to the industry, who form a matriarchy. They are Cubans, a likeable roomful of conversationalists.
>
> Their children have suffered from discrimination. One daughter has reacted by marrying an aide of Batista, and she wishes to shower the largesse of Cuba on her family.
>
> One son is bodyguard for an American racketeer. Another is a disappointed radical who yearns for financial or artistic success. A man who, for a time, was married into the family, runs guns to Castro and involves the ex-radical.
>
> In the book are a murder, love, and family tragedy, but the one thing the author makes really clear is that America has failed in Ybor City, for none of the main characters has emigrated spiritually to the United States.

You may be surprised that I have quoted such a banal piece. Surely worse things were written over the years about my father's work, and mine for that matter. Yes, far worse things.

But I remember my father leaving for his job as a junior executive at Merck, Sharp, and Dome at seven in the morning, his face smacked with after-shave, and then arriving home at six-thirty, a rumpled copy of the *Times* under one arm, his tie undone, his beard regrown, his carefully combed morning hair askew and damp with sweat, winter and summer, thanks to the ride on the IRT all the way downtown on Church Street up to 168th and Broadway. The jacket and tie would come off and he'd talk loudly and always colorfully, even when bitter, about the day's events at work, and continue gossiping and arguing and reasoning with my mother while she dried and he washed the dishes, washed them so energetically that his pants were soaked, and then he'd shut himself up in the bedroom with a cup of strong coffee, there to smoke Kent cigarettes and clack furiously on a black Royal typewriter until well past my bedtime. That went on for years—Saturdays, Sundays, weekday nights—a struggle I doubt I would have the heart or energy to make myself today (remember, I am his age now) to produce this novel, a novel of which Mr. Gilroy's sole comment of critical substance is: "The one thing the author makes really clear is that America has failed in Ybor City, for none of the main characters has emigrated spiritually to the United States."

The New York Times represented in those days the single most important review an author could receive, an importance that the passage of time has only increased. I'm sure that, to my father, a man who loved New York City, who read the *Times* virtually every day of his adult life, who took its reviews to heart, who was then naïve about critics and reviews and their importance or lack of it — to that middle-aged and yet very young novelist—Mr. Gilroy's odd line, suggestive that somehow it is my father's fault his characters didn't assimilate, must have galled. Certainly it galls me. Assimilate into what, Mr. Gilroy? The culture of Tampa in the 1950s? Is that a consummation devoutly to be wished?

In fact, my father answered that question, answered it with his later novels. Often hilariously and often sadly he told the story of how the children and children's children of those cigar-makers became indistinguishable from the other chubby occupants of modern Tampa's endless malls and fast-food restaurants, indistinguishable except for the legacy of their demanding and loopy aging relatives. But those novels by Jose Yglesias (the last written uncomplainingly during the final stages of prostate cancer that had spread into his bones) were also found wanting by the occasional reviewer, only this time by Latino critics who admired Jose Yglesias's talent but were disappointed he didn't sufficiently celebrate the enduring power of Hispanic culture.

I can hear my father complain that I have left the impression his writing was never praised. Of course it was. Right from the beginning. In fact, at the moment, beside my black laptop computer (which I like to think is a descendant of the old black Royals) lie several yellowed and very good reviews of *A Wake In Ybor City*. My point, the product warning label that I wish to slap onto my father's work, is that he wrote as close as he could bear to the truth of the community that gave him not only life, but his values, his hopes, and his most painful losses. Because of your background, your needs, your ideology, you may not find in his novels the people you wish had lived in Ybor City, but I traveled there for every summer of my childhood, and I've returned often enough as an adult to feel confident about this assurance: The people you will meet in my father's books are the people he knew.

Jose Yglesias wrote to preserve the lives of the Ybor City cigar-makers, to honor their odd island of nearly pure socialism. He wrote to remember their rescue and creation of him. He wrote to confess his love of working people and his conviction that literature exists to liberate us—all of us, including those who live in the suburban gated communities of Tampa—from our loneliness and our wearying burdens. The people he loved are gone, and my father is gone. What you have in your hands is the first product of his urgent desire that you come to know them. His novels are their only life now, and my father's last hope.

Rafael Yglesias
New York, New York
July 1998

I

Dolores got up from the glider as soon as she saw her two sisters on the sidewalk. "My tongue has been stuck to the roof of my mouth all day," she called out, "for lack of anyone to talk to!" Mina, the oldest, laughed and preceded Clemencia, the youngest, to Dolores' porch. "They are coming; the children are coming and I could not reach you on the phone." Dolores grabbed their hands to make them listen. "I have had to keep the news to myself all day!"

"You are getting to be an eccentric old woman," Mina said. "You don't even say a word of salutation first, and, besides, you already told us last night that they are coming from Havana."

Dolores appealed to Clemencia. "Last night I only said that I expected them any day, isn't that so? I did not know then that they would be here tomorrow." She looked from Clemencia to Mina and laughed and kissed them. She gasped for air, took out a handkerchief from her bosom and fanned herself with it. "Tomorrow morning they will take a plane in Cuba and in an hour and a half—such are the miracles of modern inventions—they will be here in Tampa!"

"Tomorrow?" said Mina. "Why didn't you say that immediately?" She let herself fall back on the glider and drew Dolores to it. "You never say first what is important."

"You are going to have a houseful," Clemencia said.

"Yes, yes," Dolores replied happily. "The house will be full again. Not just me rattling around by myself. After all Armando is never here after he gets up in the middle of the day."

"You sound as if they were coming to stay," Mina said.

Dolores sighed. "Ah, ah!"

Dolores and Mina sat on the glider and Clemencia faced them on the wicker rocker, and for a moment all three were quiet, thinking of their scattered children. Then Clemencia remembered that her oldest son Roberto was back in Tampa with his family. "I could tell as we came up the street," she said, forgiving Dolores her good news, "that you were impatient to tell us something."

1

Dolores first laughed, then complained. "Of course, of course, to you I seem a foolish old woman!" She paused for breath and the others waited; her shortness of breath no longer reminded Mina and Clemencia that Dolores had a bad heart condition. To them it was just her interesting way of speaking. Dolores put one hand to her very full breasts and pointed to Clemencia with the other. "You are surrounded with people at the cigar factory. You do not know what it is to click your false teeth to yourself all day. I can imagine the number of interesting conversations you have been party to today."

Mina laughed and struck Dolores' soft, round arm with her large, lean hand.

"While I," Dolores continued, "have only an occasional delivery-man or a child not of school age to talk to—"

"Enough, enough," Mina interrupted. "There's more than talk at the cigar factory. I remember the days when I stripped tobacco leaf very well, and you are a foolish old woman to envy Clemencia."

Dolores covered her face with both hands, held them still for a moment, and then lowered them to her breast where she clasped them together. "I forget how fortunate I am. I forget." She reached out to Clemencia but managed only to touch the arm of the wicker rocker. The light from the living room fell on her hand. There was a large amethyst ring on the second finger, and the half-light made the band of tiny pearls surrounding the stone glow richly.

Clemencia looked for a moment at the new ring that Dolores' daughter had sent her from Cuba, and it stopped her from patting her sister's hand. "There is nothing to apologize for," she said. "Don't let Mina make you feel that working at the cigar factory is a terrible tragedy for me. It is only bad when the cigar leaf is dry and brittle and breaks in your hand as you roll the cigar. Today was one of those days. I thought I would never make my quota."

"And if it is a damp day," Mina argued, "the leaf is gummy and impossible to spread. Don't tell me; I remember."

"Clemencia, just you wait," Dolores announced. "Everything is going to be all right. I have had a presentiment since your Roberto came back to Tampa, and now I know; my Elena will help him! I will speak to her myself. Perhaps even to Jaime. Neither of you has met him, but he is very simple and direct, a real person despite his enormous influence at El Palacio. No one is closer to the President, and yet—you know what I've told you—he is ready to do anything for us."

"This is nineteen fifty-eight," Mina said. "You cannot do things through influence any more."

"Please," Clemencia protested, "Roberto may not be interested."

"Oh, my dears," Dolores explained, "where there is love and the will to help those you love, anything—anything can happen. Look how Elena and Jaime have taken in my Clara and her little Jimmy; they are like parents to my grandchild. They are bringing them along, and they pay for everything. You'll see how Elena will feel when she sees Roberto; and, besides, Roberto has a world of experience to recommend him. After all, those years in New York have given him a knowledge of the world that counts for something. Elena and Jaime will offer him something and then—and then you will be able to stay home like Mina and me!"

"But everything *is* all right with me," Clemencia insisted. She tried to keep the irritation out of her voice, for she didn't like to be the subject of her sisters' talk. Clemencia liked best those conversations that allowed her to nod and laugh and occasionally ruminate on her own. Sometimes, when she was with Mina and Dolores, she felt again the sad delight of being the little girl in a big family, quiet and happy in the midst of talk and argument. "Roberto has his wife and two children. They need my help more than I need them. Besides, I don't think they have decided to stay in Tampa. It is only a visit."

"Oh, Roberto, Roberto!" Mina threw her arms up. "He, too, believes in the nobility of labor." She looked at Dolores and pointed at Clemencia. "I don't know whether Clemencia encourages him in this or whether the shoe is on the other foot. I never thought a nephew of mine would think that working in a cigar factory—"

"Darling, darling," Dolores interrupted, "Roberto is an idealist!"

"—is noble," Mina continued. "Look at him, working in a grocery store, and his mother in a factory. Work is not good for the workers or for anyone else, for that matter. That's where I cannot go along with the Communists—work, work work!"

"But, my dear," Dolores said, "work is like happiness. It is not *thing;* it is a point of view!"

"Work is work," Mina insisted. "And that does not make me a Marie Antoinette."

"But no one says you are," Clemencia said quietly.

The thought made Mina even angrier. "Then I wish Roberto would get a good job so you could stay home. I don't want my little sister to still be in the factory at sixty." She took out a handkerchief from her bosom and wiped her eyes. "I don't like it. You have still two years to go before social security."

Automatically, Dolores also reached for her handkerchief. "But why do you pick on Roberto? Clemencia has other children. You should be glad Roberto has brought his wife and children here to start all over again. You know he is your favorite nephew." Having ended decisively, she put her handkerchief away again.

Clemencia sighed. "He is more like Mina than her own son. The same temper, the same impatience."

"Roberto is thoroughly Americanized," Mina continued, refusing to be assuaged. "All those years in New York with Communists and Socialists, being one of them. I know what he thinks of me—a bigoted Catholic, I am sure he says to his Jewish wife, because of my little novenas."

"Nothing of the sort," Clemencia said.

"Roberto knows I do not forgive the Church its reactionary politics. I have never been able to tell him that I made a promise to the Virgin of Covadonga so she would keep him safe during the war. I only completed those Hail Marys last spring!"

"Oh how wonderful it is to talk!" Dolores said. "My Armando was out late last night and left the house early today. And yet, tomorrow Elena and Jaime and Clara and little Jimmy will be here!"

Mina paid no attention to her. "Roberto thinks he is a revolutionary because he married a Jew," she said.

"Don't be a fool," Clemencia sad. "It is none of our business whom he married."

Dolores turned away from them because she heard footsteps on the sidewalk. Clemencia and Mina also looked, always willing to postpone a quarrel for any distraction. A man and woman, followed by a young boy, looked toward the lights in Dolores' house.

"What is their name?" Mina asked, as soon as they passed.

"The husband is Gutierrez," Dolores said, "but you remember her mother's—Carrera. Her mother rolled cigars for Serafin, my husband, may he rest in peace. Then the ten-month strike came."

"Oh yes," said Clemencia, "at The Clock."

"Then he is the Gutierrez who takes the numbers for the factories on Seventeenth Street?" Mina guessed.

"The very one," Dolores said. "That is his territory. It is not a bad one. Cigar makers still play the numbers every day."

"I don't understand," Mina said, "how this Gutierrez—Cuban as he is—can still have that job. My son, Feliz, tells me that the Italians are taking control of the numbers business."

"Certainly, and that is why Tito Sanchez was killed right on Ninth Avenue," Clemencia explained. "But they do not bother with the runners like Gutierrez. It is the bankers, like Tito Sanchez, the big fish, who have to watch out." Mina and Dolores were surprised that she sounded so knowing, so she added, "That is what they say at the factory."

"Oh Italians!" Mina exclaimed. "Wherever there is an empty space, look for them wriggling in. They are never the ones to start anything themselves, but they are always taking over. Look at the Pope, he is always an Italian, though I'm sure the first one was not." Mina crossed her arms under her bosom and threw her shoulders back. "Isn't that so? They were always the first to break a strike at the cigar factories . . ." She stopped and looked at Clemencia. "Oh I'm sure you know none of this can be said of Steve. You would have to look far for a better son-in-law."

"Well, my Alice is happy with him," Clemencia answered drily.

"And there's no doubt in my mind about that," Dolores said. "You know that my Mario and he are always together in Miami—" She interrupted herself to exclaim, "Ah, if only they, too, could be here tomorrow, it would be a real reunion!"

"But you cannot deny that the Italians started all the gangster-ism in Tampa because they could not get the good jobs in the factories," Mina insisted. "Do you remember how they delivered liquor in ambulances during Prohibition? Every time you heard the sirens down Michigan Avenue you knew some Americans had ordered liquor in a hurry."

Her sisters didn't answer her, and Mina remembered a day during the Depression. Her husband, Claudio, now dead, was foreman at La Pila then, and he hired or fired cigar makers when the owners in New York decided. In bed at night he used to ask Mina which family most needed the job, but she always reported everyone destitute, so Claudio eventually had to make the decision himself. One day, while cooking supper, she stepped out into the back yard to pick some lemons from the tree whose branches spread over into the alley. She held them in her apron, and before going back into the house, she stopped a moment on the stoop to look at the sunset. The sun was like an orange at eye level over the alley, not blinding as at midday, and so she immediately saw the Italian at the back gate. He was a cigar maker at La Pila, and she started to smile and nod, but then noticed how frightened the man looked. With a quick gesture—she remembered it as an angry gesture now—he threw a fat, white chicken into the yard. Its logs were tied, and she watched it twist and beat its wings on the sand. Startled and amazed, like the chicken, Mina looked up at the man again. "For you, Señora San Martín," he had said, his voice quavering, "and your family." He ran down the alley and Mina remembered that for a week there had been rumors of a layoff at the factory. There was nothing to them she knew, for Claudio had not been taking inventory with her at night. She would not cook the chicken and she could not return it; it became a pet of the children. They called it Cinderella and finally it died of old age.

"Well, I guess we are all the same," Mina said aloud, "Cubans, Italians, Spaniards."

Dolores put her hands to her bosom. "None of us can talk. Look at my Armando, working for Wally Chase"—she threw out an arm and pointed up the street— "in that house surrounded with bushes and a bare electric wire!"

"No, Lola, no," Clemencia said, using the diminutive of Dolores. "Mina didn't mean that with her talk of gangsters. You know Armando is . . ." She looked from Mina to Dolores, uneasy because she was never so emotional; and finished, "like our own son."

Dolores pulled herself out of the glider with a series of gasping sounds. "My dears, you are my sisters, that is why we can say anything to each other." She pulled her handkerchief out again, coughed into it, and moved heavily to the door of the living room.

"What are you exciting yourself for?" Mina asked from the glider. "There's no need to act like the Lady of the Camelias."

Dolores coughed again, one hand fluttering from her mouth to her bosom. When she stopped, she waved her handkerchief at Mina in a gesture of forgiveness; it released a heavy scent of gardenias. "Armando does not have the excuse that he is Italian . . ."

Mina got up from the glider impatiently. "You know Wally Chase is retired." She pronounced it Walliché, as did every Latin in Tampa.

"Then why does he need Armando to work for him?" Dolores asked. "Such a strange job anyway. He spends all his nights there. He tells me they play cards. I tell him he's a bodyguard. Son, I tell him, you know what happens to bodyguards. They are the pads the horses wear in the bull ring. They get ripped to shreds."

Mina never teased Dolores for using extravagant language if the subject were important. Dolores wrote poetry, and such language, her sisters felt, was rightfully hers. They did not forget, however, that, of course, Dolores had never seen a bullfight.

"Come," Dolores continued, motioning them into the house. "Armando will be here soon to take Walliché his cold drink."

They followed Dolores through the living room and dining room to the kitchen. Each room opened on the next, all in a row, on the left side of the house. On the right were three bedrooms, also in a row. This was all there had been to the house when Serafin and Dolores first rented it fifty years ago. In time the privy in the back yard was replaced by a bathroom in the house, a back porch was added behind the kitchen, and the front yard was shortened by another porch. Dolores' children, as they married and left home, added other things to make her comfortable. The porches were screened, a hot water unit installed, a heater to warm the house, a fan in the dining-room ceiling to draw out the hot summer air, and Venetian blinds to cover every window. All these things made Dolores feel loved.

In the doorway of the kitchen, they paused for a moment, waiting for the fluorescent lights. The bright glare shining on white Formica always came as a shock to the old ladies. This clean, utilitarian kitchen was the one thing Clemencia most envied Dolores. For her, it was a beautiful thing in itself. Not to Mina; to Mina, each new thing in the house was a reminder of what Dolores' daughter Elena had achieved.

Dolores ran her hand along the Formica next to the sink, as if smoothing it out, and sighed again with disappointment that it was not marble. She picked up a pitcher covered with a piece of cheesecloth and brought it to the table.

"Oh," Clemencia said, "you are making *garapiña!*"

Dolores nodded, brought an empty pitcher to the table, and placed it next to the covered one.

"For Walliché!" Mina exclaimed.

"Would you believe it?" Dolores said. She put the cheesecloth over the mouth of the empty pitcher and began to pour the fermented liquid from one to the other. Whenever a pineapple peeling clogged the spout, she delicately pushed it back with her forefinger. "With all the hard liquor Walliché bootlegged in his day, this is what he likes to drink on a warm night. He sends Armando over for it

7

around ten o'clock, and the next morning around ten o'clock, too, he sends over flowers by a cracker who works for him."

"He does have a beautiful garden," Clemencia said. "Flowers everywhere."

Dolores finished pouring and took the cheesecloth and pineapple peelings away. "Beautiful, beautiful," she said. "It is a beautiful island in our block, that corner lot. But I keep thinking of the electric wire in the bushes."

Mina got up, opened the refrigerator, and took out an ice tray. She handed it to Dolores. "He brings you flowers!" she said smiling. "How courteous, how Spanish . . ."

So Clemencia wouldn't hear her, Dolores said softly to Mina, "You are a bad girl."

Mina laughed teasingly. "It is very Spanish of Walliché, very gallant to send you flowers."

"They have always said at the factory that he is very partial to Cubans," Clemencia explained earnestly. "He always worked with Cubans, all the men around him are, you know. That is why the Italians are trying to push him out."

Mina's little teasing laugh climbed the scale until her whole body shook with laughter. "Think of it; think of it!" she said. "At sixty-five, Dolores could be known as the Numbers Lady, *La Bolitera* of Ninth Avenue!"

Leaning on the sink, the ice tray in her hand, Dolores laughed until tears forced her to stop. Mina clapped her hands, delighted with herself. Only Clemencia was quiet. Startled and embarrassed at having missed the tone of the conversation, she blushed and spoke harshly. "Mina, don't play the clown! What would people think?"

"Yes," Dolores said happily. "Mama always said she was the clown of the family." She shook a finger at Mina and turned to Clemencia. "And yet she calls *me* an eccentric old woman!"

Mina snorted. "I suppose you would turn down Walliché if he asked for your hand."

"I wouldn't know if he were asking me," Dolores argued. "I don't suppose he speaks Spanish."

"Doesn't Armando know?" Mina asked.

"Do you think he tells me anything?" Dolores complained. "I know all my children like these old hands, except him. Even when they are far away I think I can tell you just when Elena and Clara are having their periods. But Armando tells me nothing. I am not complaining; he is a good boy, but he doesn't tell me anything Walliché says."

"Oh I think they say he does speak Spanish," Clemencia said. "He has lived here among us all these years."

"Anyway," Mina joked, "you poets know the international language of love!"

This time all three laughed, and they did not hear Armando, who had entered through the back porch. Mina jumped in her chair, startled, and gave a muffled gasp. Armando was short, thin, and dark. At twenty-eight his youthfulness was beginning to desert him, and without the life it gave to his skin and his movements he might become wizened, a dark little man with a crooked nose, thin lips, and large soulful brown eyes like Dolores'.

"I have warned you, my darling," Dolores said, "I am too old to be startled."

"You are right; I forgot. I was listening to your laughter." He looked respectfully at Dolores and waited. She never meant to reproach him and she coughed to cover up the little pang that her ill humor always caused her. Armando turned to Mina and Clemencia and bowed. "Will you tell me the joke? I didn't catch any words, just your laughter."

"Should we tell him?" Mina asked her sisters. "You would be surprised what old ladies can talk about."

Clemencia looked away. God knows what Mina might say.

"That's what I hope for—a surprise," Armando said.

"But I won't," Mina said coquettishly. "After all, the three of us have diapered you, and as far as we are concerned, you are still too young."

"Shall I tell you some of the things I used to overhear when I was really too young?" Armando asked.

"No, no!" Mina said, putting her hands to her face.

"Whatever it was," Dolores said, "there was never anything to hide. There is never anything to hide that is worthwhile, not from one's family, and Clemencia and Mina are like mothers to you."

Armando's manner became formal again. "Yes, they are. I never forget that."

"Never mind," Mina quickly interjected. "I like to think that I have a few things to hide."

"Well, Armando, how are you?" Clemencia sad. "Roberto asked about you."

"I am as you see me—well," Armando said. "Tell Roberto and his wife I hope they are well."

"But you are seeing them tomorrow," Dolores said. "Don't tell me that you have not arranged it. You promised."

"I am, I am," Armando said. "I've asked Walliché. He won't need me. After the party I'll go to his house."

Dolores smiled. "I knew it, my darling. I knew you would not let anything stand in the way of your sisters. There is nothing more important than family. What would Jaime have thought? He comes of an old Cuban family. It would have been an affront."

"Then you are having a party?" Mina asked.

"Of course, we must all get together the first night. I am sure Elena would have it no other way."

"And I am invited?" Mina asked.

"You are getting old and eccentric," Dolores said. "How can you even ask? We are not Americans . . ."

Armando picked up the pitcher.

"Wait, wait," Dolores said to him. "I have to put in the sugar." She took out a large spoon and stirred the *garapiña.* "Everyone must be here to meet Jaime. He and Elena are only stopping for a day or so to leave Clara and little Jimmy."

"What kind of a visit is that?" Mina asked.

"They are going to Virginia," Dolores explained, "but on their way back to Havana they will stop here again to pick up Clara and little Jimmy."

"Zoom, zoom," Mina said, "like mosquitoes."

"So you see we cannot waste time," Dolores said; "we cannot waste time. Jaime has to meet Roberto and I want Armando here to spend as much time with him—"

"Mama!" Armando said warningly. He was on his way out, but he stopped when he heard his mother. "Please remember . . "

Dolores waved him away with one hand. "I remember, I remember, that you are obstinate and hard-headed and foolish."

Armando flushed and started to leave again, but he stopped when his mother began to talk once more. "Yes, go on and play poker with that gangster when you could be managing a *finca* in Cuba."

When he saw she was through, he smiled at his aunts and shook his head, asking them to forgive Dolores.

Clemencia looked at him with troubled eyes, thinking of her son Roberto. "Good night, Armando," she said softly.

"God bless you," Mina called after him.

When the back door slammed, Dolores explained, "There is nothing Elena would not do for her little brother. And if he persists in this way, it will break her heart. There she is, married to so important a man as Jaime, a man who sees the President every day, and she cannot pull her brother up to better things. I have tried to make Armando see, but sometimes it seems there is no use talking."

"Maybe Elena will have other things on her mind," Mina suggested. "You said yourself that she and Jaime are busy people."

"Not my Elena, she will never forget her family. She is no American; she has lived in Cuba too many years." She stopped a moment to take her gardenia-scented handkerchief from her bosom, looked around to make sure they were alone, and then continued in a whisper. "I suspect that Armando is Elena's main reason for coming. This is her real home, all things considered, and she does want to see it again after so many years. Yet, when I spoke to her on the phone this morning, I could tell how much he is on her mind. She did not tell me outright that she was coming to get him—she always hides her good intentions—but a mother can tell that she has some other purpose in coming besides me and the old house!"

"What an imagination!" Mina said. "You make the whole thing sound like a novel!"

II

Two hours later, Robert preceded Shirley on the cement path to Dolores' porch, and Dolores opened her arms to welcome him. He leaned over to kiss her, aiming his lips at her right cheek. The dark brown sagging skin under her almond-shaped eyes gave her face a brooding, poetic look. Bad heart, he remembered, just as her face got closer. Dolores locked her hands behind his neck, straightened his head, and kissed him moistly on the lips, hungrily, as if he were still a child.

"Ah!" Dolores exclaimed, breaking away. "When are you going to paint me? Like you used to say before you went to New York."

"When next you write a poem for me," Robert said in Spanish, or she would not have understood.

Clemencia stepped down from the porch on the alert. She had been promised by Dolores and Mina that they wouldn't speak to Robert yet about getting a job offer from Elena, but she knew they could easily forget such a promise.

"Not so loud, not so loud," Mina called from the porch steps, jealous that Robert enjoyed Dolores so much. "Not everyone in Ybor City stays up this late."

Shirley caught only the "Ybor City" in the Spanish they spoke so quickly and lightly, and she wondered what they could be saying about the Latin section of Tampa. It sounded exclusive, and she decided she should not greet Dolores with a kiss as her husband did. She simply smiled and nodded when the old woman looked her way, but she found that was enough encouragement for Dolores to grab her hands and kiss her.

Dolores struggled with the few English phrases she knew, trying to recall the word "hello," but it would not come, like a difficult rhyme. Finally, she dropped Shirley's hands and pointed to Robert. "I love him," she said in the only English she could remember.

Mina laughed. "I love him, too," she said. "Clemencia loves him and . . ." She trailed off, her English unable to keep up with her

12

thoughts. Instead, she made a few derisive noises, pushed her way past Robert and Dolores, and kissed Shirley.

"Tell me, Clemencia," Dolores complained to Robert's mother, "is Mina making me out to be a fool again? I do not trust our sister when she speaks English."

Clemencia stood a little apart from them, wondering why she was not familiar with her son as Mina and Dolores were. "Oh, Mina's English is nothing to speak of," she said in Spanish, but Dolores had turned to Robert again.

"You should read it," Dolores was saying to him. "It will interest you."

"*Gloria?*" Robert asked.

"By Benito Perez-Galdos. It's about a young man like you who falls in love with a Jewish girl and wants to marry her. A young man who puts all conventions aside, as you did, to marry a girl outside his faith."

"But of course he doesn't get he girl," Robert said, "if I know Perez-Galdos."

"It is a very strong, passionate novel," Dolores said, putting a hand on his chest. "Don't laugh at it."

"My God, you have it all wrong!" Mina said. "The heroine is a Catholic and the hero is a Jew."

"No, no!" Dolores said.

"Pay no attention to her," Mina said to Robert. "I heard that novel read in the cigar factory several times in the days when every factory had a reader."

"I remember because she had reddish hair and a pink complexion," Dolores insisted. "He was Spanish and, of course, dark."

Mina shook her head. "You are thinking of that American girl from Georgia that your Armando marred," she answered. "*She* had red hair. Besides, there are Spanish women with light complexions and red hair, or hair any color of the rainbow."

"I had forgotten that Armando was married when he was in the Army," Robert said.

"He never speaks of it," Dolores explained. "They only spent one day in Tampa, here in the second bedroom. She was a young thing, an American cracker from Georgia. But your aunt is right; she had reddish hair and a milky body. I can understand the feeling a dark man like Armando must have for a woman like that. I saw her robe come loose in the morning. A little blue vein ran into the cleft of her breasts. Oh my dears!"

"Oh, oh, oh!" Mina exclaimed. "There, you have embarrassed Roberto."

Robert laughed. "Not at all. Lola and I understand these things." He had an image of Shirley's freckled breasts, an image so intimate that he became silent.

Shirley touched Clemencia's arm. "Were we late, Mother?"

"No, not at all." Clemencia spoke drily, unconsciously trying to influence Dolores and Mina, not liking the tone their conversation with her son had taken. "You did not have to come, really," she said in English, trying to soften her manner. "We could walk."

"Not me," Mina said, turning to Shirley. "I like to be driven in a car."

Dolores took Robert's arm and walked to the car. "Did your wife call Clemencia 'Mother'?"

Robert nodded.

"If that is a Jewish custom, it is a nice one," Dolores said. "After all, it is an old race, and they can probably teach us a lot."

Robert looked down at Dolores and saw that she was peering at him with that eager look that signified she was having a *special* conversation, one between artists. He nodded and turned to see if Shirley could have overheard. They had been in Tampa two months now, and he was still apprehensive when anyone spoke to him about Jews. He kept waiting for open, coarse anti-Semitism that would force him to come to his wife's defense. Feeling Dolores' weight on his arm, he hoped it would not come from his darling old aunt.

"Oh, no!" he moaned, then laughed because he had spoken aloud.

"And why not?" Dolores asked pleasantly. "Haven't you always been like a brother to Elena?"

He tried to retrieve the words she had been speaking and make himself hear them again. "Did you say Elena is going to be here? In Tampa?"

They had reached the car, and Dolores turned to the others. "Clemencia," she announced, "I am telling Roberto that Elena will arrive tomorrow and that I expect we will see him here tomorrow night." She saw Clemencia's alarmed look and so only added, "How happy Elena will be to see you!"

"The store does not close until late," Clemencia warned.

"It is absurd," Mina said. "Whoever heard of keeping a grocery store open at night? Only in the Negro section do they do that."

14

"It is not Roberto who does it," Clemencia said. "El Rubio likes to catch every bit of business on Saturdays."

Dolores turned to Robert. "It does not matter when you get here. The important thing is that you must come."

"I'll come; I'll come," Robert said gaily.

"The important thing is he must find another job," Mina said. "El Rubio is working him to death at the grocery store." She grabbed Robert's arm and shook it a little. "You don't need all those brains to sell toilet paper to cigar makers."

Clemencia turned to Dolores and whispered, "I told you she wouldn't be able to hold her tongue!"

They had forgotten Shirley. She walked around to the front door of the car and opened it. Only when they spoke slowly and evenly did she understand their Spanish. In a group Robert's family spoke too quickly, with so many stops and starts that she could not tell when a sentence began or ended. They would also grab and slap one another so frequently that it was impossible to concentrate on the words.

Shirley sat in the front seat of the car and watched her mother-in-law look at Robert with somber black eyes, just like Robert's. Two months in Tampa had made Shirley very conscious of family ties again; she was an orphan, but it was a long time since she had brooded about it. As if she had divined what Shirley was thinking, Dolores leaned into the car, took her face between her hands, and kissed her.

Slowly, carefully, gravely, Dolores looked into Shirley's eyes and said in English, "Good night." Proud of her achievement, she continued in Spanish to Robert, "You tell your wife she must come early tomorrow. Elena will be happy to know her and so will my Clara, who is closer to her in age. They both speak English." She gave Shirley's cheek a soft pat. "She won't have to listen to just a lot of old women talking in Spanish."

"Clemencia," Dolores called, forgetting her promise, "speak to Roberto." She stepped back from the car, and Shirley leaned out and waved at her as they started off.

The scent of gardenias that Dolores carried remained with Shirley. "She is such a sweet person," she said to Clemencia and Mina.

"Sweet? Who is sweet? Dolores?" Mina laughed. "As soon as you get gray hair people call you sweet. I have gray hair. So does Clemencia."

Robert laughed. "All right. All right. You're sweet, too."

"That is better," Mina said.

"Mama," Robert said. "What are you supposed to speak to me about?"

Mina started to answer for her, but Clemencia touched her arm, and, instead, Mina pointed to the house on the corner. "Look, all the lights are on at Walliché's house."

"Aren't they always?" Robert asked.

"Yes, like a carnival. He is like a little boy who will not go to sleep unless he knows all the lights are on." Mina shook her head and sighed. "What a way to live—scared of every dark corner."

"If I were he, I would move to another city where people do not know me," Clemencia said. "Now that he has retired, it does not matter where he lives."

"Retired?" Mina said. "Gangsters never retire."

"You told Dolores yourself," Clemencia protested.

"I don't want to worry her. You would say the same thing, too," Mina explained. "Dolores exaggerates, but she is really sensitive and must be protected from her imagination."

They were silent a moment. "Poor Lola," Clemencia said, after she had thought it over.

Shirley turned in her seat and tried to divert the two old ladies. "I got the impression that Dolores stays up very late herself."

Mina laughed. "I used to call her Stalin, when he was alive. You see, she writes late at night. If I know her, she is making a cup of coffee now and sitting down at the kitchen table to write."

"Poetry?" Shirley asked.

Clemencia nodded.

"Poetry, plays, prayers," Mina explained. "No novels. They are too . . ." She broke off, conferred hurriedly with Robert in Spanish, and then turned to Shirley. ". . . prosaic; she says novels are too prosaic."

"That's interesting," Shirley said, "but what are her plays about?"

"Greek gods, statues, kings! But none of that matters. They are all about love. Dolores—I had better tell you—is very romantic." Mina stopped and looked at her nephew behind the wheel. "But this is not exactly true. Your husband will be laughing at her . . ."

Robert laughed.

"There, you see!" Mina leaned forward and tapped him on the head. "To tell the truth, Dolores is writing a play about Saint

Sebastian. It is all in poetry, and it is very beautiful. Tonight she recited a long speech that a beautiful Roman girl says when she sees Sebastian wounded with all the arrows. She is not a Christian, but she loves him. He is such a beautiful young soldier, and, after all, they are of the same class. But, of course, her love is doomed because Sebastian is a saint and must be martyred. 'Love me and I will love your God,' the girl says. It is very pretty."

"My God!" Robert said. "It sounds interesting."

"You are not serious," Mina complained. "You are laughing at her."

Robert laughed again. "You're to blame. You made me laugh."

"Well, you must admit it is a lot of foolishness," Clemencia said.

"Oh all artistic things are," Mina said. "But after all, Lola does not have a family to support. She does it for her own . . . gratification. Like a true artist, after all is said and done, a true artist." She looked at Robert, for she had hoped to arouse him with that speech. When he said nothing, she worried that she might have hurt him. "My dear Shirley, please learn Spanish. I get a headache when I speak so much English. After five minutes I begin to get dizzy."

Clemencia started to tell Mina privately, in Spanish, that she should give her tongue a rest, but Robert laughed and said, "I remember the day when I first realized I was thinking in English. I was thirteen and a half, and I was looking at a sketch of the Parthenon in our junior-high school library . . ." He broke off and looked at Shirley, who was watching him with interest. "It was not while looking at a girl."

"What? What?" Mina asked.

"What I meant to say," Robert explained to his aunt, "is that Dolores could be a very successful writer, if only she wrote the same things in English. Not as verse plays, but as novels or movie scripts. Americans like historical novels. Their authors are very successful."

"Roberto!" his mother complained, "you are not being nice about Dolores. What will Shirley think?"

"Besides, it is not true," Mina said. "I cannot believe it. Americans? Impossible!"

Robert shrugged his shoulders. "Why not? They're as smart as anyone else, or as dumb."

Mina and Clemencia were startled—that their Roberto should compare them to Americans! In the dark, Clemencia again put a warning hand on Mina's knee.

"My dear, I hope I have not offended you," Mina said to Shirley, after a pause. "I know you have an admiration for literature. Clemencia has told me how you read books. I was talking about the Americans here."

Shirley was delighted. "You must not apologize to me. Certainly not to me."

Mina leaned over and touched Shirley's blonde curly hair. "Besides, I do not think of you as an American."

"Of course, of course," Clemencia agreed.

"Neither do Americans, really." Shirley turned and looked at the two old women. They were smiling at her, although they looked a little puzzled by what she had just said. With a burst of courage that made her voice harsh she explained to them. "They think I'm just a Jew."

"Aiee, aiee," Clemencia murmured.

Mina's eyes widened in her head. "Barbarians! Barbarians!"

Robert brought the car to a stop in front of the old house where Mina lived with her son Feliz and his fourth wife. "I almost forgot," Mina said, pretending she had just thought of it. "I was talking to Feliz today and he wants to add another bedroom to your house."

Clemencia remained still. She was tired of trying to head off Mina.

"You need it," Mina said boldly to her. "With one more bedroom you will all be comfortable—one room for the children, one for you, and one for Roberto and Shirley. It makes sense."

Clemencia looked at Robert, hoping he would agree, now that Mina had let it out. "I will think about it," she said.

"No, we can't afford it," Robert said.

Mina turned to him, happy she had gotten a foot in the door. "It is free; Feliz will do it for nothing—on Sundays. You will help him and the lumber will come from one of the houses he is building. Why not?"

"We can't accept it," Robert said. "There's no need."

"Oh, dear Virgin!" Mina groaned. "Feliz is your cousin, your mother's nephew, my son!"

"It is very nice of Feliz," Clemencia said.

"I didn't say it was not," Robert said. He hit the steering wheel lightly with the palms of his hands. He didn't like his cousin Feliz. "Despite what you two may have told each other, we're not staying in Tampa. We came down for the winter because Paul had an ear infection. I am working at the grocery store because I need the money. Do we understand each other?"

"Very well," Mina said. "If you don't like living down here, then you should talk seriously to Elena tomorrow night. She can get you a good job in Cuba."

Robert laughed. "I hadn't heard about that plot. Is that what you were supposed to speak to me about?"

"There is no plot," Clemencia said.

"Of course there is," Mina said. "Think it over. Stay here with your mother or go to Cuba and get a good job."

Robert shook his head. "Well, anyway, thank Feliz for me. If he were home I'd do it myself."

"They are not out," Mina said. "They just go to bed early."

Robert looked at the dark house. "But all the lights are out."

"That's the way Feliz is," Mina said. "He doesn't like to leave any lights on. But he is generous, believe me. Roberto, think it over. He will be more than happy to build that room. Frankly, I would rather you did not go to Cuba. I did not want to say it in front of Dolores, but I don't like that Batista and all the graft and corruption."

Mina pulled herself out of the car with an effort and waited for Robert to say something encouraging. Finally, she kissed Shirley good night. When the car moved off, angry tears welled up in Mina's eyes. What did it matter that Roberto was such a pleasure to talk to, she asked herself. He was a fool. It was Clemencia's fault, she decided; Clemencia should make him see that it was his responsibility to take care of her in her old age.

Clemencia waited until they were at the corner of their block before she spoke. "I think Mina has been talking to Feliz about the room for a long time. She is disappointed that you did not appreciate it."

Robert looked at his mother; he had to clear his throat before he spoke. "I appreciate it, Mama, and I'm sure Shirley does, too." He realized, as soon as he said it, that he hadn't consulted Shirley at all, that he didn't know what she thought of any of his plans. He turned to her and saw that she had hurried from the car because Paul was still up.

Paul ran down the steps with the girl from next door, who was baby-sitting. "I hope he gave you no trouble," Shirley said.

Paul wouldn't let anyone but Robert pick him up, and not until the girl had left and Shirley's voice got sharp did he go inside. "You know, Daddy," he called out to Robert, who sat on the porch with Clemencia, "I can blow my nose all by myself now."

Robert laughed and stretched his legs and looked over at his mother. "I hope you have been teaching him Spanish. I never have time."

"He just laughs at me," Clemencia said. She wanted to ask him what he was going to do. It was spring now; they might go back to New York if they didn't change their plans.

"How old is that oak tree?" Robert asked, before she could think of how to say what was on her mind

"Older than you, Roberto."

"I remember the trunk," he said, recalling the drawings he had made of it years ago. "But not all the branches."

Clemencia took a deep breath. "Roberto, why don't you stay in Tampa? It would be good for the children."

"It's too late to discuss it tonight."

"You have not changed." She leaned over and tapped his knee. "You arch your back like a cat, ready to fight. You were always rebellious. I am not surprised you turned out to be a Socialist or a Communist or whatever you call yourself."

Robert looked at her steadily. "I'm not interested in politics anymore. I just want to make a living."

"Good." She looked out at the street as if someone might be listening and lowered her voice. "Good. Those Americans are too stupid to accept communism. You would only be wasting your time."

"Latins aren't any smarter," he said. "Spaniards have Franco and Cubans have Batista."

"Oh, if you're going to talk politics, I'm going inside," she said irritably. "You know I don't know a thing about it. Your father talked politics and for three years before he died he was on the cigar factories' blacklist."

"He was not a good provider, was he, Mama?" She looked shocked, so he quickly added, "He was like me."

"What are you saying?"

"I didn't mean to ruffle your feathers," he said. "I was only trying to apologize for having sent you no money all these years."

"When your father died, every cigar maker in Ybor City was at his funeral. No priest was there and no foreman from the factory, but every worker was there. Every flower in Tampa was on his grave that day."

"I remember," Robert said.

"And what is wrong with your cousin Feliz helping you build a room?" Clemencia said and got up. "What do you think families are for? Feliz may be a foolish man, but he is not an exploiter." She stepped back and shook a finger at him. "I will tell you what your father said—families are people who do not exploit each other."

Robert got up, too, and put an arm around her waist.

"Don't kiss me now. I am not a sentimentalist like your Aunt Mina." She went inside and left him alone.

It took Robert a while to get over his irritation. Finally, he decided that his mother was really only thinking of him; she had let him go easily enough when he was eighteen. She had had his younger brother and sister to take care of then. He went inside to talk it over with Shirley, but he found that she was already in bed. He took off his clothes in the dark and lay beside her. Their apartment in New York was sublet for the next three months, they had just enough money for the trip back; and according to the doctor the fluid in Paul's ears had completely dried up.

He turned on his side to go to sleep and that woke up Shirley.

"Is everything all right?" she asked automatically.

"Well, we have to decide," he said. "The old ladies are right about that."

"Oh," Shirley said. She'd been thinking of the children. "Well . . ."

"What's the matter?" he asked. "Did you have to listen to too much Spanish tonight? I guess you couldn't stand it as a steady diet, could you? I mean, the old ladies talking all that Spanish would make you feel apart."

"Oh no, I think they're dears."

He didn't say anything. After a while she asked, "Who's Elena, exactly?"

"You know, Aunt Dolores' oldest daughter." His voice became lively; he was grateful she wanted to talk. "She's set up most of her family. She's generous and they all depend on her."

"Is she going to do something for us? Is that why they want us to meet her?"

"That's what the old ladies think will happen."

"What can she do for you?"

"You know, her husband is a kind of presidential secretary. He has been writing the speeches for all the presidents for the last twenty years, and so he has all the privileges that go with such a

21

position. I guess there's hardly a job in Cuba he can't get for a friend."

"Oh."

"Of course, there's nothing they can do for us. And I'm not going to ask them." He put a hand on her hair and lay on his side, looking at her. "Unless you want me to."

She smiled. "And I thought there was more between you and Elena."

"She's my cousin, remember! Still, there's more than the old ladies imagine. She lived in New York for about a year, just after she divorced her first husband. She had an affair and they used my apartment."

"I don't believe it—a Spanish girl from Tampa?"

"I didn't myself when she asked me. But she told me straight out. I was working at a summer camp, and I never saw him." He stopped a moment. "I didn't even know any of the details, like his name. I was too shy to ask."

"You've spoiled my fantasy," Shirley said. "I'd decided she was the older woman who taught you about sex, who sacrificed herself for your manhood, and you came out of it the accomplished man I met."

"Oh, that's better," he said, and pulled her toward him. They could decide some other time.

III

DOLORES stood in the doorway of his room, and Armando had the feeling that it was not the first time that she had come to look in on him this morning. He did not open his eyes until he was certain she had gone. The bedroom was in half-light; it was almost midday, but the drawn shades made it a warm, brown, indeterminate time. Hung throughout the room were clues of the day, long yellow slivers of sun that entered where the shades did not quite cover the old windows. Armando threw back the light cotton blanket and tested the temperature of the air with his nude body. He did not like to walk into the day until the chill of morning had gone from it. It was the one resolution he had made in the Army that he had kept, but in those days he thought he would always have Katie beside him to warm the bed.

Like a slim bright dagger, a strip of sun lay across his chest. In the shade of the room his body was a comforting light brown, except where the black pubescence flowered, but the streak of light showed his skin pale. He decided he must go to the beach and lie in the sun. With one hand he felt his stomach muscles. They seemed firm, but, to make sure, he lifted his legs straight up in the air and slowly let them down. He scarcely felt the strain. In one movement he rolled out of bed and walked to the back window. He pulled up the shade and stood in the sunlight, half-expecting to see Pinta, the cow, in the back yard, the way it used to be when he was a boy.

He must ask his mother what had happened to Pinta . . .

"Armando," his mother said.

He didn't turn. "Yes, Mama?" He couldn't ask her about Pinta. She would only talk and talk, the way she gossiped with his sisters and joked with his brothers when they were in Tampa.

"I thought I heard you," Dolores said, watching the dark outline of his body against the sunlight.

With deliberation, he turned and picked up a robe from the straight-backed chair by the bed. He drew it on slowly without looking at his mother, remembering this was the day when he was to stay away from Walliché's.

"You will be wanting coffee and a roll," she said. "It is late. Maybe you will let me cook some eggs for you, too."

He shook his head. To herself, Dolores rehearsed a speech to Mina. "There he was, Mina, just as I brought him into the world, Like my Saint Sebastian, smooth and delicious. And like all my boys so well-equipped for the game of love." What could that American girl have been thinking of, to leave him when he is so beautiful?

But Dolores said nothing and only sighed.

"I know," Armando said in reply to her sigh. "I haven't forgotten. I'm picking up Elena and the others at one-thirty at the airport. Don't worry."

"Good, good," she answered. "After all, Jaime is not Americanized like us. He is no stranger to courtesies. Wherever he goes in Cuba there is a presidential car to meet him." She stopped because he didn't seem to be listening. "But you must eat before you go. Let me give you eggs with your coffee."

"No," he said firmly, and walked past her to the bathroom. He closed the door and looked down at the washstand. He must keep away from Walliché's today, and he must, for peace of mind, stay away from his mother until the others arrived. He could tell she planned to lecture him about Elena's offer while he ate breakfast. He smiled, knowing how much she would enjoy learning that he plotted to outwit her—if he let her know the way his brothers did.

On his way to the kitchen he noticed she had put the old Madeira linen tablecloth out on the dining table. Walliché's flowers were all over the house—everything must be all right there, he told himself, if there had been no message—and she had placed bottles of liquor and wine on the sideboard. That would be his job tonight, to serve the liquor.

To serve the liquor and avoid their plans for him. Walliché wasn't the only thing on his mind today; whatever happened, he didn't want to be judged by Elena. That was why he had never applied for a job; he didn't want anyone to look him up and down and decide what he was worth.

His mother put down the phone and served him his coffee and roll. Back on the phone, she finished giving the grocery man his order and explained to him that her daughters were arriving from Cuba. Then she called a Spanish restaurant and ordered pastries.

She had not finished when he started to leave. "Armando," she called. He stopped on the back porch. "You are leaving now?" He nodded without turning. "But it is early."

He nodded again and went out into the back yard. She has given me up, he thought, and he was sorry he was making her sad. He could hear her on the phone again as he crossed to the old barn. It was a garage now, and he kept his car in it.

Whenever he had not been to see the girls for a few days, the garage reminded him that it was here that he had first put a hand under a girl's dress. He backed out the car, undecided about where to go, since he had agreed to stay away from Walliché's house. The girls would laugh if he showed up so early in the day, and it was better, in case they checked, if he didn't use them as an alibi. Just for a couple of hours he had to be seen somewhere; the rest of the day would he no problem: He'd be with his family. Impatiently, he turned the car into the street and stepped hard on the accelerator, heading for Seventh Avenue, where the shops, restaurants, and Spanish clubs were. He'd have coffee in the espresso shop and talk to the men. It was lunch hour, and the shop should be filled with people he knew, or who knew him.

At the espresso counter he saw El Chulo, the numbers man. El Chulo immediately detached himself from the others. "A dollar on the usual," Armando said.

El Chulo mumbled, "Two-four-eight?"

Armando nodded and put a bill on the counter. Two-four-eight, the last three digits of his Army serial number. "Have a coffee with me."

El Chulo accepted, and Chapitas, the counterman, put demitasses in front of them, wiped the counter, and looked from one to the other. "Tell me what Armando played," he said to El Chulo, "and I'll put a quarter on it myself."

El Chulo said nothing. He knew Chapitas was referring to Armando's connection with Walliché and that was the last thing in this world he wanted to meddle with.

Very slowly, Armando stirred the coffee. "You should be inside the restaurant serving Spanish bean soup to the tourists." He put the spoon down on the marble counter so carefully that it made no noise. "I've never hit the right number once, Chapitas. What makes you think my guess is better than yours?"

The old man thought it over and then laughed. "Come now," he said, "don't treat me like a dog from another neighborhood. Your old man was my friend, and you'll always be his youngest son to me."

It was time to move off, Armando decided, but he wanted to stay until he'd shown Chapitas that he had not been made uncomfortable. And if his sister Elena asked him what he was doing, what would he say? And what of his plans for the future? Armando looked into his coffee and let Chapitas and El Chulo drift away, embarrassed. His plans, he told himself were just as good as hers. When he looked up, he saw his old school friend, Arturo.

Arturo threw his arms up, opened his eyes wide, and grinned. Faithful to their old high-school ritual, Arturo crouched, threw one arm straight out and walked to him, wobbling from side to side. The coffee shop was full with the lunch crowd, and he stumbled against others as he made his way to Armando.

"Mando!" Arturo cried.

Armando was supposed to duplicate Arturo's gestures, but not until he was quite close did Armando relent. Then, he only held out the arm stiffly.

Arturo hit him a couple of taps on the chest and feigned two passes. "How's the old man?"

Armando nodded. It couldn't have been more than a week since he had last seen him. "How's business?" he asked.

"Slow," Arturo said seriously. "It always is after Easter. In a couple of weeks we'll start with the bathing suits and Palm Beach suits. It'll pick up."

A silence fell between them. Chapitas came over. "Coffee?" he asked.

Arturo nodded and turned to Armando. "And you?"

Armando shook his head.

"It looks like one only," Arturo said to the old man. "How are you, Chapitas?"

"Playing twenty-six, like everyone else." Chapitas went away and came back with a demitasse. "We're playing every possible combination of twenty-six in honor of the rebels in the Sierra Maestra," he explained. "The most popular combination is seven-twenty-six. Understand? Seven for July." He laughed and wiped the counter. "We're great revolutionaries here in Ybor City."

Arturo raised a hand to get his attention. "Why not two-six-seven? Only Americans put the month before the day. Eh?"

Chapitas mockingly considered the point. "Ah yes," he said, "You may have something there. We don't know what we are any more—Cubans, Spaniards, or gringos." He gave the counter another wipe and moved off to another customer.

Armando listened to them and wondered how the old man and Arturo thought of so many things to say to each other. "How are the kids?" he finally asked.

Arturo looked at him with a smile. "Oh they are wonderful." He stopped a moment to consider what he had said. "They're a bother, of course," he added proudly.

After a moment's silence, Arturo tapped him again on the chest. "You look fine, you lucky guy."

"Fine," he said, feeling he had said this before. "Fine." He put down the empty cup. "See you." He meant to walk straight out, but he turned, put out his hand, and said good-bye again.

"Come to the house," Arturo said to him.

Armando nodded. "Sure, see you." He walked past the men at the counter to the sidewalk, avoiding Chapitas' eyes. Jesus Christ, he thought, everyone is worried about me.

Behind the wheel of his car, he wondered again where to go before picking up his sisters at the airport. He had more than an hour, enough time to satisfy himself with the girls, and they were as good an alibi as any, after all. With a laugh, he switched on the ignition and started the car. He drove to the corner, meaning to turn right and head for the railroad tracks where they lived; but he had to stop for a light, and he suddenly remembered his former wife, Katie; how light and fresh her skin had been. "No," he said aloud, and turned left down Fifteenth Street.

He had to drive slowly because the narrow streets were full of cigar makers walking home for lunch and children chasing each other. In front of El Recurso Clinic, the Soler girl in nurse's uniform waved at someone across the street. Probably she had just finished assisting Dr. Ortiz at an operation upstairs in one of the bedrooms of what had once been a rooming house. She was small and pretty, with black hair and dark eyes and good legs. He could understand the rumors about her and Dr. Ortiz, but for himself he would prefer if she were like—he was surprised to find that the image in his mind was not Katie. It was Shirley, sitting on Clemencia's porch the night he had gone to pick up his mother and to meet Robert for the first time in many years. Shirley had looked straight at him and extended her hand and asked him direct questions, all things he imagined only New York girls did.

27

His mood suddenly lifted and he hurried as much as he could down Fifteenth Street. Maybe Shirley would come with him to the airport. He had just decided to ask her when he saw a man in a long white grocer's apron waving at him. A Negro woman wearing a blue handkerchief on her head stood next to the man and smiled. He slowed down—the more people who recognized him the better— and realized the man was Robert. He had never seen Robert at the grocery store, and he smiled to think that with the long apron on Robert looked quite at home in Ybor City with all the other Latins.

Armando stopped at the curb and leaned out the window. "I'd forgotten you work here," he said.

The Negro woman looked at him, a loose smile showing a mouthful of gold teeth. "Bebito!" she said with an American accent.

Armando recognized her accent first; it was a childhood friend, the colored woman who had done their washing.

"Hello, Graciela," he said.

"I am seeing all my children today," she said. She grinned and waited. Armando leaned down and embraced her. She still smelled of yellow soap and boiling water. "You are both my children."

"Did you know Roberto was back in Ybor City?" Armando asked.

"Oh, they all come back," she continued in the same comical Spanish. "I was not surprised. I went in to buy cigarettes, and there was one of my children."

Armando looked over her head at Robert, and they exchanged smiles.

"He did not let me pay for them. He is just like my daughter, Tina; she doesn't let me work. How are your mothers?" She looked from one to the other and laughed to herself. "You thought I would forget. I know you are not brothers. You have different mothers. Tell them I am coming to see them. They remember Graciela. Yes, indeed they do; they do. And Graciela remembers, but she is too busy. There are so many people I must visit. I walk all over town. Don't tell me I am too old."

"Where are you going?" Armando asked. "I'll take you."

She turned to Robert, her gold teeth gleaming. "See, he'll take me. My children don't forget."

A woman walked into the grocery store and the screen door slammed behind her. "I have to leave you," Robert said. "Don't forget, Graciela, come see us."

Graciela nodded. "I don't forget, never. I have a very good memory."

Robert nodded good-bye.

"I was thinking of dropping by your house," Armando said to him, "forgetting that you were at work. I thought you could come to the airport to meet Elena and Clara."

"Do that," Robert said in English. "Shirley and the children are home. She'll be glad to have company."

Before Armando could answer, Robert had gone inside. Armando forgot for a moment that Graciela was there. He could only think of the astonishing suggestion Robert had made, that he should visit Robert's wife while he was away. What made him so trusting? It was the same quality Shirley had. She could look straight into his eyes and ask him questions and yet not be flirting. Robert's suggestion put the stamp of innocence on his own feelings about her. But here was Graciela. She had stopped talking and was looking up at him, an uncertain smile on her face, trying to discern whether he really meant to take her in his car.

He took her elbow and tried to hurry her. "Let me take you around the other side."

Her body began to shake and she moved slowly. "You remember Graciela, Bebito. I can walk. I can walk."

He ran back to his side of the car and took off fast with her talking beside him. He was sorry he was so sentimental—niggers weren't good witnesses either—and wished he could be going straight to Shirley's. He drove fast up Twenty-second Street, in the Negro section, not listening to her chatter until she yelled, "There! There!"

He stopped at a Coca-Cola sign with the words "Palm Cafe," and waited anxiously for her to get out. There were two wooden benches outside the building, and two Negro men stood at the window counter. They watched Armando when he drew up. "That's right. Let me out here, Bebito," Graciela said. She opened the door and the suddenly turned to him and asked very clearly, without the grinning and shaking that had gone with her reminiscing, "What are you doing free in the middle of the day? Are you out of a job?"

"No, I work nights," he said, one hand on the wheel ready to make a U-turn.

"It's good to be free, isn't it?" Graciela said, and let him see all her gold teeth. "I'm going to sit on that bench there for a while."

He was in too much of a hurry to look back as he made the U-turn, but the two Negroes had watched them both and Graciela called out, speaking English for the first time, "Good-bye, honey!"

On the corner of Michigan Avenue he stopped at a filling station for gas; the station attendant there knew him and would remember him. To make sure he asked the attendant for the time, and then hurried to Clemencia's house to see Shirley. When he slowed down on Michigan Avenue to make the turn, he found himself directly in front of Mina's house. She was on the porch with a gallon jug, watering the potted plants on the veranda, and he could see that she was disappointed by his not stopping. He was sorry that she had recognized him; he'd rather she did not guess where he was going.

Shirley was out front settling an argument between the children, and after she got over her surprise at seeing him, she waved at the woman across the street before going inside. "The sun is getting too hot," she called out to the woman.

The old lady laughed from her porch and nodded, but she obviously did not understand Shirley. Armando translated, and the old woman answered rapidly and at length. Shirley watched Armando answer for her until, after several false stops, their conversation came to an end and the old lady went inside.

"It's a pity I didn't catch it," Shirley said. "What did she say to you?"

"She agreed," Armando said.

"What?"

"That the sun is hot today." It was not until she laughed that he realized how funny his description of the conversation was. "Latins talk a lot, don't they?" he said, pleased that she had laughed.

She shook her head. "Others don't talk enough. Come." On the porch, she turned. "Is everything all right? Does your mother need anything for tonight?"

"Oh no," he said quickly, glad she'd asked. "Thank you. I'm on my way to the airport to pick up my sisters and Jaime and little Jimmy. I saw Roberto at the store, and I thought you might like to come for the ride."

"That's nice, but there are the children." She looked at him a moment. "Anyway, I'm sure you'd rather have your sisters to yourself for a while today."

He couldn't tell her that he didn't look forward to talking to Elena, and that there was never much one could talk about to Clara. It made him frown.

"But if you have time, why don't you come in and have coffee with me," she said, to make up for what she feared had been some unfriendliness on her part. "Please do. That way I can keep an eye on the children from the kitchen."

He held the screen door open for her, and after she passed him, he quickly looked up and down the block. Just before he stepped inside, he wondered if he should tell her what people in Ybor City would think of a woman asking a man into the house while she was alone. But there was no one on the block to see him. His palms began to sweat.

Coming in from the sun, he found the house dark and remembered the summer he went to Niquita's house every day just after lunch. He was fourteen and Niquita thirteen. When no one was in the street to se him, he'd enter the dark house and go straight to the second bedroom. There she waited for him, her skirt lifted to her chin, staring at the ceiling with shining eyes. Without removing his pants, he would play on the bed with her for an hour and most of it was spent fighting to lower her panties. They did not kiss or laugh. They were very serious.

"Never fear," Shirley said. "I'm not giving you American coffee." She turned on a light under the small pot. "I'll warm it up a little more. I was just going to have some." She sighed, went to a cupboard, and took out two demitasses. "Sit down." She looked at him and then pulled out a chair for him. She brought out two small spoons and put them next to the cups. "Sugar?" She kept moving about the kitchen until she brought the coffee pot to the table and sat down.

With every move she made, Armando abandoned each subject he thought of for conversation. When she was seated, he said immediately the first thing that came to mind. "I guess you learned to like it here in Tampa . . . Cuban coffee, that is."

Shirley brushed her hair back with one hand. "No, we always had it whenever we ate out in the Village. Or the Spanish restaurants around Fourteenth Street. Or for that matter, any French restaurant midtown, except that they are too expensive for us."

His pale skin flushed a little. "You have everything in New York, I guess."

31

"Not at all." Shirley smiled. "Here you drink it the way it should be done, not like a special treat when you eat out in the Village."

The look on his face didn't change, so she asked, "You've never been to New York?"

He shook his head.

"Then you don't know what I mean by the Village?"

He blushed. "Is that where you live?"

"No, The Bronx," she said. "The Village is downtown Manhattan, and it's supposed to be, well, Bohemian and artistic. A lot of young artists live there, or used to. Now it's no longer inexpensive, but a lot of the college kids go down there to the coffee houses and . . ." She broke off and laughed at the expression on his face. "It's not so wonderful."

"Oh I don't know enough," he said.

Shirley didn't hear him, and she said, almost to herself, "Robert lived there before we were married . . . in a cold-water flat."

"It sounds like a very nice place."

She put down her empty cup. "Yes, the truth is it's a very nice place." She pulled up a strap of her house dress and got up, taking her cup to the sink. Over the sink were windows looking out into the back yard. Light fell on her bare shoulders and arms, and when she moved forward to look at the children playing, a streak of sunlight made her hair golden.

Armando held his cup in mid-air and watched her. He felt as if he were stealing something, and he put down the cup suddenly, making a clatter. Shirley turned to him. "Take some more coffee," she said. "In New York, it's not peaceful, the way it is here."

He tried to say something, but his throat felt constricted, the way it did when he was a boy and tried to keep from crying. His eyes kept returning to her smooth, round, light arms, knowing they were soft and giving. In the crook of her right arm he could see tiny blue veins just below the surface. As if catapulted by something other than his limbs, he was at her side, the little cup shaking in his hand.

Shirley suddenly yelled, "Viola! Listen to me, don't you start it." She turned back into the room and found herself looking right into Armando's eyes. A tremor went through her.

The front door slammed.

"Excuse me," Armando said, and held out the cup guiltily. They heard a woman's voice. "Is anyone home?" Shirley turned to the door and waited, her body trembling with relief.

32

Mina walked into the kitchen. "I thought he was coming here," she said. "My dear, I decided to come because Latin men cannot be trusted, especially those of Cuban descent, like him."

Without looking at Armando, Mina went straight to Shirley and embraced her. The old lady's arms stopped her trembling, and for a moment Shirley thought she had mistaken the look in Armando's eyes. Then she looked at him and saw how pale he had become.

"You see how suspicious old ladies are," Mina said. "I saw the car outside and I said I had better go in and save that innocent. My sister Clemencia is working at the cigar factory, and I must take her place." She sat at the table and laughed. "And all he wanted was a cup of coffee. Well, I want one too."

He was able to leave in a few minutes. He calmed down enough to be sorry that he hadn't gone straight to the girls and, instead, had chased around town for a whole hour. Shirley, he decided was just like all the other women; she had suspected the worst; she hadn't given him a chance. By the time he was back in his car on the way to the airport, he had achieved that very cool, angry feeling he wanted to have when he met his sister Elena. He wasn't even worried about alibis; whatever happened to Walliché, it wasn't his business.

IV

ELENA did not recognize the short, dark man in the sports shirt at first glance. Not that she gave him a second glance, but he waved and she looked again. "He's changed, he's grown much older!" she said aloud, though only little Jimmy was at her side. Then she saw that Armando had not aged that much; he simply was on his guard and it made him look hard. She instinctively made it difficult for him; she let go of little Jimmy's hand, walked quickly across the airport waiting room, and threw her fur stole around his shoulders to draw him to her. It was the kind of demonstrativeness she'd learned to curb in the last few years.

Armando held himself stiffly, but she kept an arm around his waist and made him stay at her side while they waited for her husband, Jaime, and Clara. Jaime wore a white linen jacket and looked so unruffled that Elena almost laughed at the effect he had on Armando. But it was Clara who really startled Armando, although she had been gone only two years. She looked like an actress to him; her dress was short and tight, particularly around the hips, the way Havana women wore them. Elena saw him look at Clara and said, "How do you like the change in your sister?" Then she laughed and brought her husband to her side too, keeping the men to herself.

Little Jimmy had been tugging at Armando's hand, but he wasn't noticed until he punched Armando in the thigh. "Uncle!"

"Ah!" Elena said. "He's happy to see his uncle. See, Jaime, how affectionate he is!" She disengaged a hand and put it on little Jimmy's head. "You're going to see so many relatives you're going to forget Jaime and me."

Then, before anyone could think of the next move, Elena took charge of getting the luggage out to the car. Armando was dispatched to the loading platform, where the porter was heading, and little Jimmy was told to hold his mother's hand. Elena rearranged herself, took a swift look around the waiting room, and put an arm through Jaime's. On the platform she made the porter sort out the

34

luggage. Some bags were to be taken back and checked for the next day's flight to Virginia, while the rest were to go in Armando's car. She sent one porter off with tickets and instructed the others on how to handle the bags that were to stay in Tampa. Armando returned with the car while she was giving these instructions, and he could not help but look impressed.

"Armando, darling," she said, with laughter in her voice, "give them the key to your trunk." When he was out of the car, she took one of his arms and kept him at her side again. "Don't let anyone tell you Latins aren't efficient."

That finally made Armando smile. He realized she held his arm to teach him that only porters carried bags and opened car trunks. She loved seeing the knowledge reflected in his eyes; she smiled and remembering from whom all this came, reached out and pulled Jaime down toward her, kissed him lightly on the cheek, and said, "Aiee, *mi negro!*"

"We'll come back to Tampa later," she explained to Armando, "to visit some more and to take Clara and little Jimmy back . . ." She looked at his brown eyes, resisting her with so much effort, and plunged right in. "And you, too, if you want."

Without giving him a chance to answer, she turned away and motioned to Jaime to take care of the porter who had finished loading the car. Almost as if it were an afterthought, she said in a lower voice to Armando, "Don't think for a minute that I'm letting you go. I've got you now." And with that she disengaged herself from Armando and began to thank the porter who had checked their bags on the Virginia flight and who was now back with her tickets and check stubs.

Little Jimmy grabbed Armando's arm. "I want to sit next to the window," he said. "Can I sit next to the window, Uncle Armando?"

Armando picked him up and carried him happily to the car. Clara followed. "I see you are going to spoil him too," Clara said. Armando turned to answer her and noticed that the bright sunlight showed up layers of green and blue mascara around her eyes; and her lips were too red. "Has anything interesting happened while I was away?" she asked, aware that he was staring.

He shook his head slowly without taking his eyes off her. They were the youngest in the family; they had been very close once—too close.

"Don't you like the way I look?" Clara asked.

"I hear you're getting married again," he said, then playfully threw Jimmy into the car.

Before she got into the car also, Clara held Armando's arm a moment. "Has little Jimmy's father been asking about me?"

Armando shook his head. "I have little occasion to see him."

Elena and Jaime waited until a porter opened a back door on the other side of the car, and that gave Clara a second longer with Armando. "There's no need to talk of it now," she said hurriedly. "You can give me his messages some other time." She took a nail buffer from her bag and sat moving it back and forth over her fingertips.

"Fifteen years!" Elena exclaimed from the back seat when they were all settled. She held on to Jaime's arm, sorry that little Jimmy wasn't also in the back seat with her. "Fifteen years ago this airport was not here. And that highway! Is that the miserable narrow road we used to take to Clearwater Beach?" She leaned forward and put an arm on Armando's shoulder as he approached the highway. "Look, a gray hair! My youngest brother has a gray hair!" She laughed as if it made her happy. "Someday, you'll come back like this and you will know what a strange sensation it is."

Armando looked at her hand and saw a narrow gold bracelet shaped like a snake. The body of the snake was tight around her wrist but its head swung loosely away from the wrist; it had tiny emerald eyes and a ruby tongue. "I was away in the Army for three years," he said, "in the Korean War."

Elena pointed across the highway toward the turquoise bay. "See that part where the land sticks out," she said to Jaime. "Where it's thick with pines and palm trees. They made a movie there once with Lupe Velez. They came all the way from Hollywood to make it here. I was fifteen or sixteen then and I used to wake each morning and say to myself, Lupe Velez is in Tampa, just like me."

"Where, Auntie, where did they make a movie?" little Jimmy asked.

Elena leaned forward, took his head in her hands, and turned it toward the wooded corner of the bay. "There, darling, in that clump of trees. They spent thousands and thousands of dollars to make it."

Clara put the nail buffer back in her bag and looked up at the rear-view mirror. "I was only five years old then," she said. Her nails were dark red, almost black, and she inspected them frequently with a serious, intent gaze.

"Those were the days when Gary Cooper was courting her . . ."

"Who?" Jaime asked. "Clara?"

Elena laughed. "No, no, no! Lupe Velez. Gary Cooper was madly in love with Lupe Velez. He came here to visit her and every day the newspaper had something new and delicious to report. I was beside myself; I'd find excuses to go downtown and walk by the Tampa Terrace Hotel, where they said he was staying. But I never saw him."

Jaime put a hand on her arm. "Lucky for me."

Elena leaned back and held on to him. "Frankenstein would not have looked at me then. I can afford to tell you that now." Delicately she pulled back the snake's head from the bracelet and read the tiny face of the watch it concealed. "I did get to see Lupe Velez and that was much more important. The movie people put up a platform in Tampa Bay Park one Sunday, and all the people connected with the movie were introduced to the public. I went and found to my surprise that Lupe Velez was a lady, not at all the wild girl that she played in the movies. She spoke so sweetly and wore a simple light green dress and was charming and demure. She was absolutely lovely, a revelation to me."

Clara looked straight ahead and spoke loudly. "I never thought Lupe Velez was very beautiful. Someone once told me at a Cuban Club dance that I looked like her. I didn't dance with him again."

"You should have married him," Elena said. "Beauty comes cheap. What was important about Lupe Velez was something else. She was a Mexican girl; she had been nobody; and there she was— a real lady! Even the Americans admired her, though of course all of Ybor City was there to greet her, too." Elena turned to Jaime and put a hand on his knee. "Ybor City, my sweet Negro, is the ghetto where all the Latins live in Tampa."

"How can I forget," Jaime said, "where you were born?"

Little Jimmy climbed on the seat and asked Elena, "Auntie, will I see my father today? I want to see him."

Elena leaned a little forward and paused a moment. "Darling, Uncle Jaime and I will be gone only for two weeks," she said finally. "We will be back before you can miss us." She put a hand on his head and shook it playfully. "If I knew you were going to miss us so much, we would have planned to take you to Virginia."

"Of course you will see your father," Clara said. "Nobody told you you can't."

Elena stared at Clara in the rear-view mirror, and Clara lowered her head with a frightened look. It had been settled that Elena

37

and Jaime were to legally adopt Jimmy if his father went along with
it, and Clara was not to encourage her former husband to see the
boy. Jaime knew how angry Clara's remark had made Elena, and
he pulled her toward him affectionately. In a moment Elena was
laughing again. Armando knew nothing of the arrangement, but he
saw how relieved Clara was to hear Elena laugh; it made him tight-
en with anger.

"Lupe Velez stood in Tampa Bay Park, made a pretty speech,
and then blew a kiss to us all," Elena said, winding up quickly the
story that Jimmy had interrupted. "She was a conquistador!"

Jaime mocked her. "Like Ponce de León?"

Elena took his hand and played with it. "The movie turned out
to be a big disappointment to me. It was called *Hell's Harbor*, and
Lupe Velez played the same wild girl again."

"Ponce de León had his disappointments, too," Jaime said. "He
drowned in your Mississippi, didn't he?"

Armando cleared his throat and spoke to his brother-in-law for
the first time since they had shaken hands. "As a matter of fact,
there is a plaque on a tree in that park commemorating where
Ponce de León met an Indian chief."

"Very interesting," Jaime said politely.

Elena laughed. "No one remembers the Indian chief's name—
only Ponce de León's." They were in the city now, and she was
looking out at the houses. "My God, Michigan Avenue has not
changed. Hell's Harbor is right; it's the same ugly place."

"It does not look so bad, my dear," Jaime said, loud enough for
Armando to hear. "Cuba is no paradise either." He stretched his
legs as much as he could in the back seat of the car. "I think I
would like to soak in a tub of hot water as soon as we get to your
mother's home."

It was while Jaime was in the tub that Elena and Armando
quarreled. Dolores came out of the kitchen, where she had been
keeping Clara and little Jimmy out of the way while Elena and
Armando talked in the living room. Armando had left. "He refuses
to come to Cuba!" Elena said to her mother. "What will Jaime say?
He was prepared to be very generous."

Dolores put her hands together as if in prayer. "Perhaps you
approached him too directly. He is a grown man and he has to be
handled delicately."

38

"Delicately! He tells me that he will not be bossed," Elena said, and smoothed her hair, trying to act indifferent. "Delicately! It's more likely he'd understand a threat at gun's point. He's no young innocent, Mother."

"He'll think better of it, you will see," Dolores pleaded. "I know how men are. You will persuade him yet. I have a presentiment about this."

When Jaime came out of the bath, in a red silk robe, smelling of cologne and pink-cheeked from his shave, they told him Armando had been called away. Elena kept her promise to Dolores to say nothing to Jaime, but holding anything back was so alien to Elena that her constraint was obvious to her husband, and her manner left everyone subdued, even little Jimmy.

Elena held her head high at dinner, turning her face slowly and with great condescension toward anyone who spoke—her indignant-hen look, Dolores had always called it. Elena's new haircut, close-cropped, with wisps of hair straggling on her face, made her seem even more like a bird. It made her eyes, black and almond-shaped like Dolores', even larger, but unfortunately, this cap of hair also enlarged her nose. It was too much like a beak, Dolores decided vindictively, as she watched the meal she had so carefully prepared going unnoticed.

Nothing was said about the chicken soup. To Dolores this was the most potent of soups, so full of nourishment that she, Mina, and Clemencia always made it for their children when they arrived from a trip. She knew the soup would set all the juices flowing again and would bring back to the body all the strength drained from it while away from home. The butcher had sent her a chicken so young and tender that it dissolved in the soup perfectly; no globule of fat floated on the surface. After the soup she set before them black beans and rice. The rice had emerged beautifully, each long grain separate. It was not until she cut the roast eye round of beef that the food began to catch their attention.

"I feel as if I had not left Cuba," Jaime said.

Dolores had stuffed the roast with raisins, olives, and bacon, and when she cut it, the stuffing released a sweet aroma.

"Oh Mama," Clara said, "how delicious that looks. Just a little for me. It will make me fat."

"Grandma," said little Jimmy politely, "you are a good cook."

Tears came to Dolores' eyes. "Thank you, angel," she said. "I cooked it for you."

Elena leaned across the table and patted Dolores' cheek. "And for me too, Mama, because you know I love it."

Elena's good humor made everything right, although Dolores still missed Armando and Elena wished she had him back so she could try again. Still, they knew he'd be back, and whenever Elena looked at her mother, they reassured each other about him. They had just finished dinner when Mina and her son Feliz and his wife arrived, and they all stayed in the living room, talking and embracing. With them, Dolores forgot to think of Armando.

Mina had started Jaime talking about his farm when old Consuelo appeared at the door unexpectedly; there was a doorbell on the front porch, but no one ever used it. Elena did not see Consuelo and so she picked up Jaime's conversation when he paused at the sight of the old woman standing in the doorway. "Farm, he calls it!" Elena said. "It's a *finca* with hundreds of acres."

"Lola, my sister!" old Consuelo called out to Dolores. "Forgive me. I did not know you had company." In a faded gingham dress that reached almost to her ankles, she stood there like a reproach. She lifted her long bony hands to shield her eyes, and the pink palms were startling against the gray folds of skin on her face. "My nieces," she said shyly, and peered around the room.

Dolores crossed herself, but the surprised look on Jaime's face decided her. She got up and went to her. "My dear Consuelo," she said, and extended an arm. Consuelo grabbed it. At her side, Dolores felt how frail Consuelo had become in the last few years. Her hair had finally turned gray but it was as tightly curled as ever—though thinner—and it still looked like bunches of raisins stuck to her head. Once it was her hair that immediately gave her away, but now the thin ashen flesh had become black along the many deep wrinkles. Consuelo was an old Negro woman; there was no denying it.

"Heh, heh, heh!" Little gasps of helpless laughter escaped her. She stopped looking around and finally noticed that Dolores was leading her to a chair. "Thank you, sister," she said, and the tears began to run down her face.

Mina got up determinedly. "Consuelo, you remember me?" Consuelo nodded and stopped crying. "Well, then, let's go into the kitchen and have some coffee." Dolores looked at Mina with admiration for having thought of this solution, and together they led old Consuelo away.

40

"Well!" Elena exclaimed. She put a hand to her head and smoothed down the hair framing her forehead. She looked around the room, first at Feliz, then at his wife, then Clara, and finally at Jaime. "There," she said to him. "Now you know everything about me. I have nothing more to hide."

Jaime looked at her with a smile and waited for an explanation. Clara put down her nail buffer. "It's an interesting story, Jaime . . ."

"Don't tell him," Elena said and laughed.

"Uncle Cheo, after his first wife died, had the influenza during the epidemic and Consuelo was hired to nurse him. She did such a good job that she had a baby by him," Clara said.

"Your very first day in Tampa and you found out everything," Elena said to her husband.

Clara took one last look at the mother-of-pearl polish she had just painted on her nails. "Uncle Cheo didn't marry her, of course, and when he went off to Miami, he left us old Consuelo and her mulatto baby as relatives."

Mina came in from the kitchen and asked her son Feliz for a cigarette. "Poor Consuelo," she said.

"What's the matter with her?" Elena asked harshly. Thinking better of it, she put an arm around Mina. "What would Mother do without you, Aunt Mina!"

"Consuelo has not eaten all day," Mina said. She took the cigarette Feliz gave her and held it to her breast. "Her pension check is more than a week late . . ."

"Oh, oh!" Elena gasped. "Tell Mama to give her money. I'll pay."

Jaime got up. "Señora San Martín," he said to Mina, "please reassure her."

"It is all right," Mina said. Her eyes glistened with tears. "We already gave her some."

"What's the cigarette for?" Feliz asked.

"For Consuelo. She's finished eating, and she likes a cigarette with her coffee." Mina was startled when they all laughed, but in a moment she too, laughed with relief. "Never mind, I intend to smoke panetellas when I get old enough."

Mina returned to the kitchen as if propelled by their laughter. Only Feliz did not laugh; he always felt his mother lacked dignity.

Jaime turned to Feliz. "She's a charming woman, your mother."

Feliz smiled cautiously. He took two cigars from his breast pocket and held one out to Jaime. "Would you like one?"

41

Jaime took the cigar and turned it in his hand, noticing that it had no paper band or cellophane wrapper. "It looks excellent. Is it freshly made?"

Feliz leaned back proudly. "Today fresh from the factory. An old friend of my father brings them to me. They're completely handmade, from the first piece of filler to the leaf wrapper."

Jaime brought it to his face and smelled it carefully. "Havana?"

"Oh yes," Feliz said. "There are still one or two factories that use only Havana tobacco. Not just the wrapper, but the filler, too."

"I see that you know your cigar making," Jaime said politely.

"His father was a foreman at a big factory all his life," Elena said. "He kept the whole family working, thank God."

Jaime turned to Elena and asked, "May I, my dear?"

Elena looked puzzled for a moment. "Of course, of course, you may smoke it in front of us. We are all used to cigar smoke here. It's perfume to us. Isn't that so?" And she turned to Feliz's wife, Teresa.

Teresa was delighted that Elena should ask her. "Oh yes, indeed," she said. "You are so right. It is like perfume to us." She did not look at Feliz because he knew she hated cigar smoke. Feliz had never, however, asked her for permission to light a cigar. Nor would he ever, Teresa thought.

"You're very kind," Jaime said. He hesitated a second and Feliz handed him a wooden match. "Thank you," Jaime said. He neatly punctured the end of the cigar with it.

Feliz did not puncture his cigar with a match. He bit into it and tore a small piece from the end. Then he rolled the end in his mouth, wetting and reforming it. His thick, purplish lips puckered into an O and alternately gripped and let go of the end of the cigar. Having twirled it several times in his mouth, he took it out and looked at it. The end of the cigar was dark with saliva. With his thumbnail he scratched the wooden match until it popped into flame. He put the flame to the cigar first, as if warming it, and still holding the flame at the end of the cigar, he moved the cigar around in his mouth. He twirled it slowly while he puffed and exhaled bluish-gray clouds of smoke.

"Ah!" Feliz said, "in my father's day, the Ybor City factories knew how to make cigars. Alfonso the Thirteenth used to buy Tampa cigars. But the cigar owners didn't know how to advertise, or were too stingy. Instead they began to bring in machines like the

American factories use up North. That was the beginning of the end."

Clara went back to examining her nails, buffing them to a high shine. She did not like gatherings where there was no man who belonged to her.

"This is an excellent cigar," Jaime said.

"Because it's made the way a cigar should be made," Feliz explained, and hoped his mother would stay in the kitchen so he could hold the floor. "It's made by one man from beginning to end. No breaking up the process into bunch-makers who take the bunch, put it into a mold, and press it; and rollers who open up the molds and then wrap an artificially cured leaf—a leaf that has an even green color but no taste around the bunch. No, sir, I won't speak of those machines into which you throw tobacco at one end and even-size brown pieces of rope come out the other! They can't be called cigars. A cigar is an object that a man builds up in his left hand with the help of right hand that knows how to select and place every piece of long filler—I said *long* filler—into the hollow of that left hand." Feliz held out his left hand, half closed, and moved the fingers over the thumb. "That left hand has to know how to shape the cigar and how much pressure to exert on the tobacco to let the cigar burn evenly later. An honest brown leaf that has been carefully selected should be stretched over it and then it will burn like this." He held up his cigar at an angle. "That ash will hang on to the very end if it's a good cigar."

"Bravo!" said Elena.

"I am convinced," Jaime said. "I'm afraid that feeling the way you do, you must not enjoy working in the new factories."

"Oh me!—never!" Feliz said. "I don't work in the factories. I'm in construction. I build houses. Cigar factories are dying. There's no future in them."

"That's a pity," Jaime said. "Elena, you never told me."

"Let them die," Elena said. "They never did anybody any good. The whole town living on cigar making, worrying that in London, New York, and Madrid fat old men with the money to pay for them still wanted to puff handmade cigars!"

Clara looked up vaguely. "I think it's nice that a man smokes a cigar."

Elena looked at her sister Clara and laughed. "I'm sure you do." She studied Clara's sleepy eyes, her long, pointed breasts, her rounded thighs, and ended with a glance at the smooth round calves. "Yes," Elena sighed and turned to Feliz's wife. "We all like men who smoke cigars, don't we?"

Clara moved in her chair. "I wonder if Jimmy is all right."

"He's all right," Elena said quickly. "I kissed him good night, and there wasn't anything more he wanted."

Dolores, returning from the kitchen with Mina and old Consuelo, called out to everyone. "Elena and Jaime are like another set of parents to that boy!"

The men got to their feet, and Elena, arms outstretched, welcomed the three old ladies into the living room. She selected seats for them. "Now, Consuelo, do you remember me?" she asked, after settling her in a chair between Dolores and Mina.

Consuelo's face was alive with happiness. Food and recognition had revived her. Her head bobbed up and down in affirmation.

Elena pointed to Jaime. "This is my husband," she added.

Jaime bowed. "Jaime Campos, your servant."

Old Consuelo nodded and murmured her name under her breath. The others, now the ice was broken, began to talk to Consuelo, and Elena threw herself on the sofa next to Jaime. "I *am* sorry you know she is not a blood relation," she said to him softly.

He looked at her big black eyes. "And why, may I ask, did you want to keep me in ignorance?"

"Because I know about you nice Cuban boys. You like a drop of black coffee in your hot milk."

"It's been a long time since I was a boy."

Elena put a hand on his thigh and breathed into his ear.

"Take care," Jaime said. "I am not that old."

"You're wicked," she said and laughed out loud.

Dolores turned to Elena, delighted to hear her laugh. "We were saying, Elena, that Jaime should feel at home in Ybor City."

Jaime moved forward on the sofa, leaving one arm behind. Elena leaned her body against it. "I already do," he said. Out of sight, his hand slowly moved up and down Elena's buttocks. "I have, in the course of my work, had to read Marti's speeches carefully, and some of the most important of them he delivered here to the Cuban colony. He gave voice in Tampa to very important objectives of the War of Independence." Between forefinger and thumb he pressed the familiar flesh. "So you see, Ybor City, as you call this Latin colony of Tampa, is part of the history of Cuba." He gave one last squeeze. "*Cuba Libre*—that was his slogan, and Cubans everywhere responded."

Something in Elena's satisfied smile irked Clara when she looked up. Why must Elena always insist on giving the impression that she took care of Jimmy? "And now," Clara said, "Cuba Libre is just a rum and Coca-Cola drink."

Aha, Feliz thought, that Cuban has his ladle in several pots. Lucky for Jaime to have two such women in one household.

"I remember Papa talking about it," Clara continued. Everyone looked at her in surprise; she seldom talked, at least not about such topics. "He used to take me to that factory on Sixteenth Street near the Cuban Club. When he was just a young boy, he saw Marti there. Marti stood at the top of the steps and talked, and all the cigar makers emptied their pockets for their Cuban brothers. That's why those speeches were important, because they made Cubans help Cubans."

Elena clapped. "One thing you must say for us Latins, whether Cuban or Spanish or in-between, we are all orators." She looked at Feliz and winked. "Eh?"

"It's true, isn't it?" Clara asked. "That's what Papa told me." She looked around at the others.

"I didn't say it was not," Elena answered. "I guess it is."

Triumphantly, Clara took the nail buffer out of her bag, and with half-closed eyes she returned to her nails. She smiled to herself, remembering that it was Jimmy's father, Esteban, her first husband, who talked like that. A crazy radical, but how he loved me, she thought. He does still, I'm sure.

"We might as well be Cubans," Elena continued. "God knows the Americans in Florida didn't want us."

"More reason to pity them," said Mina.

Elena laughed and with a wriggling motion got off the sofa, excited by the idea. "Look at us here—Teresa, Clara and these wonderful blooming roses—" she pointed at the old ladies. "Nor would I want those American girls to have a chance at these two men!"

She stood in the middle of the room, arms out like an entertainer, and all around her they looked up smiling. Jaime did not quite understand why the North Americans should matter at all, why one should even guess at what they thought of Cubans, either in Cuba or here in Florida; he simply admired his wife's energy and her manner which, he guessed, was very North American, for no proper Cuban matron would act in this way. He congratulated himself; it was like being married to one's mistress.

45

The screen door squeaked and Armando stepped into the room. "I'll drink to that," he said to Elena. Stiff-necked he swept the room with his eyes, then closed them for a moment to regain his balance. "Stay away from American girls; I'll drink to that!"

"I don't think you need a drink." Elena covered her eyes in mock horror, hoping to create a distraction. She was glad Armando was back, but she was afraid he might become maudlin about that American girl who had left him.

"Everybody needs a drink!" Armando threw one arm up oratorically. He saw his mother looking at him with an anxious smile. Next to her, old Consuelo grinned and bobbed her head, her enormous, brilliant false teeth threatening to fall out. He shook his head and saw Teresa. Who is she, he wondered. Oh, Feliz's wife. Third or fourth? His arm fell to his side; he had forgotten what he meant to say.

"He is right." Jaime stood up, put an arm around Armando's shoulder, and together they walked to the dining room. The bottles of liquor and wine were neatly arranged on the sideboard. Feliz immediately left the women and joined them.

"Ah, Domecq Fundador!" Jaime exclaimed.

"The best, only the best," Armando said. He looked at his brother-in-law steadily, then nodded his head. Jaime was all right. All right.

"When it comes to cognac," Feliz said, "it has to be Spanish. The French have been overrated."

Jaime nodded solemnly, wishing Elena could see how well he was acting.

"Oh I admit their wines are better, but everyone knows they have to import the grapes from Spain," Feliz continued. "But even with wines, they have yet to come close to Spanish sherry. Of course, that's only for women."

Elena called from the living room. "Jaime, my sweet Negro, bring me some crème de menthe." She beckoned Feliz's wife to sit with her and Clara. "Talking of American girls, Roberto has married a New York girl, I understand."

Clara looked up. "Jewish?"

Feliz's wife nodded and tittered. "But she's very nice. I don't know her very well . . ."

"She can't be worse than that stupid Georgia cracker Armando married," Clara said.

"Oh no," Elena said. "Jews are very worldly."

Feliz's wife nodded vigorously, hoping to please. "Your aunt likes her very much," she said, and looked at the old ladies in the corner.

Dolores was talking breathlessly across Consuelo to Mina. "There may yet be news about Clara. A young man called her from Cuba as soon as they arrived from the airport. She was not in the house five minutes before the phone rang. He comes from one of the finest families in Cuba."

Mina raised her eyebrows. "Yes?" She looked over at Clara. She poses like a movie actress, she thought. Mina did not like women who spoke so little. It meant they thought too much about themselves.

"She deserves some happiness after her two marriages," Dolores said. "You know what her life with Esteban was like."

"I always liked him," Mina said.

"Everyone did," Dolores said enthusiastically. "He is so *simpatico*. But so wild. Threw up one job after another. Always talking radical politics and disappearing for nights altogether. Distributing leaflets, he said. More likely running after other women. There was talk, you know."

Mina laughed heartily. "I liked Esteban."

"They say at the Cuban Club canteen that he is involved with those foolish rebels in Cuba, buying guns and sending them over on fishing boats."

"Good for him!" Mina said.

Dolores shushed her. She drew a handkerchief from her bosom and fanned herself. "Very foolish. Things are fine there. Elena says so."

"Well," Mina said placatingly, "those men at the Cuban Club no doubt have to think up stories to entertain themselves. They can't just play dominoes all night."

"And Clara's second marriage to that poor boy was a terrible trial to her," Dolores said. "All he had time for were his studies. They really make medical students study too much. Clara might as well have been a widow. He stayed up all night at his desk with his books. The most revealing and expensive pink nightgowns were no help. My dear, Clara spent a fortune on them. You know how well pink goes with her coloring. She would walk up and down before him," Dolores held out one arm languidly, "but nothing happened. She took to smoking cigarettes in order to bend low in front of him for a light, hoping to inflame him. But . . ."

Mina snorted. "He was impotent."

"What? What?" old Consuelo asked.

Dolores put a hand on her arm. "We are talking about Clara."

"Oh Clara!" Consuelo nodded. "Oh yes, Clara . . ."

Dolores breathed heavily and turned her eyes full on Mina. "Do you really think so? I know that's what Elena says, but how can it be? Look at the girl." They turned and looked at Clara. Her right leg, brown and stockingless, was exposed beyond the knee. "Those calves, those buttocks!" Dolores exclaimed. "I am her mother, but I have to admit they make me want to reach out and—"

Dolores stopped abruptly. Jaime stood before them, holding three dainty glasses of liqueur. He had overheard them but gave no sign. "Here is something for you to sip."

After they had shyly taken the glasses from him, he held up a warning finger. "It looks like water, but it has a tangerine flavor you Floridians will like. Like you, too, its looks are deceptive. There is alcohol in it."

Mina looked at him boldly. "Ah, but has it been so well-aged as we?"

Jaime laughed and moved away to the dining room. He had underrated these old ladies, he thought. The black-garbed, middle-class ladies of his mother's family, always in mourning, would never say these things. Was it because these women were working class, or had they inherited the liveliness of the *majas*, those Spanish women in mantillas who threw roses at toreros? Bold, vivacious, eloquent . . . Jaime was jolted out of these thoughts by the sight of Feliz drinking a third jigger of cognac in one gulp. With horror he imagined the fine liquor being flung to the back of the throat and swallowed with the burning sensation any whiskey could have produced.

"A-a-ah!" Feliz slapped Armando. "That will hold me." With a movement of his head he beckoned Jaime toward them. "I was telling the youngster, here, that we all make mistakes with our first women." He made his face solemn and explained. "That is what he was referring to when he came in, you know, when he said he would drink to American girls. That is, to having nothing to do with them. His wife was an American."

Jaime looked politely at Armando. Idiots, Armando thought, that's not why I'm drunk.

"No need to be downhearted; we're men here," Feliz said, encouragingly. "Look at me, I've been married four times. My mother says I've made a hobby of marrying." He stopped to laugh. When Mina had said it he had left the house in anger. "So you can say I've made at least three mistakes."

He poured another cognac and held the jigger poised. "Embarrassment was the cause of my first marriage. In those days there was a dance every Saturday night at the Centro Asturiano— my old man was Asturian, you know—and that night I wore my first white linen suit. Every girl in the place gave me the eye, but Onelia interested me most of all. It was her prominent breasts that attracted me. I was eighteen and breasts were very important. Anyway, I had a job persuading her to spend an intermission with me in my old man's car. I had parked it behind the Centro, where it's dark, with this thought in mind. Actually, she was very stiff and little happened. It was all very awkward, just a few kisses after much begging. Getting out of the car—I was holding the door open she stumbled and brushed against my leg. I didn't give it a thought. Two minutes later, we walked onto the canoe floor and every man in the place knew. God knows how many others! I had to go home immediately. Right on the fly of my linen pants there was a bright smear of Onelia's lipstick!"

"Marvelous! Marvelous!" Jaime exclaimed.

Feliz nodded, threw back his head, and swallowed the cognac.

Armando was so groggy he had not really been able to listen; he just nodded foolishly, but a noise at the front door revived the whole suspense of the day. The look of expectation on his face made Feliz and Jaime turn toward the living room. Clemencia had arrived with Robert and Shirley. Armando recognized them right away, and now he was hopelessly awake and jumpy again.

Jaime and Feliz left him in the dining room, and he hung back a moment. Maybe he should go over to Walliché's now. How long could he stay away without it seeming really suspicious? He looked toward the back of the house; he could leave through the kitchen and not be seen. The noise of individual greetings reached him from the living room like a series of explosions. He swallowed a drink of cognac the same way Feliz had, and, sober again, he went to join the others. He had told Walliché he would be with his family; there was no reason to worry; it made sense.

"I'll be right back. I've got gifts for everybody," Elena said on her way to the dining room.

"Elena, Elena," Mina called, "you should not have done it."

Elena was already out of the living room, near Armando, but she turned around and answered Mina. "Never mind. Now that I can afford it, I do everything I always wanted to do." She turned back again to head for the bedroom. There was a happy smile on her face when she bumped into Armando, and she threw an arm around him and kissed him.

She dragged Armando with her to the bedroom. "Help me," she said. "And don't mind me. Forgive me for fighting with you. Of course, you must do what you want. I'm just bossy, that's all."

"I like bossy women," Armando said, and smiled because he'd suddenly discovered the way to act with her. "You're my favorite sister," he added.

They were alone in the front bedroom. On the bed, thrown open was one of her long, leather suitcases. "My little baby," she said. 'That's what you used to say when you were a kid. 'My favorite sister!' It used to make me so happy. Why, why don't you let me help you? Never mind, don't listen to me. I *am* very bossy."

He shook his head. "As soon as I find a girl like you," he said, "I'll marry her."

She came away from the suitcase and gave him another kiss. "See these," she said, and held out a group of neckties. "They're Italian, of the best silk. That's for the men. For the women, French perfume. In Cuba they make only sugar, but there is nothing in the world that you can't get in Havana. It's the age of gold."

She led him into the living room, she carrying the ties, he the boxes of perfume. The others had begun to settle down. Dolores, Mina, and Clemencia were sitting near the dining room; Consuelo was at the other end of the living room, where she blinked and smiled at Robert and Shirley, one of whom she did not know and the other she did not recognize. When Mina turned to exclaim at the things Elena was carrying, Clemencia first noticed Consuelo.

"Oh, there is old Consuelo," Clemencia sad to Dolores. "How nice of you to invite her, Lola. Since her son died, she has been all alone in that furnished room."

"Don't you find her aged?" Dolores whispered, ashamed to say that she had not invited Consuelo.

Clemencia looked at Consuelo again and nodded.

Dolores' eyes brightened. "Really, tell me, don't you think she looks like a cockroach? I know it is very bad of me to say so, but when I look at her, that is what I think of. That wispy mustache . . . really, it is like the feelers of a cockroach!"

A startled laugh escaped Clemencia. She looked at Consuelo again and saw, to her horror, that there was a resemblance. "I must speak to her," she said in a strangled voice, ashamed to have laughed. Dolores squeezed Clemencia's hand and let her go across the room to Consuelo. With an indulgent smile on her face, Dolores watched Clemencia hesitate a moment and then, overcoming her distaste, kiss Consuelo. Dolores turned to Mina, who was at her side. "My dear, I wonder if you realize that our Roberto gets his sensitivity, his artistic gifts from Clemencia. He does, you know."

Mina sat up straight in her chair. "You old fool," she said. "Did you just discover that? Who did you think he got it from? You?"

Dolores smiled to herself, and with one hand tapped Mina's arm reprovingly. They settled back to watch Elena go around the room distributing the ties and the perfume.

Elena stopped before she got to Shirley and Robert. "You must forgive me. I'm acting like a Santa Claus." There was a look of doubt on her face; she was unused to hesitating.

Shirley recognized the look. She knew it well: the fear of rejection, something she did not expect to find among Latins. "You must not stop now," she said. "I don't want to be left out." She put out her hands, took the box, and exclaimed, "I *thought* it was Chanel! I've never had any. I know it only from ads."

"Oh yes, Elena, yes," Feliz's wife called out. "It's wonderful!"

Elena turned from one to the other. "Really? You like it?" She smiled happily. "It's nothing. We decided to go on vacation so suddenly I didn't have time to get something different for everyone."

"No, no," Teresa insisted. "This is perfect."

"And look at those ties," Mina said. "All these men are going to be as handsome as gigolos."

"These men! These men!" Elena made a gesture as if she were embracing them all. "The older they get, the handsomer they become."

"Don't tell them," Mina said.

"In Cuba the women know how to manage them," Elena said. "They wear their dresses tight and drench themselves in perfume. At every gathering the air is so thick with delicious odors that the men are as powerless as drowsy flies. You can just reach out and get one."

Boldly, Mina took her up. "Is that how she got you, Jaime?" she asked Elena's husband.

"Oh I couldn't even fly," Jaime explained, gallantly waving the hand holding the cigar. "I was underfoot, waiting to be swatted—by her, of course."

"Don't believe him," Elena said. "I worked like a dog to get him. And now I've got him, I'm not letting him go."

There was a loud burst of laughter, and as it died down Armando asked, "Drinks? Let me get you drinks." He felt so good he could even look at Shirley and Robert, sure that she would not have told Robert how he'd acted that afternoon.

"Oh that's nice of you, sweetheart," Elena said. She perched on the arm of the sofa near Shirley and Robert. "I should have brought one of the maids to help here, even if Jaime and I are only spending a day and then going on to Virginia. There's still Clara and Jimmy staying behind, and Mama can use the help. It was foolish to stop myself, but I didn't want to startle the neighborhood. You can imagine what they'd say—that I was putting on airs."

"My dear, there were other problems," Jaime said. Everyone listened, not knowing how to comment. "We must not let your mother think that we put our vanity before her well-being."

"How can I help adoring him?" Elena asked everyone. "Doesn't he speak beautifully? Because of him, the President speaks as well. Every president for the last twenty years has spoken beautifully for the same reason. If Jaime didn't write their speeches they couldn't stay in office. The President just won't let him retire."

Clara raised her eyes and, finding no one in the room who interested her particularly, addressed herself to me whole gathering. "Elena couldn't bring a maid because they are all colored, and not one of them would come here or to Virginia. You can't treat Negroes in Cuba the way they are treated here. Isn't that so?"

Some looked at old Consuelo, others at Elena. "Yes, that's right," Elena finally said. "It wouldn't be so bad here in Ybor City, but in Virginia . . . well, you know how Negroes have to act there."

"Yes, I know," old Consuelo suddenly said. "These American Negroes are terrible, terrible. When I see one go by it makes my soul shrivel and I want to say an *Ave Maria*. They are bad, bad; they will do anything." Her voice began to crack and she paused a moment and began again loudly. "And to think that when my son Reymundo was alive—may-he-rest-in-peace—they turned him away from a Cuban Club dance right here in Ybor City. They thought he was one. In his native town they mistook him for one! Oh it was a terrible night. I remember when he came home." The tears began to run into the wrinkles of her face. "He told them, I am a Villanueva, you have made a mistake . . ." Consuelo spread her hands out in front of her and let them drop into her lap. "But it was no use his talking. They did not let him in."

"Oh Consuelo, my dear, my dear!" Dolores got up and went to the old woman with arms outstretched. "Don't torture yourself, my dear. The world is a harsh place and we must put up with it." She embraced Consuelo and stood by her. Mina came over also, and Clemencia brought a glass of water. The old women talked rapidly, not giving Consuelo a chance to recollect her sorrows.

"We all loved Reymundo, you know that," Mina said, and although the tears continued to trickle for a moment, Consuelo was soothed.

Jaime turned to those around him and, in a confiding voice that the old women could not hear, continued the conversation. "In Cuba, as you know, one has to be careful. The President himself is the subject of all kinds of rumors when it comes to this. He looks as if he may have Chinese blood in him, and many say that his family picture is tarred by all kinds of brushes, but as a Cuban poet of questionable politics said in a charming verse, when the bongo drums sound in Cuba there is hardly anyone in the island who doesn't respond with his very blood."

"It's like jazz in me United States," Robert said. "The whole world thinks of jazz when America is mentioned, but it was the Negroes who gave us that." He suddenly realized that Jaime had not been talking about Cuban culture.

"Shirley," Elena said. "I have a feeling your husband is going to talk politics. I want a chat with him." She got up and took Robert's hand and pulled him from his seat. "I'm taking him away. Jaime, you talk to Shirley about Cuba. She has never been there. Wouldn't she be a success walking down a Havana street—with that fair coloring!" She threw up an arm and blew Shirley a kiss. "The sayings they would call after you! Cubans even have a special word for that, *piropos*."

Elena took Robert to the dining room and poured out two drinks. "Scotch, for you," she said, and handed it to him.

"With water," Robert said, and went to the kitchen for it.

Elena followed him. "With water?" She laughed and looked him up and down.

"What's the matter?"

"Nothing, nothing. Scotch and water. That shows how far behind you've left Ybor City, you don't drink whiskey straight."

"I don't know. Ybor City has left me behind. I'm still working at the grocery store where I used to deliver groceries as a kid. It was a cooperative then, forty cigar makers owned it. Now one of them owns the whole thing, and on the side he plays the stock market."

"Listen to you! You speak English without a Spanish accent."

Robert sipped his drink. There was too much to say.

"So you stayed in New York and married a Jewish girl"—she looked at him mischievously—"probably the only one without money." She saw the shocked look on his face and laughed and patted him on the arm. "I have nothing against Jews."

"I have nothing against money," Robert said. "It's a great problem-solver."

"Absolutely!" Elena took his arm and walked him to the back porch. "It never occurs to me any more that someone I meet may be thinking of me as a Cuban nigger, the name the Americans used to call us poor Latins. Instead, I can see them thinking that I'm someone it pays to be nice to because Jaime is in a position to bring their affairs to the attention of the President."

They sat in aluminum chairs, their backs to the light from the kitchen, and looked out into the night. "How's that?" Robert asked.

"Well . . ." Elena paused a moment. "Say some American businessman wants to sell potatoes in Cuba. It may require a presidential dispensation to allow them to be imported, or it has to go through the Ministry of Commerce. Jaime can see to it that the application doesn't stay at the bottom of the pile somewhere. We're going to some swank resort in Virginia tomorrow. Well, we're guests of a businessman, of course, and I can tell you any of the big families here in Tampa would be delighted to be introduced to me there." Elena chuckled and looked at him. "Especially in the dresses I'm going to wear."

"It must give you a kick to remember that you come from this side of Nebraska Avenue in Tampa," Robert said.

"Roberto, my boy, they would be delighted to cross over to Ybor City to see Jaime and me if they knew we were here," she said firmly, like a schoolteacher. "People with money are very democratic; they're ready to be friends with anyone with money. What's more, that businessman would love to get invited to our country place in Cuba, probably more than I want to go to Virginia."

54

Robert turned and looked at her. "Don't he angry, but what—what fun do you get out of it?" She looked at him in the dim light, and he held her gaze. "A bunch of rich old bores, aren't they?"

Elena smiled indulgently. "Except for one's family, poor people aren't more interesting than rich ones. Much less, as a matter of fact. How the rich made their money is much more entertaining than how the poor stayed poor. Believe me, I'm happy now and I'm not protesting too much, either. I say this because I have the feeling you disagree with me, and also because I'm a bossy type. I want all my family to follow suit, and you're my cousin, don't forget." She finished her drink. "The only thing Jaime and I lacked was children and now Jimmy—Clara will get another husband and she won't want Jimmy. She's a fool, but of course you know that."

She turned to him for agreement, but he could think of nothing to say.

"What fun do you think it was for me to be a bilingual secretary in New York? You remember . . ."

Robert nodded and smiled.

"Don't laugh at me," Elena said. "After that experience in New York, I was through being a poor Latin girl. The men I could meet in New York wouldn't marry me. They'd keep me, all right, but they wouldn't marry me."

Robert had finished his drink, and he felt uneasy. "They wouldn't marry me either," he said. He got up with a laugh, ready to go inside.

"I'm not through yet," she said. "I'm like your older sister, you know. You haven't told me anything about yourself, but I can tell. You're here—no money, two kids—working in a grocery store. Don't turn down my offer like my brother Armando."

"What offer?" he asked, surprised.

"Come to Cuba," she said, "as the travel posters say. We have a *finca*, several hundred acres of sugar cane, a big, big house and grounds with fruit trees and walks and flowers, and God knows what else. We need someone to manage it."

"Me?" He could not believe the offer would come just like that.

"You don't have to know anything about farming. All you have to do is deal with the American sugar people. They are the ones who take care of the sugar cane. Everything else is a matter of common sense and seeing that things get done. I have to be in Havana with Jaime all week, and when we are out at the *finca* for weekends, we don't want to do anything but relax. Well?"

He turned the glass in his hand and looked away. "You are very generous, Elena."

"Of course I am, but I'm offering it to you, and you're family, so it has nothing to do with generosity. You and Armando are the only ones who don't seem set. The others all know they can come to me if they want help, but they have jobs that seem to satisfy them. Anyway, you do need to do something else. It's obvious. Don't tell me you're doing what you want to do."

"No, I'm not," Robert said. "But I didn't come down here to stay."

Elena got up. "Well for God's sake, why don't you say yes and we'll celebrate. I don't understand all this hesitating. When something good comes by, you grab it. We're only going to be here until tomorrow morning and then in two weeks we'll stop by again on the way back to pick up Jimmy and Clara."

She held her empty glass away from her and with the other hand straightened her dress. Robert was afraid he had offended her. "Elena, old girl," he said, "you make me feel like a little boy. I appreciate what you're offering me. Let me discuss it with Shirley. All right?"

"I don't understand," Elena said. "Tell me, why does my brother Armando turn me down? Why does he prefer to hang around that small-town gangster? Forget that I'm his sister and that maybe he resents me and likes to think that I want to boss him around, but, my God, anyone would jump at the chance!"

"I don't really know Armando," Robert said. "It's another generation, even if he's only ten years younger."

"Oh you too, you too," Elena said, still exasperated. "You don't respond with eagerness either." They were standing close to each other, and she reached out and grabbed his sleeve. "What have you been doing in New York all these years? Mama says you're an artist and a Communist and a Socialist. An idealist, she says. Well, why aren't you a practicalist?"

Robert laughed.

"You know what I mean. If you're an artist, why aren't you selling paintings instead of groceries?"

"It's not so simple," Robert said.

"Very well. If you're interested in politics, why aren't you a politician? I refuse to believe that you're one of those ordinary people who do nothing. I don't care what people think of the President in Cuba. Jaime's family, you know, is very snobbish about him. He doesn't come from the right kind of people, they think. More power to him, I say. He was only a sergeant in the army, but look at him now!"

"If you put it that way you're right, of course," Robert said.

"What other way is there to put it? Tell me."

"Maybe there is no other, but things just don't happen that way. You ask me what I've been doing in New York for twenty years. Well, I'll tell you, even if I resent your asking me."

"Resent? Why do you resent it? Am I a stranger?"

"I guess because I'm a little envious that I haven't done as well as you, that I'm not a success. That's what the great pressure is, you know. I want it, too. I want very much to be a success now, believe me. Sometimes I think even my wife wants me to be a money-maker."

"Don't kid yourself," Elena said, "every wife wants that."

"Well, all right. But I was telling you what I did in twenty years. I went to New York when I was seventeen. I got a job and met a lot of artistic and political young people, and so I got excited about ideas and girls, although I spent most of my time just working to make a living. That went on until the war. So you can put down three or three-and-a-half years to screwing."

Elena laughed. "Three-and-a-half years?"

"All right, all right . . . Then came the war, and for four years I had an exciting time. I'm ashamed to say I enjoyed it. When I came out I met all my old friends, all left wing and still interested in every-thing. I went to art school for a year. It was difficult. I had always talked art and never really practiced it. I was in my middle-twen-ties. I met Shirley and we got married. The job I got in a commercial art studio was not bad-paying. I drew hands and feet all day for mail-order catalogues. I enjoyed the marriage and the kids, and then—you know—the Red scare. I had always talked like a Communist, and when the studio decided to stop dealing with the union I was fired. I couldn't get commercial art jobs, partly because I wasn't good enough, and so I took jobs in department stores as a salesman. And that's how people don't make money. What bothers me is that my ideas have always been so big, and such good ones, too, really, and yet I haven't done anything myself. In three years I'll be forty . . . I'm afraid the truth is that I'm just not talented."

"Nonsense!" Elena said. She slipped her arm through his and walked him to the kitchen. "You're smart. You've got to set your mind on something and you'll do well. Then you can spend your spare time painting, like my mother spends hers writing poetry."

Elena misunderstood his bitter laugh. "I mean it," she said. "With money, everything is possible. Jaime plans to retire soon; that's why we've been trying to put away as much money during the last few years as possible, and why not? Everyone is doing it. Anyway, Jaime plans to write a book on the Indians of Cuba. Don't ask me any details—it's over my head—but I'm sure it's very worthwhile, like your painting."

Robert felt depressed and drained. "I know we're cousins," he said, "but we'd better go back or they'll think there's incest going on."

"Oh if you can talk like that you'll be a great success in Cuba," Elena said. "But before you go back in there, promise me you'll not forget our conversation."

"Very well," he said.

"You have two weeks," she repeated. "Remember."

"In two weeks," he said.

Elena did not hear him. She had caught sight of the men at the sideboard. "I'm breaking this up," she said, and took Armando and Jaime away.

Feliz watched her, his face flushed, his eyes shining. "Her flesh still looks firm," he said to Robert. "My wife tells me that she goes to the beauty parlor every day to get her breasts massaged."

"Feliz, I've been meaning to thank you," Robert said, "for offering to build the room. Aunt Mina told me last night."

"Oh, not at all," Feliz said.

"But there's no need. We're not staying."

"I didn't think you would," Feliz said. He gripped Robert's shoulder. "Let's have a drink. You don't belong in a small town, I always said that. Back to New York, eh?"

Robert didn't answer because his Aunt Mina called them into the crowded living room, and Feliz always immediately did anything his mother asked.

Dolores was standing in front of her chair, and when she saw Feliz and Robert come in, she held out her tiny cordial glass to make a toast. "Now that I see you all before me, I wish I had written a poem to tell you how I feel having you all here for this one night. But no words can tell you what an old woman thinks when she sees her children grown and in the flower of life . . . And when we look at you, we think of those who are not here: my son, Cheo, and his wife and children, all alone in Chicago; my Mario and his wife and children in Miami; and Clemencia's Alice and Julian and their families who are also there. How I hope that they are together tonight and thinking of us . . . the way we old women always think of them."

"Are they the only ones missing?" Elena asked. "It seems to me we were more. I remember big crowds when we got together."

Dolores took out her handkerchief. "Yes, dear, there were more. I don't forget them. I don't want to see anyone cry tonight. No, not a tear. Remember. But I want to drink too to your fathers. Mina, my darling, to your generous Claudio. Clemencia, to your great-hearted Bernardo. And to my own sweet Serafín. Children, children, let me tell you unashamedly that your mothers loved your fathers and had we not you to live for, we would hasten to join them in a better world. Mine was a Cuban, Mina's an Asturian, Clemencia's a Galician; but like all of us here, they belonged to the family of Latins." She stopped a moment and looked around the room until her eyes fell on Shirley. "Someone translate for her."

"There's no need." Shirley announced. She turned to Robert. "Next year in Jerusalem, right?"

"Shirley, my dear, your people, too, are from the Mediterranean, and it is proper that through your children's veins should course the blood of sister races that have often mingled in the past." Dolores' breath was short but no one wanted to stop her. She held out a warning hand as if she expected that they might. She brought it down and held out the glass to finish her toast. "I drink to us all here. We are one big family. We are all the children of Cervantes . . ."

Dolores stopped when she heard the police sirens. It was on the street outside that they sounded, slowly dying down as the cars passed the house, leaving everyone in the room quiet. Then they heard people calling to each other in the street. Armando was the first out of the house; Feliz followed him; but the rest hung back, then straggled worriedly out to the porch. Feliz came back alone, his eyes popping with the news.

"My God!" he announced, "they found Walliché dead in his house!"

"Murdered, most likely," Mina said.

Everyone looked at Feliz. He nodded. It was true.

V

"Dead?" Dolores covered her face and shivered. "Armando! My boy! Where has he gone?"

"Call him back, Feliz," Mina ordered, but Feliz was gone again. Involuntarily, she took Dolores' wrist to feel her pulse, as she noticed pale blotches appearing like danger signals on Dolores' face. "Someone, get Armando."

"No, no," Dolores decided. "Armando must go. It's only right." She sat back heavily in her chair and moved her head from side to side. Spittle foamed at the corners of her lips when she spoke. "And Walliché's flowers are still in the room. He sent them this morning."

"Ah, ah," Mina murmured.

Clemencia shook her head, afraid that Mina was exciting Dolores.

Dolores took out her handkerchief. "Then, it's only a short time since he. . . *aie!*" The handkerchief dropped from her hand and her head fell back on the chair.

Robert picked up a newspaper and moved toward Dolores to fan her with it, but his mother and Mina blocked his way. Mina held Dolores' head and Clemencia waved a handkerchief to give her air. He didn't seem to be needed there, so he started out to the porch to see what was happening. He laughed when he thought that he was acting just like Feliz, and he noticed that his laugh startled Elena. He stood in the doorway of the porch and looked back into the living room.

Beyond Elena, Robert saw Mina wave an arm at Clara and call out, "The nitroglycerin pills are in the bathroom." Clara looked at her mother, dropped the ever-present nail buffer, and ran to the bathroom.

Jaime leaned forward and grabbed Elena's arm. "My dear," he said, his voice harsh and impatient, "what is your brother involved in? Who murdered this man, Walliché?"

For a disoriented moment, Jaime's fear thrilled Robert. Could Armando have killed Walliché? Was this the reason the room had

60

become so quiet at the news of his death? He let the screen door slam behind him and bumped into Shirley on the porch. Together, they heard Elena's reply, "Don't be a fool! What are you imagining?"

"They are all terribly upset," Shirley said quietly.

"Yes, yes," Robert answered distractedly. "Go in and help Dolores. I'm going to see what's doing with Armando."

The street was filled with police cars, and in front of every house there were people on the sidewalk talking to others on the porches. Robert walked into the middle of the street and looked toward Walliché's house on the corner. The high dark hedge surrounding it looked black; only at the gate, in the middle of the hedge, was there a crowd. They were looking at the bright lights in the house and grounds.

A car turned into the street and caught Robert in its headlights. It moved slowly, and he leaned against a parked police car to let it go by, for the street was narrow. He held his breath as the car drove toward him, feeling momentarily cornered. It had happened to him once in New York nineteen years ago; Barcelona was falling to the Fascists, and, along with a group of young people who had been demonstrating before the Spanish consulate, he had been chased to the subway entrance by mounted policemen. He had not made it to the stairs and had had to squeeze himself against the sidewalk railing. He had looked up at the rearing horses, expecting them to come down on him with their hooves, and heard, as if they were his own, the screams of women.

"Roberto!" the man at the wheel of the car said. "Roberto, I heard you were in Ybor City." He spoke in Spanish and squinted through horn-rimmed glasses at Robert. "It's you! You don't remember me."

"Yes, yes," Robert said lamely, and then remembered. "Esteban?"

Esteban nodded. "I'll give you another clue. Clara's first husband, little Jimmy's father."

"Of course, of course." Robert stepped to one side to show he was in a hurry.

"And what are you doing back in Tampa?" Esteban asked, ready to talk.

"That's a long story," Robert said. "Right now I'm busy . . ."

From the parked car, a policeman spoke in English to Esteban. "All right, mister, you can't park here."

"Listen, all I want to know now is about Jimmy," Esteban said. "Is it true he's here with his mother?"

Robert nodded and looked at the police car, eager to get away.

Esteban kept his eyes on Robert, ignoring the police. "Is she up? Were you just there?"

"Yes," Robert said hesitantly. "But—"

"But what?" Esteban insisted. "Has she got a new man with her?"

"No, it's not that," Robert said. "Just now isn't the best time." He moved his head around to point out to Esteban the extraordinary activity on the street. "Don't you know what has happened?"

Irritated, the policeman called out again. "Okay, friend, time to move on."

Esteban put out an arm and held Robert by his belt buckle. "Why would they care? What have they got to do with this gangster getting his—" He broke off and struck himself on the forehead. "Of course, the fool—" Esteban looked quickly at the police car. "Her brother!"

Robert put a finger to his lips.

"No need to worry about these big-balled boys," Esteban said, nodding toward the police car. "One thing you can count on is they haven't bothered to learn Spanish."

The policeman stuck his head out of the car window. "All right, Mac. Get on with it." He kept staring at Esteban, waiting for some response.

Esteban still paid no attention to the officer. "And Jimmy is with her, right?"

"He's asleep," Robert said. "I'll see you another time. I must go."

"I'll see, I'll see," Esteban said. He put the car in gear, turned his face to the police car and grinned idiotically. "No speak English," he said, and pulled away noisily in low.

"Your friend can't speak English," the policeman called out to Robert, "but he sure can speak one mess of Spanish. You Latins sure talk a lot."

Robert walked away from him and moved on to the sidewalk by the hedge. A hand tapped him on the shoulder. It was Feliz; his eyes were wide with fear. "Where's Armando?" Robert asked.

"Who was that in the car?" Feliz questioned. "Who were you talking to?"

"Clara's first husband, Esteban. Why?"

"Another madman!" Feliz's voice was hoarse with impatience and the need he felt to whisper. "He's mixed up with the Cuban rebels. Stay away from him."

"Some other time tell me about him," Robert said. "What's happened with Armando? They're worried about him at the house."

"I know for certain that Esteban is raising money for the rebels," Feliz insisted. "I don't know why we are mixed up in all this. Let's go back to Dolores' house."

"But we came to be of help to Armando," Robert reminded him, feeling warm toward Feliz for the first time. "Where is he?"

"I don't see Armando from one year's end to the other," Feliz said. "Why should I be with him now? Now, when it will do no one any good to be hanging around Walliché's house! We shouldn't be seen here!" He pumped his arms as if they were his legs taking him away from the scene. "There are people in Ybor City who have long memories. The months go by and then—poom, poom—they shoot you down right at your doorstep."

Robert shook his head. "Come now, man."

"Listen to me, Roberto. You've been up in New York where such things don't happen. But this is Tampa!"

Robert put a hand on his arm. "What happened to Armando?" he asked.

"He went into Walliché's house with a couple of detectives," Feliz said calmly, as if he had been slapped. "He must be mixed up in it in some way; what did you expect?" He shook his head from side to side. "I'm sorry, I'm not playing this hand. I'm going back to the house. I've got to take the women home."

"Okay," Robert agreed, glad to be rid of him. "Tell them I'll be back as soon as I know something." He saw Feliz start to turn away as if released from a trap. "Detectives?" Robert held him. "How do you know—if they were in plain-clothes?"

Feliz stopped only long enough to explain. "Everybody knows them," he said impatiently. "They're as bad as racketeers. They're detectives like you and me; they couldn't detect an eclipse of the sun at midday."

Robert turned his back on Feliz and walked to the gate. A policeman stood in the shaft of light that cut onto the sidewalk from the floodlit yard. He made a move to stop Robert from entering.

"I don't want to go in," Robert said. "I'm waiting for a relative who's inside."

"What?" the officer said.

"There he is." Robert nodded toward the house. Armando had come out, followed by a plain-clothesman. The detective took Armando's arm and they stopped to talk.

"Oh," the policeman said to Robert. For a moment he and Robert watched the other two under the bright lights. "Just like a night ball game," he went on, ready to chat.

Everything looked all right to Robert. The plain-clothesman seemed to be talking casually to Armando, and Armando nodded just as easily. As they drew close, the plain-clothesman said, "Like they say, it's more a question of formality, but every little bit helps."

"Armando," Robert called, alarmed at what he heard. "You don't have to answer any questions."

The detective looked sharply at the policeman at the gate, then at Robert "Who are you, mister?"

Robert ignored the detective. "Armando," he tried again. "You have a right to a lawyer."

Armando looked too startled to speak.

The detective moved between Armando and Robert. "You from around here?" He brought a hand to one hip. "Why are you talking lawyers? Who asked you?"

"I don't have to tell you—" Robert began, and then stopped when he saw the detective's face scowling.

"He's my cousin, Casper," Armando finally said.

Casper moved back a step. "Well, that's different now. He just didn't sound like he was from around here."

Armando suddenly burst into talk. "His name's Robert Moran. I bet you know him, Casper." Armando's accent became Southern as he talked. "Robert went to Patrick Henry High School."

"Well, for Christ's sake!" Casper said, and turned to Robert. "I'm Casper Friend. Remember? We was classmates at Patrick Henry." He offered Robert his hand. "Long time, no see."

Confused, Robert took it, feeling queasy. It was strange to be shaking a cop's hand.

Casper pumped Robert's hand and, without letting go, turned to Armando. "You know this boy and me both tried out for the football team. And you know what? We none of us made it!" He laughed heartily. "Yes sir, yes, yes."

"Yes, yes," Robert echoed, trying to think of a way to get Armando away from there.

"Say, let's not stand here," Casper said. He playfully pulled them along the sidewalk until they were close to the police car.

"Look, Bob," Casper explained, "Armando is just coming along with me to the station so's we can take down his statement That's all. Isn't that so, Armando?"

Armando nodded, but did not look at Robert. He had fallen silent again.

"Well, Casper, I just wonder if that's necessary," Robert said, listening to his own speech take on Casper's pattern. "You know he's not mixed up in it. He doesn't know—he *can't* know anything about it because he's been home all evening."

Casper listened to him professionally, not showing if he agreed, only keeping his eyes on Robert. With Casper looking steadily at him Robert found that the force seemed to be going out of his voice, and he stopped talking when he saw Casper had not been moved.

"Why sure, sure," Casper said reasonably. "Of course, Armando's not mixed up in it. But it wouldn't look good, would it, if he didn't cooperate with the authorities? I understand of course, but that's 'cause him and me are old friends. Anyway, there's nothing to worry about. Armando wants to see we all do well by Wally Chase. He was a good old egg, and we're going to do our best by him."

Casper put a hand on Armando's shoulder. "Isn't that so, boy?"

Armando nodded.

"The way I see it, anyway, it must have been because of a personal feud," Casper said. "Otherwise he wouldn't have been cut up this way.

"You ask Armando here," Casper continued. "We played lots of poker with old Wally, but it wasn't easy inside to identify him." He gestured over his shoulder to the house. "Whoever did it sure worked him over. It was done with a knife, sure sign of a personal feud. If there's a bullet in him, the medical officer is going to have one hell of a time finding it. That was some mess!" He leaned down suddenly and ran his hand along the cuff of his right trouser leg.

Robert involuntarily strained to see what Casper was wiping off his cuffs, but only saw Armando bring his hands together to control their trembling.

Casper pulled himself up, looked at the two of them coldly, and in a stern voice said, "We got to get going." With one hand he pointed to the police car and with the other he took Armando's arm.

Robert felt checkmated. "I'm coming with you," he announced in a strangled, small boy's voice.

"Oh hell, man, you can't do that," Casper said. He pulled open the back door of the police car and, without looking at Robert, motioned to Armando to get in. "This car can only take people on official business."

"I'm coming in my own car," Robert announced. "I'll wait for you outside the . . . station, Armando."

Casper's voice began to sound impatient. "We'll drive him back, too," he said. "No need to bother yourself."

"No, I'll come wait for him." He turned to Armando. "Okay?"

Casper looked from one to the other and shrugged his shoulders. "Suit yourself." Armando nodded to Robert and got into the car without looking back. A smile broke out on Casper's face. "Well, Bob," he said, extending a hand, "take care of yourself now, hear? I remember you all right—used to wonder how you could be Spanish with a name like Robert Moran."

"It's Spanish, all right," Robert said.

"I know, I know. That's what you used to say." Casper got into the car beside Armando and closed the door.

Just as the car started up, Armando leaned across Casper and said good-bye to Robert. "I'll see you later," he said, but it sounded more like a request than a promise.

Robert saw Casper frown. "I'll wait for you in my car," Robert promised loudly over the sound of the police car's engine, and started back to the house.

He walked fast, his head down, as if he were in New York, to keep the groups on the sidewalk from stopping him to ask questions. Shirley was waiting on the porch steps, and he shook his head to show that he didn't want to talk until they were inside; but there was an argument going on in the living room, so they stood together for a moment on the porch.

"Armando is in some kind of trouble," he told her. She put a hand on his chest, and he added, "Maybe not . . ."

Inside, Elena argued loudly with Clara in Spanish. "You are responsible; you don't interest yourself in what the boy eats."

"Listen, honey," Robert said to Shirley, "I promised Armando to pick him up at the police station . . ."

"Did they arrest him?" She bit her lips. "Don't tell the old ladies."

"Oh no, nothing like that, they just wanted to talk to him. Just to get information . . . Anyway, that's what they say."

Shirley nodded. "Don't worry about me. Mother and I will either stay here for a while or go back to the house on our own. Don't worry."

Together, they went inside. Clara sat by herself, refusing to look at Elena, who paced the living room angrily. Little Jimmy lay on the sofa, and Jaime sat at his side, rubbing the boy's stomach.

"Let him turn over, Jaime, and he'll lie on his stomach," Elena said to her husband.

"No, please, Auntie," Jimmy said. "I want to see everybody. It's not fair."

Elena knelt in front of him and hugged him. "My baby, darling, darling, of course." She grabbed his head and kissed his cheeks. "Jaime, rub his stomach."

"It's nothing Jimmy ate. Don't blame yourselves," Clemencia called from the door of the bedroom. "It's the water, the change from Cuba here. All the minerals are different and they affect the stomach. I shall never forget how I suffered on my honeymoon because of the change of water—though we only went to Sarasota." She stopped when she saw her son Robert in the doorway,

Elena saw her look and turned to Robert. "Isn't Armando with you?"

Robert shook his head. "They asked him to identify the body, and then he went down to the police station with them." He tried to keep his voice level. "How is Lola? I want to tell her there's nothing to worry about."

"Mother is all right," Elena said, studying Robert. "She's inside."

Clemencia nodded to reassure Robert. "I'll tell her you're here," she said, and went back to the bedroom.

Feliz left the liquor on the sideboard and came to the living room. "There, I told you nothing was wrong. Nothing to worry about." He turned to Robert. "But you know how women are!"

Elena looked at Feliz angrily and then turned her back on him. "Then what is he doing at the police station?"

"Nothing's wrong," Robert repeated. "The police thought he could give them information—you know how it is. I'll be going downtown soon, and he'll come home with me."

Elena shook her head. "I don't like this." She turned to her husband. "Jaime, call the Streeters. They own half of Florida."

Jaime shook his head. "I don't think it's wise."

"Elena, this isn't a situation of that kind," Robert said. "I spoke to them. They didn't take Armando to the station by force. He went quite willingly. Let me go down and get him. You'll see. If I'm wrong, then . . ."

"Then get a lawyer," Elena said sarcastically. "I don't believe in lawyers."

"Come, come," Feliz said, smiling confidently, "Armando is only giving evidence. The fact is he knew Walliché, and the police naturally want to ask him questions. I see it now. It's like on television. He may know something he doesn't know he knows."

"My dear, he's cooperating with the authorities," Jaime said to Elena. "Why should that worry us?"

Elena thought it over.

Clara answered for her in a clear, sure voice. "Because Elena knows that in Cuba when the authorities take someone to the station you often never hear of them again. That's why."

Little Jimmy whimpered, then moaned loudly. "Mama, Mama!" he called. "I'm afraid."

Clara got up from her chair. "What? What's the matter?" she asked him resentfully, ashamed that her son's complaint put her in a bad light before the others. "What are you afraid of?"

"There, there, big boy," Jaime said. He kept an arm around Jimmy, holding him to the sofa.

Elena stepped between little Jimmy and Clara. "Watch what you say in front of him," she said to Clara. "He loves his Uncle Armando. He's a sensitive child."

"Auntie, Auntie," little Jimmy called.

Elena wheeled around to him. "Yes, sweetheart, lamb of my heart." She put a hand on his forehead and stroked it. "Your mother was only fooling. She was talking about the movies. Everything is all right."

Little Jimmy looked up at her with big, troubled eyes. "I want a Coca-Cola," he said. "It will make me feel better."

Elena leaned down and kissed Jimmy's forehead and then looked up at her husband. "He has no fever," she said to him. "What harm can it do?"

"No," Clara said from her chair. "No Coca-Cola. It will blow him up more."

Elena paid no attention to her, and Clara appealed to the others. "It's not right. The child doesn't know whom to listen to," she said to Shirley. "He'll grow up spoiled."

"They mean well," Shirley said consolingly. "They love him."

"Listen, Clara," Robert interrupted to get her off the subject, "did Jimmy's father come to see him?"

"Esteban?" Clara said. "What does he care about Jimmy?"

"Well, I saw him in the street just a while ago," Robert said. "He was on his way here."

"That's just like him," Clara said slowly. Her face began to relax and she put a hand on one hip. "He starts for a place and never gets there."

Robert shook his head. "I told him Jimmy was asleep and that tonight was not a good time for him to visit."

Clara thought it over. Her eyes closed a moment, and she smiled to herself. "He's still after me. I know him. He wants to see me again. He can't leave me alone." She looked up and noticed Shirley. "Please excuse the way I talk, Shirley, but that's the way he is. He's irresponsible and, like all Cubans, he's only interested in women."

God damn it, Robert thought, they are not interested in what's happening to Armando.

"Well, anyway, you were right to tell him we are here," Clara continued. "He's Jimmy's father, after all."

"Robert," Shirley said, "Mother's calling you."

Clemencia stood in the doorway to the bedrooms and waved at Robert to come to her.

Elena, on the way to the kitchen to get a Coca-Cola, stopped. "What?" she asked Clemencia. "Is Mama all right?"

Clemencia nodded. "She wants to see Roberto."

"Of course, of course," Elena said. She waited until Robert got to them. "Clara made me forget, Roberto. Please treat my mother carefully." She put an arm around Clemencia while she talked to Robert. "Lie to her the way you did to me. Armando is her baby, you know."

Robert shook his head at Elena. "I wasn't lying, believe me."

Clemencia shook her head, too. "If Roberto says not to worry then you are not to worry."

"Aunt Clemencia," Elena said, "your Roberto is still the smartest and kindest of all the children. But you and I can see through him."

"Don't be foolish," Robert said. "Why do you insist on being so tragic? I'll go get Armando as soon as I speak to your mother."

"All right, everybody, here, here!" old Consuelo called out in a high, cracked voice. She came into the dining room with a large tray filled with tea cups, and Elena jumped nervously when she heard her voice. Consuelo put down the tray and looked happily around. "It's *tilo, tilo*. There's nothing like it for the nerves." She looked slyly at Clemencia and giggled. "I am not completely useless after all."

Clemencia went over to the table and picked up a cup. "That's very good, Consuelo. I'll take one to Dolores. It will soothe her, I'm sure."

Robert followed his mother as she carried the aromatic cup of tea into the bedroom. Dolores was sitting up in bed wearing a pink bed jacket and resting her head against the propped-up pillows. Mina sat by the bed and fanned her with an ivory fan. The room was filled with the gardenia scent that always followed Dolores. Its sweetness retreated from the sharp odor of camomile tea, and the mixed fragrance made Robert feel foolishly faint for a moment.

"No, no," Dolores said to Clemencia. "I can take nothing nothing." Then she saw Robert and made an effort to sit straighter and to hold out her arms. "Roberto, Roberto." She let her arms drop to her side. "They tell me you went out to find my son. Where is Armando? Is he in trouble? The foolish boy!"

"Tut, tut, tut," Mina said. "Calm yourself."

"No, no, there's nothing to worry about," Robert began. "I was with him."

Dolores' eyes brightened, and without waiting to hear more, she lifted an arm to him. "Roberto, my darling, my darling. You are courageous like Elena." She turned to Clemencia. "These two are brave—they carry their hearts in the very center of their chests, for all the world to see."

Mina stopped fanning. "Let him talk, for God's sake!"

"There's nothing more to tell," Robert explained. "Armando is not involved in any way. They wanted to ask him some questions to help them in their investigation, and I'm going downtown to pick him up. I'll bring him home soon. So you see, there's nothing to worry about."

"Then Walliché is dead?" Dolores asked. "Murdered?"

Robert nodded.

"He was kind to Armando," Dolores said in the soft tone reserved for the dead. "Armando was right to offer his services."

Mina resumed her fanning. "Promise me you will not write a poem eulogizing that old gangster."

Dolores continued softly. "Who are we to judge?"

"This sounds as if you *will* write a poem," Mina said, and looked closely at Dolores. "That's like the fools who rushed to church every time the Pope got the hiccups. I'm not that kind of Catholic, I'm glad to say."

Robert chuckled.

Mina looked up at him and waved a friendly hand. "You *are* right. We are just foolish old women."

"A little kindness is never too much," Dolores said reprovingly.

"Yes, yes, Mina," Clemencia said. She always tried to be scrupulously fair, so she added, "Though no one should waste tears on Walliché."

"I think I'll take the *tilo* after all," Dolores said.

This made them all happier. "Good, good," Clemencia said. "I'll get a cup for Mina and—" she laughed impulsively like the little girl she often felt when she was with her older sisters, "for me. I guess we have all become more excited than we should. A little *tilo* will calm us."

"As for me," Mina said contritely, "I should live on *tilo* only, but I am afraid that not all the *tilo* in the world will wash away my temper." She looked up at her nephew. "You thought we did not know Shakespeare? The Americans have one or two good things, I must admit."

Dolores put a hand on Mina's arm. "Do you think little Jimmy can come in here with me? Perhaps *you* would ask my daughter. When he was a baby, he used to sneak into my bed when he was frightened."

"He is not such a little boy any longer," Mina said. "Let him be."

"But they are only letting him stay for two weeks," Dolores said. "And he used to tell me he loved the way my bed smelled. Ah!"

Mina shook her head. "Just get used to the fact that the grandchildren don't belong to us."

"Very well, very well." Dolores looked up at Robert and smiled. "I shall never get used to it."

Clemencia came back with two cups, gave one to Mina, and sat down on the other side of the bed.

"Now that you're all settled, I'll go," Robert said.

Dolores held him a moment. "Do you know when the funeral is? I want to send flowers. We must."

"It won't look right. Only other gangsters will send flowers," Mina said. "Besides, there is no family to notice whether you send flowers or not."

Jose Yglesias

Clemencia put down her cup emphatically. "Certainly there is.
The Chases and the Streeters are his family. They own the orange
groves and the canning factories and the beaches up and down the
coast. They are very respectable. Now that he's dead, they will probably give him a grand funeral."

"Oh they were always hand in glove," Mina said. "That was just
a pretense that he wasn't allowed at their Bayshore homes—the
better to cover up their dealings. What are they all but successful
gangsters!"

"Let us be just," Dolores said. "It's a fine family Walliché came
from. He would have been like them but for some youthful folly I
am sure—an excess of energy. That is all he suffered from, and it is
the old story—he took one wrong step and then another until there
was no turning back."

Mina clicked the ivory fan shut. "It is plain to me that money is
the only thing that makes those Americans respectable, and
Walliché was just as respectable as his cousins and nephews. They
are like the great old Spanish families: one for the Church, one for
the Army, one for the Government. They kept everything in their
grasp."

"Yes, yes," Clemencia agreed.

"And if the king or just a duke looked lecherously at one of their
daughters, then—bing, bang—there went their so-called
respectability. A royal bastard made a respectable family complete."
Mina laughed and struck herself with the fan.

Dolores put a hand to her bosom. "But what has all that got to
do with Walliché?"

"It is very simple," Mina explained. "Instead of having a son in
the Church, these Americans have a son in the rackets. It is very
profitable missionary work."

Dolores extracted a handkerchief from her bosom and delicately wiped the tears of laughter from the corners of her eyes. "We
should not be talking this way at a time like this." She sighed and
then started. "How did he die?"

They turned to Robert. He was at the door, on his way out.
"Roberto?" Dolores asked. "How did he . . ."

He lied. "I don't know. Later, maybe I'll know."

"I'll be up. Come and tell me," Dolores said.

"Did you hear a shot this afternoon?" Clemencia asked. "That
would have been it."

"Oh my dears, this afternoon I only had ears for my children. Roberto . . ." She started to wave him back. "Very well, go."

His job was done, Robert decided. All he need do now was pick up Armando and bring him home, but Clara stopped him in the dining room and took him aside. "Tell me," she said self-consciously, "what did he say about me? What did he ask you?"

Robert didn't understand for a moment.

"Esteban," she said. "He must have talked a lot about me if you're acting so innocent."

"Actually nothing," he said—almost harshly because he was embarrassed. "He wanted to see Jimmy."

Clara smiled. Robert could see her take what he had said and pass it through a test, as if she were reading tea leaves or looking up images in a dream book. "I see his game," she said and put a hand on Robert's arm to make him see it too. "He asks about Jimmy only to learn about me. Whom did he expect to see at this hour? I hope he's not insinuating that I don't take proper care of Jimmy. Let him come around. I'll show him I'm not pining away." Her body trembled with excitement. "Roberto, I talk to you as if you were a woman." She took her hand away. "Please don't mind."

Robert shook his head quickly. "How is Jimmy now?" he asked. With Clara he was always changing the subject.

"Oh Jimmy is all right," she said half closing her eyes and feigning modesty. "It's the excitement of the day, the airplane, and all the people. Elena and Jaime take all his complaints too seriously. It comes from having no children of their own."

Clara was startled when Elena spoke over her shoulder.

"You're right, Clara," she said. "He's all right now. He probably just wanted some attention."

Changing her tone quickly, Clara added, "Elena is too good to him. Better than I."

Elena put an arm around Robert and drew him away. "I'm not going to keep you,' she said. "I just have a question for Jaime's sake. Is there likely to be any publicity? Jaime will have to get away. He can't get involved. We're due to leave for Virginia tomorrow morning anyway . . . What do you think?"

"I don't know anything about that, but why don't you go to our house for the night," he suggested. "That way Jaime would never be mentioned . . . although I don't know why. No reporters seem to be around."

73

"Good," Elena said, squeezing his waist. "Jaime will go there, but I'll wait here. Maybe I shouldn't. Armando always gets angry at anything I say. But I won't say anything. I'll make him no offers. I'll just see how he is . . . It's so frustrating!"

Robert smiled, shook his head, and started to leave.

"Roberto," Elena called, "this is very good of you."

Robert suddenly realized he was doing it to please Elena, not to help Armando, and it made him hesitate.

Feliz saw Robert hesitate, and he came after him, saying to Elena as he passed her, "I'm going with him."

"Good," she said gratefully.

Robert had hoped to be alone. On the porch he said to Feliz, "You don't have to come. I'm only going to park near the police station and wait for him." He saw Feliz waver when he said *police station*. "There's nothing else we can do."

That last decided Feliz. "One never knows. Something may come up." He followed Robert to the car. There were fewer people in the street. "Look," said Feliz, "there's only one police car now. Right in front of the entrance." He did not get into the car but strained to see down the street. "The lights are out too! That means they have taken the body away!"

"Let's get along," Robert said.

Feliz responded quickly. "Yes, yes," he said, "we must get on." He settled himself in the front seat next to Robert. "Armando will tell us all about it later. Then it will be our duty to advise him. I don't mind telling you that's why I am coming along with you. He needs some sober advice or he may come back and get the women all upset again. Let him tell us as much as he wants about the whole thing—that is only right—but we must see to it that he puts things in a common-sense light to the women. They must not be alarmed."

Feliz cleared his throat and nodded to himself. "And after all, there's no reason to worry on Armando's account," he continued. "The boy was ill advised to have been so intimate with Walliché, but we all know he is not involved in the gambling, and certainly not in this murder. He spent the whole afternoon with his family and this evening at the party. We all know that. I must say that it is all very interesting, and if it were not for Armando, you and I would never get a chance to learn about an event like this at first-hand. You'll see how we shall be bothered all week. Every cigar maker in Ybor City will be seeking us out to get the details. I shall be forced to go to the Cuban Club every night."

Feliz took out a cigar and began to light it. "Of course, Armando has been most foolish, but this experience will make him grow up. After all, it's only luck that he was home and not with Walliché when it happened. He is an innocent; you must come to that conclusion when you think about this boy. Why, should the occasion arise, I would not be unwilling to tell the police so. That's the kind of character the boy is—an innocent, I am sure that you would join me in pointing out to the police that we were with him at possibly the very moment that Walliché was—"

Feliz stopped abruptly. "Roberto!" he said hoarsely. He threw away the match with which he was about to light his cigar. "What did Armando say to you? God damn it, man, what are you involving me in? You knew all along that Armando was away."

Robert stared at him. "Away—where?"

"Oh, oh," Feliz moaned. "Of course, you didn't know. You arrived later."

"What are you talking about?" Robert insisted, and slowed down the car.

"That Armando was not home all the time. He came in after we arrived—drunk and hysterical!"

"So?" Robert waited.

"It's you who are the innocent," Feliz said. "I tell you, he could have been . . . there!"

For Feliz' sake, Robert turned to him and shook his head. "Don't be foolish," Robert said, "Armando's our cousin."

VI

When he came out of the police station Robert felt almost sheepishly foolish. "I have to admit," he said to Feliz, "that I was worried there for a moment—after what you told me."

Feliz had waited in the car while Robert went inside to talk to Armando, and now he looked at Robert expectantly and chewed his cigar. "What are you telling me?" he asked. "Out with it."

Robert went around to the driver's side and got in the car before he answered. "Everything's all right," he raid, and smiled.

"You *are* an innocent," Feliz said. "How can everything be all right?"

"I'll tell you." Robert looked around before making a U-turn, and Feliz looked nervously around, too. "Our cousin was out at a whorehouse, that's where he was!"

Feliz breathed a loud sigh and Robert looked at him, and then the two laughed together. "Why didn't I think of that?" Feliz said.

Robert told him Armando had set his mind at ease immediately. He'd called Robert into the little office at the station where he and Casper were talking, and the two of them laughed at Robert's worried look. Armando told him to go back to the house and reassure the family. "He looked very cool," Robert said to Feliz, suddenly puzzled about the change he'd found in Armando. "Anyway, he walked out with me and told me about his alibi."

"I advise you not to tell the women about this," Feliz warned. "They would not understand."

"Well, well," Robert said. He'd turn into Michigan Avenue and soon they'd be back in Ybor City. "So it turns out that all the sensible things I told the old ladies were the truth after all." But why, he asked himself, did this strike him as less plausible than the suspicions they had both felt? "He said he'd be back at the house soon."

"I think we owe it to the family to wait for him and hear the whole story," Feliz said. He took out a match and lit his cigar butt. "Not that he need explain anything more. On the one hand,

76

Walliché had many enemies, and, on the other, it makes sense that a youngster like our cousin should be out enjoying himself with the girls. He could not have saved Walliché anyway, not if they were really out to get him."

"I've never seen anyone out of a job look so happy about it," Robert said.

"I was talking to him earlier tonight and I remember saying to myself, this Armando is a fool about women all right." Feliz contentedly blew out a puff of smoke. "Would you think it to look at me that I, too, could be a fool about women?"

"Oh, we all have been," Robert said. He'd begun to like Feliz for the first time tonight.

"You say that only to be courteous," Feliz answered. "I can tell about these things. You don't fool around with women." He took the cigar out of his mouth. "I'll tell you something I've never admitted. It's true what my first wife said I did to her. You heard the gossip, don't say you haven't. My mother didn't speak to me for a whole day when it got out, and I had to listen to many jokes at the Cuban Club at my expense. All on account of my first wife's vindictiveness. But, after all, I was only eighteen and I was very curious. I put her on the kitchen table and examined her with a flashlight. I don't know what I expected to find!"

Feliz reached out and slapped Robert's shoulder. "I can still remember her laying on the table and whispering loudly, 'Feliz, pull down the blinds. Pull down the blinds,' she said, but then she went and spread it all over Ybor City. I could have told them all how she was worried about the blinds, but I didn't. You and I were taught to be gentlemen, but I always have been a fool about women."

Robert shook his head sympathetically. "The things we did when we were kids!"

"I'm telling you in confidence," Feliz said. "After all, she is the mother of my oldest boy, and I could not defend myself. You know how gossip travels through Ybor City, and I would rather explain to him what I was doing with the flashlight than why she was worrying about the blinds. I may have to yet. Every time I see the boy and he starts to ask me a question, I say to myself, aha, here it comes! It's a very gossipy town. It is my contention that it is due to cigar makers sitting down all day with nothing to do with their heads but wag their tongues. A construction man has other things to do. All this interest in gossip strikes me as effeminate, don't you agree?"

Robert tried hard to keep a serious face, and seeing Esteban on Dolores' block gave him a chance to cover up his amusement. "There's Esteban," he said.

"What does he want?" Feliz asked. "Pass him by, that will discourage him." He kept his head pointing straight ahead, but rolled his eyes to watch Esteban. "Cubans are insufferably curious."

Esteban came straight to them, but spoke only to Robert. "I had decided not to come tonight, as you suggested, but I heard . . ."

Elena came down the porch steps and Esteban stopped. "Isn't Armando with you?" Her eyes finally settled on Esteban. "Esteban! At such a late hour!" Then she remembered that she counted on him for little Jimmy. "It's been so many years—forgive me, there's been so much excitement here."

"Well, it can all end now," Feliz said. "Armando will be along in a minute."

Elena looked at him hard. "Why not now, with you?"

Feliz could not think of an answer, and Robert explained. "He preferred it that way. But, believe me, everything is all right. I spoke to him."

Esteban finished his inspection of Elena. "Then perhaps I've only come with gossip," he said, "But I thought Armando ought to know."

"Know what?" Elena asked, looking around, and then raising her hand to warn him. "Not here." She turned and led them up to the porch. "What did you hear?" she asked before they had stopped, unable to wait.

"To begin with," Esteban said, "there was birdseed in Walliché's room, scattered all over the place."

Elena held the screen door open and did not give Esteban time to greet Clara, who was sitting on the glider. "What does that mean?"

Esteban nodded to Clara. "It means that Walliché had been turning people in to the police, and that's why he was murdered. Birdseed means he was an informer, that he sang."

"What has that got to do with Armando?" Robert asked. "I just saw him; he was nowhere near Walliché's today."

Esteban explained. "The story is that Armando is involved just because he was not there."

Feliz snorted. "That does not make sense."

Esteban took another look at Clara before he explained again. "They say Armando was paid off to be out of the way tonight."

"Elena!" Clara cried, alarmed.

Elena shook her head. "Let's not talk about it here."

"Of course, of course," Feliz said, and held the front door open for her.

Elena ignored him, but went in. "Come, Roberto," she said.

After Robert went in, Feliz followed, deliberately preceding Esteban. Esteban paid no attention to the snub, he walked to the glider and leaned over Clara. He reached out slowly with one hand while he smiled into her eyes, and caressed one of her breasts. "I love those darling pears!"

"Take your hand away, Esteban," Clara said. "Don't be an idiot at a time like this."

He tried to undo the top button of her shirtwaist. "Do not seal me away from paradise!"

"Esteban!"

In the living room, Elena heard her exclamation and looked at Robert. "They're already arguing. She'll spoil everything."

Robert did not understand her, and she did not explain. He motioned to the porch. "Do you think there's anything to what Esteban reports?"

Feliz moved closer to them. "Gossip, gossip—pay no attention to him," he said. "You yourself saw that the police have nothing against Armando."

Elena continued to ignore Feliz. "It's very likely. He was probably paid off." She saw the shocked look on Robert's face and added, "Or warned off."

Clemencia came out of the front bedroom and stopped when she saw the look on Robert's face. Robert shook his head and smiled. "Everything's all right, Mama."

Elena turned around and Clemencia spoke to her. "Jimmy threw up again. He heard you and wants to come out."

Elena put a hand to her forehead to control the throbbing in her head. "Clara!" she called. She turned to Feliz. "Look, you can help me, take Consuelo and your wife home." Then she explained to Robert, "Shirley and Jaime have already gone to your house. Mina and your mother will stay, of course, until Mother is feeling better. Help me quiet things down here so that Jimmy will go to sleep."

"Anything you say, Elena," Robert answered, and she put a hand on his wrist to thank him.

Feliz agreed to go, but he was very disappointed. "I think it's just a stomach ache," he said, hoping he could stay until Armando came and told his story.

Clara came in from the porch after she checked the buttons on her shirtwaist. "You're making too much noise. Jimmy will wake." Elena motioned her toward the bedroom. "Take care of him; he's sick again." To Feliz she explained, "That's all it is, but the excitement doesn't help." She relented enough to smile, and Feliz began to round up his wife and Consuelo. Elena walked Clara to the bedroom door. "Please don't antagonize Esteban," she whispered.

Without being asked, Esteban came inside. "With all the excitement," Elena said to him, "we've forgotten the ordinary courtesies."

"What is this about Jimmy?"

Elena stared at him a moment and then realized that he had a right to ask about his son. "It's just a stomach ache, nothing more."

Esteban nodded and started toward the bedroom, but Elena reached out and held his arm. "For his sake, wait until tomorrow."

Esteban hesitated and looked at Robert. Robert nodded, urging him to stay in the living room, and Esteban said, "All right, until tomorrow."

Elena took a look around the living room and sat down in a chair. "Now all we've got to do is wait for Armando." She put a hand up to her temples and closed her eyes for a second.

Robert smiled sympathetically. "He's going to be surprised that you're worrying about him. I'm convinced he has nothing to worry about."

Feliz had collected his wife and Consuelo, and now he supported Robert. "Of course, of course, the police never do anything about this kind of occurrence. They just let things take their course."

Elena looked up at him and thought over what he said.

"If you like," Feliz added, "I'll stay here until Armando comes."

Esteban sat down too. "Everyone agrees that the police aren't going to catch anyone," he said. "But if they're saying Armando was out of the way on purpose, then Walliché's gang may want to get even."

Robert shook his head at Esteban, hoping to keep him from saying more in front of Elena.

"Don't worry about me," Elena said. "I can figure it out. If Walliché's gang doesn't get to Armando, then the others may want him out of the way because he knows too much."

"Come, come, we must go," Feliz said to his wife. "There's nothing to worry about." His interest in staying had evaporated, and in a minute they were out of the house.

Elena looked at Robert and Esteban after watching Feliz hurry his wife, and all three laughed simultaneously. "Let's have a drink," Elena said good-naturedly, and Robert got up to make one for each of them. "The fact is, Armando is in danger."

She took the drink from Robert and shook her head at him. "Don't treat me like the old ladies, Roberto. We've got to face facts; I have to decide what to do about Armando." She stopped because Esteban was there.

"I'm just waiting for Clara to come out," Esteban said, as if he'd read her mind. "I want to ask her about Jimmy."

Before Elena could answer, Clara came back. She had combed her hair and put on more lipstick. "Jimmy is asleep," she said. "You're making too much noise."

Elena got up and led them to the porch. "Armando has to go to Cuba," she said. She looked at Clara and Robert. "When he comes, I hope you will support me in this." She sat down on the glider next to Clara before Esteban could get to her. "I appreciate your coming, Esteban. If you'll stay a little longer, you can tell Armando what is being said."

Esteban smiled. "I understand," he said.

Elena ignored his ironic tone. "And he's got to take the next plane to Havana; he's endangering the whole family." She stopped at the sound of a car. She and Robert got up at the same time, but she was off the porch before him.

Armando stepped out of the car and waited for it to pull away before he walked to the sidewalk. Robert noticed it was not the detective, Casper Friend, who had driven him home, but he said nothing to Elena. He was puzzled by the turn things were taking. If Armando really were involved, then why the hell, he asked himself, was he being so solicitous about his cousin? He knew the answer: because it was family.

Elena threw her arms around Armando on the sidewalk. "Are the police through asking you questions?"

Armando ignored her and looked at Robert. "What are you all doing still up?"

"Never mind that," Elena said. "Are they through with you?"

Armando smiled at her. "I'm through with them. They've got nothing on me."

Elena hung on to his arm, and she went up the porch steps with him, sorting her plans. "Then you're free. Good, I've some ideas for you . . ."

On the porch Armando stared at Esteban and Clara. He smiled a thin smile. "I'm sorry I can't stay and talk," he said sarcastically. "I've got some things to do."

Elena put a hand on his arm. "Esteban is here because I want him to tell you what is being said in Ybor City . . ."

"Tell him, Esteban," Clara said. "Tell him!"

"Don't yell," Elena warned. "I don't want the old ladies out here."

Esteban broke in quietly, looking at Armando in a detached way. "Armando, the story is that you were purposely not at Walliché's tonight—*that's* what is being said."

Armando looked at him for a moment, then said harshly, "Yes?"

Esteban suddenly got up and stood in front of him, and it looked as if they were going to fight. "Look, I don't say it. That's the rumor—that you were paid off."

Clara jumped out of the glider and threw herself at Armando. "You must get away, little brother. Please go away." She began to sob and hid her face in his shirt. Her sobs, instead of being muffled, got louder.

"Stop her," Elena commanded.

Clara stopped crying. "Don't stay here; you're putting us all in danger," she pleaded, her voice rising to a shriek. "Don't stay here for your own sake!"

Elena reached out and pulled her head back. "Do you want to kill Mother with your screams? That's what you will do if you keep this up!"

Clara whimpered and let herself be pulled back to the glider. After Elena let her go, Clara sat down and covered her face.

"Take it easy, Elena," Robert said, breaking his silence. "The old ladies are as strong as oaks."

Elena motioned him to follow her into the living room, where Armando had gone. Robert hung back; he didn't like the way his cousins were acting, and it occurred to him that perhaps Feliz had been smart to get out of the way. Esteban whispered to him, as soon as Elena was inside, "You go in with them. I want to talk to

you later, but right now I want to stay here and console this one."
He looked at Clara, lying back on the glider, one arm over her face.
"She was a little green when I last had her, but now she is perfectly ripened."

Embarrassed, Robert walked straight into the living room without looking back. At first sight, Elena and Armando looked like conspirators. Elena glanced over her shoulder when Robert walked in.

"The four o'clock plane this morning?" Armando said. "You've thought of everything."

"Look, maybe we're all overexcited," Elena said, referring to Clara's outburst, "but you should be out of the way now—"

"We're your family," Robert interrupted, surprised to hear himself talk this way, "and we know you're innocent, but you're in danger from one gang or the other . . . The police are no protection."

"And in Havana you can go see a friend of a friend of ours," Elena said. "I'll give you his name and address and he can tell these people here—" she stopped, looked at Robert, and dared the rest— "he can call them off."

But Robert didn't hear her because his mother came out of Dolores' room and motioned to him. She and Mina, she said, had decided to stay until Dolores was all right. She kept Robert with her in the kitchen while she made more *tilo*, and explained, "We don't want Dolores to suspect that we are worried about her heart, Roberto. Tell the others to conceal all they can."

"Latticini, isn't it?" Armando said to Elena as soon as Robert had walked away. "I have his name and address too. Even his private telephone number."

"What does that mean?" Elena asked, dropping her pleading tone.

"It means I'm taking that four A.M. plane to Havana," Armando said. He looked at her as if she were a little girl. "Aren't you glad? We've got the same friends. You'll be able to show me off in Havana; I won't be an embarrassment to you."

"You can stay at my apartment," Elena said, ignoring his sarcasm.

"I was counting on you for that," Armando said. "I've only one more thing to do."

"What's that?" Elena asked.

"I want to tell Casper I'm leaving."

Elena pulled him back. "Who's that?"

"A detective . . . a policeman; no use antagonizing them," he said. "I know about these things."

"You're not telling anyone," Elena said, slowly, with hardness. "*I* know about these things."

He started to leave her, but she pulled him back again. "What the hell are you . . ." he exclaimed angrily.

"You are doing it the way I say. You're going to need Jaime and me; don't wait 'til you get to Havana to find out." She let go of his arm, but held him with her eyes. He made no move to get away and her voice softened as she gave him instructions. "You have at least two hours. You can pack, say good-bye to Mother, and Roberto will drive you to the airport. He'll make the reservation in someone else's name and charge it to my air travel card."

Armando fell back on his ironic manner. "What makes you think he'll want to run the danger?"

Elena took him seriously. "Don't worry about him. He's family."

"All right," Armando said, deflated. "I'll pack now."

"I'll give you Jaime's personal card, and you'll be able to skip Havana customs when you show it to them there."

Robert followed Clemencia out of the kitchen. She was carrying a tray with three cups of *tilo*, and she stopped a moment when she reached Armando. "We knew you would be all right," she said to him with a confident smile. "You've never given your mother any trouble and you never will."

Armando looked down, embarrassed, and let her go ahead to Dolores' room before he turned to his own to pack.

Elena took Robert's arm. "One more favor, Roberto. Will you wait and take Armando to the plane? We're making you stay up all night, and I'm afraid you're going to think we'll be terrible people to work for."

"Is he going?" he asked, and saw that she no longer looked troubled. "Sure, I'll be glad to take him."

"Someday I'll pay you back," she said, and took his arm the way she had some hours ago, when she had urged him to come to Cuba. "Don't forget our offer."

"You worry about your family, don't you?" he said kindly. "You'd better stop or one of these days one of us is going to disappoint you."

"Look at our mothers; look how they worry about each other. They're an inspiration to me." Elena opened her eyes wide in explanation. "I must do something for Mina and your mother. They—"

There was a loud murmur from the porch. "Esteban!" they heard Clara call out.

Elena shook her head indulgently and called out loudly to them, "Shh!" Then she smiled and explained to Robert,

"They never got along. Now they're probably quarreling about Jimmy. I don't know why; neither one cares about him."

"Shh!" Esteban repeated softly on the porch. He had opened the top of Clara's shirtwaist dress and was stroking one of her breasts. He held the nipple between forefinger and thumb, and when she didn't move, he leaned down and put his lips to it. Above his head Clara looked out into the night like a startled animal. He put his hand under her skirt, and he sighed when he felt no girdle. Clara began to moan.

He lifted his head and kissed her ear. "Are you sleeping in the last bedroom?" he asked. With her head turned slightly away, she looked at him with half-closed eyes, calculatingly. The light from the living room shone on her breast, and he could see the clear line where her suntan ended. She's been wearing very brief bathing suits, he thought. Boldly he took her hand and pressed it to his crotch.

Clara moved her body away, but her hand stayed caught between his legs. He brought his lips back to her breast and with a hand under her skirt stroked her bare thighs. Her body seemed to collapse and quiver under him, and he quickened his caresses as he felt her trying to gather her strength to resist him. With a start her body stiffened, and she sprang away from him. "Not now!" she protested. Her voice was like a little girl's.

"It's always time, my honey nipple," he said from the swing, watching her stand in the doorway to the living room, buttoning her dress. "Do not cover it, little girl. It's like seeing the sun go down. You are covering my joy, the light of my life."

By the time she had finished straightening her dress, she was smiling proudly to herself. She could still feel his lips on her breast. In order not to look at Esteban, she turned toward the living room and saw Robert's mother rush out of the bedroom. "Clemencia!" she called. "What is it?"

Startled, Clemencia stopped and looked to the porch. "Oh it's nothing, Clara," she said. "I've only come for a glass of water."

Robert and Elena came out of the kitchen, and Clemencia explained. "Dolores became excited. Armando just told her he is leaving."

"Oh, I should have been there to tell her!" Elena said, and hurried to Dolores' room.

"Poor Lola," Clemencia said, forgetting that Clara was in the room. "It is time she stopped having trouble from her children." She went on to the kitchen, and Robert and Clara were uncomfortable for a moment until she returned. Clara lay down on the sofa, and Robert followed Clemencia.

In the hallway leading to the bedroom, Robert said to Clemencia, "Mama, what would you think if I went to Cuba and took a job with Elena and Jaime?" He laughed a little, anticipating her disbelief. "I've been thinking about it."

"That is up to you," Clemencia said, looking down into the glass she was carrying. "Elena is very generous." When Robert said nothing, she started toward Dolores' room, but then turned again. "Roberto, you must tell me, is Armando in any trouble? Is that why he is going away?"

"Oh no, Mama. You mothers always imagine the worst."

"But he's going in such a hurry," she said.

"Well, Walliché was his friend, and what happened was a shock," he explained lamely. "It's not happy here for him. He might as well go now, and he'll surely stay out of trouble, if there is any."

"Well, you stay with him, Roberto," she said, not entirely convinced, "until he is well out of his trouble. All right?"

Armando was seated on the bed facing his mother. She held one of his hands. "Oh my dear, thank you," she said to Clemencia, reaching for the water. "I need this." She held the glass in one hand and noticed that Armando was alarmed to see her hand shake a little. "It is my shortness of breath," she explained. In front of the children she never admitted she had a bad heart. "It must be going to rain; the air is so oppressive." She turned to Mina and Clemencia. "Can't you feel it lying heavy on your chest?"

"Oh yes," Clemencia said. "Spring is always humid."

Mina only nodded. She could not contradict Dolores at this moment, but it had been a clear, dry spring.

"With all of you in Cuba," Dolores said to Elena, "I think I'll go visit you finally. But in the fall. It will be easier to travel then."

"And you will bring Clemencia and Mina with you," Elena said, and looked at Robert. The idea delighted her. "You will be our guests. I'll arrange it."

"Oh no, no," Mina said.

"I won't hear of it," Elena said.

"But we have none of us ever been out of Tampa," Clemencia said.

The old ladies looked at each other, excited. "Do you think, Elena . . . really?" Dolores said.

"It's settled," Elena said. "But now Armando must pack."

Clemencia and Mina got up to help.

"No, no," Elena said. "Armando just has to throw a few things together. When Jaime and I come back from Virginia we'll take anything else he needs. Isn't that so, Armando?"

Armando nodded and let Robert lead him out of the room. Elena followed, and they met Clara and Esteban in the living room.

"I have decided to go with Armando to the airport," Esteban said.

Elena did not want to antagonize Esteban, so she gave Robert the lead. "Good," Robert said. Esteban winked at him, and Robert looked away.

"Very well," Elena said. "Only we know Armando leaves soon, and until he is on the plane no one else need know."

"Don't carry on so," Clara said to her. "Whom are we going to tell? There won't even be an opportunity."

The telephone rang loudly in the kitchen, and with a gesture to the others to stay where they were, Elena went off to answer it. They waited a little fearfully to hear her replies. She spoke in English, and the tone of her response was polite and reserved, not alarmed in any way. Clara laughed with relief.

"My advice to you, Armando," Esteban said quickly, while Elena was still in the kitchen, "is to stay away from the farm in Cuba. Stay in Havana."

"The farm?" Armando said. "Why should I go to the farm?"

Eyes shining, Esteban explained: "The countryside is full of rebels."

"There's nothing to worry about," Clara said.

"That's what the French nobility said before the revolution," Esteban answered her. "Those bearded boys are going to clean things up in Cuba."

"I don't know anything about politics," Armando said.

"Come now," Robert said deprecatingly, "nothing is going to happen."

"Oh they are dangerous enough," Clara explained. "They are barbarians. They come down from the hills unshaven, murdering everyone who stands in their way."

"Barbarians! Barbarians, you say!" Esteban exclaimed indignantly. "That's what comes of your mixing with all those racketeers in the Palace. You probably wouldn't recognize a genuine man if he appeared naked before you."

Elena came in from the kitchen smiling. "I don't know about that. I think even *I* would." She didn't want a fight and, although she wished Esteban out of the way, she didn't want him to be angry either. "Roberto is right; nothing is going to happen. Besides, Jaime doesn't get involved in politics." She laughed. "Politics makes for short-lived careers."

Robert looked at Armando and warned, "Armando had better pack."

"Yes," Elena said. She took Armando and Clara with her, but turned back at the door to Armando's room. "That phone call was from one of Walliché's cousins, the Mr. Chase who is frozen orange juice. He wanted to know if Armando would be pallbearer at the funeral—because he was such a good friend of his cousin's."

"Maybe someone is checking on Armando," Esteban suggested.

"What did you say to him?" Robert asked, ignoring Esteban.

"I told him my brother was with the authorities, helping them solve the crime." She said it in a mimicry of her polite manner. "He left me a number where Armando could call him in the morning. I extended my condolences and told him how sorry my whole family was to lose such a good neighbor."

"Elena!" Clara protested. "It is not nice at a time like this!"

"Don't be a fool," Elena said, then laughed. "Oh yes, I also managed to let him know that I would be seeing his cousins, the Streeters who are banana boats, in Virginia. His voice didn't show it, but I know he was surprised. I don't want him to think he is doing our family such a big favor by letting Armando be pallbearer for the black sheep of his family."

"Good," Robert said. "That's the spirit."

"I'm only sorry," Elena said, encouraged, "that I could not think of a way to tell him that his bank would not give me a job when I finished business school many years ago—more years than I care to count." She did not have to explain to Robert that she did not get the job because she was Latin.

"I understand Walliché was not like that," Robert said. "I don't imagine that he was very much like his cousins."

"You have to say that for him," Clara interjected. "He was not high-faluting."

"The trouble with evening up old scores," Elena said with a sigh, "is that you don't really feel like doing it when you're in a position to be able to. What the hell, there's no profit in it. They are probably nice people, like us."

With that, Elena took Armando and Clara inside to pack.

Esteban had been waiting to get Robert alone. "What did you mean about the rebels?" he asked Robert. "Do you really think nothing is going to happen in Cuba or were you trying to keep Armando and his sisters from worrying?"

"Well, what can happen?" Robert asked.

"You have lived in New York and yet you are so provincial!" Esteban said. "I did not expect this attitude from you. Why, don't you know that a famous correspondent from the New York newspapers was with them in the Sierra Maestra, and he wrote about them and published photographs for all to see? I tell you, something is going to happen, and the rebels are going to clear out that whole gang."

"What can happen that hasn't happened before?" Robert put it as mildly as he could. He did not want to patronize Esteban, but it was amusing that Esteban did not see how provincial *he* was.

"They'll get rid of the tyrant," Esteban said. "That's what will happen."

"And the sugar plantations will still belong to the Americans," Robert said. "And your rebels will become respectable men."

"You can't give up before you begin," Estaban said. "How do you know what will happen?"

"You have to learn from history," Robert said, suddenly impatient. "Other revolutions have foundered because the conditions under which they began did not let them come to a—well, a successful conclusion. They died of internal contradictions, and when you take a little colonial country like Cuba, its revolutions are bound to end up respectable. Its leaders become respectable because the economic conditions of the country do not allow them to become anything else but opportunists." He spread out his hands and changed the impersonal tone of his speech. "Look, Cuba is just a little country, a colony of the Americans."

"That's just a way of doing nothing," Esteban answered. "Do you know that the Western Hemisphere is mostly Latin? Not Yankee!"

Their conversation suddenly struck Robert as ridiculous, and he tried to change the subject. "What did you want to talk to me about?"

Esteban was disconcerted that Robert could move away so easily from their argument. "What? What did I want to talk to you about?"

"A while ago, you said you wanted to talk to me alone, about something serious."

Esteban shook his head. "We've talked, and you're the wrong man."

"Why am I the wrong man?"

"Because you don't think Cuba is important," he said harshly. "I can't ask you to do something for people for whom you have no sympathy. I wanted you to drive down to Sarasota with some things."

"Then what Feliz says is true, that you're involved in raising arms for the rebels! I thought it was just one of his exaggerations."

"Unfortunately, types like Feliz always hear everything; they spend their lives at the club canteens gossiping, and they know everything," Esteban said irritably. "They specialize in knowing everything and staying out of trouble. Your philosophy belongs in his mouth, believe me."

"He has his good side," Robert said, remembering Feliz' stories. "He's not a bad man really."

"He is useless," Esteban said. "Don't talk to me about him."

Robert felt Esteban's disgust was directed at him, too.

"Come, tell me, what did you want me to do?" He paused and said cajolingly, "I don't believe in selling groceries but I sell them."

"There's no money in this," Esteban said. "No one gets paid."

"Oh, for God's sake! What do you want me to do?" Robert threw up his hands and laughed.

Elena came out of the bedroom. "Please go in and hurry Armando. There's only an hour or so before the plane leaves, and I can't push any more."

Robert went into the bedroom, and Elena was left alone with Esteban. She sat down in a chair in the living room and took out a cigarette. "What a family for talking!" she said. She looked at Esteban and thought how Cuban he looked: big eyes, black curly hair, a mustache and sideburns, hairy hands. Like the many white Cubans on the streets of Havana, he was just a talker, too.

"It's nice of you to offer, Esteban," she said, giving up the idea of talking to him about the adoption. "But you don't have to stay."

For a moment he considered her. He probably could put sex as a straightforward proposition to her. She'd either say yes or no without his having to put a hand on her. He wouldn't have to take her gradually, nor tell her stories, nor breathe into her ear. She has great potential, he thought; she has Clara's hips. But there was no time. "You're leaving tomorrow?" he asked.

"Yes," Elena said, as if she were saying no to his conjectures.

"I'll stay and see Armando off," Esteban said, deciding to give her up. "Who knows, maybe Jimmy will wake up. If he's sick, I should be around."

"There will be plenty of time during the next two weeks," Elena said amiably.

"Why only two weeks?" Esteban asked.

"Didn't Clara tell you? They're going back to Cuba with us."

"Maybe she is," Esteban said, sitting up straight, "but Jimmy is not. She was supposed to have gone for two or three weeks and she stayed for two years—without my permission."

"But Jimmy loves it in Cuba!" She protested more strongly than she had intended. "He has a farm to play on." Remembering she had planned to take a disinterested tack with Esteban, she threw up her hands as if she were giving up, and smiled at him. "Of course, that is for you and Clara to decide. I just thought you should know Jimmy loves it there."

"Clara loves it there, you mean. Let her go," he said. "Jimmy can stay here with his grandmother. I want him near me."

"But what can he do here? He leads a healthy life there." She stopped a moment to hold her temper in rein. "If it's Clara's super-vision you're worried about, believe me, he's not neglected. Jaime and I love him as our own." It was no use putting it off, she decid-ed. "We would like to adopt him."

"You will excuse me," he said angrily, "but that's what I'm afraid of. He's mine, not yours."

Tears came to her eyes, and she looked away a moment. "When Jaime and I die, we want our money to go to him. Jaime has other relatives who could challenge such a will, but not if Jimmy were legally our own. That's all I'm saying—that he should be ours legally." She saw the astonished look in his eyes and added, "It's for his good."

"I'm his father," Esteban said. "I will decide what is good for him."

Elena tried to moisten her lips, so dry now with anger that they stuck together and kept her from answering. "Since when have you cared so much for him? You don't deserve him. You've never paid for his upbringing."

"That's the kind of idea I don't want him picking up." He brought one arm up in an obscene gesture. "He's mine because I fathered him."

"You disgust me," Elena said. "Only what you pay for is yours."

"That's the philosophy of the upper class!" He laughed mockingly. "Go make your own."

"You're an irresponsible fool. Like all Cubans."

"I'll say that for you; you're not a Cuban," he said. "You're a Yankee who can speak Spanish."

Elena got up and started for the bedroom. "I'm talking about Jimmy, not politics. It's his well-being that concerns me. I don't know anything about politics."

"I heard you before. I heard how you and your husband are not involved in politics. Tell me, how much money are you taking out of the country? How much real estate do you own in Miami?"

Elena flushed with anger. If he said another word she was sure she'd hit him. She turned again to the bedroom, but the others were coming out. "I cannot stand this man," she said to them, "and his infernal politics!"

Robert looked from Elena to Esteban. "What is it, Esteban?" he asked. "This is not the proper time for politics."

"This is not the proper time. This is not the proper time!" Esteban said in disgust. "Are they so well-mannered in New York? I thought you were a progressive. I thought you had a mind for big ideas. She wants to take my son away from me, and you ask me if it's the proper time to discuss it!"

Clara moved away from Armando and shook a finger at Esteban. "Why are you discussing it with her? I'm the child's mother, not her." She looked around at the others, not quite daring to look in Elena's eyes. "If you have anything to say about Jimmy, you say it to me. It's disgraceful to air things this way." She was on the verge of tears. "If you have no pride, I do. It's undignified."

Esteban held up an arm. "You are right, Clara," he said contritely. "It offends my dignity, too."

Elena turned to Robert. "Holy Virgin!" she exclaimed. "I wash my hands of them!" She turned into her mother's bedroom and left them.

"You are right," Esteban continued to Clara. "We will talk about it later. Now we must get Armando off. Let no one say I don't finish a job when I begin it. I'm not irresponsible."

Armando put down the suitcase he was carrying. He seemed not to have heard them arguing. "I forgot something." He left them in the living room and went back to his room.

Armando went straight to the dresser and looked around to make sure he was alone. Then, quickly, he opened the drawer where he kept his handkerchiefs. The Beretta was still hidden under the pile of white handkerchiefs. It was a small revolver, so delicately made that it seemed almost feminine. Since he had first gotten it, it had lain in the drawer, a silly secret amongst the handkerchiefs. It was so light in his hand he scarcely believed it could shoot; not like the Army rifles he had used in Korea. He had never carried it or used it.

He could not have explained why it made him suddenly sad to see it lying in his hand. Good-bye, he said to himself, not quite knowing why. He moved his head around to the window looking out on the back yard, and it occurred to him then that he might never see the place again. Good-bye, he said. He felt the tears begin, and he turned abruptly and put the pistol in his jacket pocket. Robert was standing in the doorway. "Walliché gave it to me," he said to Robert. "I almost forgot it."

Robert stared at his pocket. The bulge it made was unnoticeable. "Please do not be alarmed," Armando said.

"What do you need it for?" Robert said. "Leave it here."

"It's all right," Armando said with a stubborn look, and started walking out of the room. "It's just a good-luck piece."

Robert gave it up. "We have to go now. It's time. We have to take your bags to the car."

Getting the bags to the car was an adventure. Elena insisted on going first to see if anyone was out in the street. When she returned, she did not let any of the men carry the suitcases. She gave one to Clara, who was pale with fear; the other one she took herself. Robert and Esteban watched her lead Clara to Robert's car.

93

In the darkness of the porch, Esteban turned to Robert. "What a woman! You have to hand it to her; she's got two pairs of balls!"

Elena led them back to the living room, where Armando had remained. Knowing that Armando carried a pistol reminded Robert again that he was involved in what might be a dangerous adventure. Why was he doing it? With the exception of Elena, none of them seemed to know what they were about, and not one of them, not even Elena, had stopped to reflect. They simply plunged in, and he had been carried along.

When he saw Elena, Armando knew it was time. He got up and went to his mother's bedroom to say good-bye. No one followed. Elena wished she could do this for him, but she only went as far as the door in case she was needed. She turned her head away from the others and covered her eyes with one hand, her head lowered, waiting to hear her mother burst into laments.

"Well, my old girl," Armando said in the bedroom, "I'm off." He tried to do it the way his older brothers would have. "I'm off to Cuba. I've been passing for white long enough. I'm off to the land of my forefathers, and I'll be sending you my little black bastards to keep you company."

Dolores threw out her arms.

"But give me a little time," Armando warned.

His mother kissed him directly on the lips and pressed her hands against his face. He turned away from her, smiling, and found Clemencia ready to hug him. She kissed him, too, and said, "You are a good boy."

Mina saw the tears in his eyes. "God bless you," she said.

"Wait, wait," Dolores called. She removed a chain and medal that hung around her neck. "Take my Santa Eulalia." She made him bend down, and Mina helped clasp it on his neck. Dolores kissed the medal and pushed him away.

When he was gone from the room Clemencia began to cry.

"Look at her," Mina said. "And I'm supposed to be the sentimental one."

"Cry, cry," Dolores said, throwing a gardenia-scented handkerchief to Clemencia. "It is good to let yourself go. Don't be ashamed. You need to cry more."

"Yes, but why now," Mina said, "when everything is turning out so well?"

Clemencia wiped her eyes with the handkerchief and wondered why she had burst into tears. "I don't know," she said truthfully. "Perhaps I was thinking Roberto will soon leave."

Dolores did not seem to be listening. "I know, my dears, why Armando decided to go right away. They think an old mother does not notice, but I know." She looked at Mina and waited for Clemencia to finish wiping her eyes. "Walliché's death was too violent a shock. Armando has too big a heart. He cannot endure all this; he's a sensitive boy. Yes, it was better for him to go now."

"Romantic nonsense," Mina said, priding herself on her level-headedness. "The boy was offered a good job and he took it. After all, Walliché's death left him unemployed."

VII

ROBERT had to admit to himself that he was frightened; he drove away from Dolores' house expecting that they would be shot down by machine-gun bullets any moment. Armando's car was the only other one on the block; and it looked ominous, as if it were hiding an army of killers. Armando was wedged between Robert and Esteban in the car, and Robert listened to their talk and wished he could ask them to be quiet without giving himself away. Before making the turn at Michigan Avenue, he had to stop to let a lonely car go by on the avenue. He watched it approach and pass, feeling all the while like a stationary target. He was surprised to be still alive after it had passed.

Once he turned on to Michigan Avenue Robert felt better, but he was eager to get beyond Nebraska, where he would be out of the Latin section. Unconsciously, he had decided that once they were away from there, nothing would be likely to happen. He passed his Aunt Mina's home and saw that Feliz had left a light on for his mother. Elena had told Robert she would take Mina and his mother home in Armando's car. "Good-bye," Elena had whispered in his ear, then she had kissed him on the cheek. "If all goes well, I'll see you in two weeks, and then you're going on to Cuba with us."

There had been last-minute instructions for Armando, and Robert had heard enough to learn that Elena must be wealthy indeed. Clara and Elena had kissed Armando, and then Elena had turned to Robert. "It's been a long day. How we have imposed on you! I'm going right to bed and I hope Jimmy isn't sick again, for I'm going to share the front bedroom with him in case he is." Then, they had gone quickly to the car. It was three in the morning, and all the houses on the block were dark. Not even Walliché's death could keep anyone up that late.

Thinking about it now, it seemed to Robert that Elena's offer of setting him up in Cuba depended on whether he completed his job of getting Armando safely on the plane. And why not, Robert asked himself defensively. Why not? Self-interest is a healthy motive; it is even the basis for revolutions. To be frank, he could only now begin to consider her offer seriously because he had begun to earn it. Tomorrow was Sunday, and he decided to get up early and offer to take Elena and Jaime to the airport. He was sorry he had not thought of it earlier and told Elena.

Armando had stopped talking for a moment, but he soon began again. "It may be years before I see you again, Esteban," he said. "Now, tell me, why didn't you and my sister Clara get along?"

Esteban looked at Armando blankly, taking a moment to awaken from a reverie. He had been wondering if Elena was giving him an invitation when she said she was going to sleep in the front room. It was true she was speaking to Roberto, but he had been standing close by and she had not lowered her voice. No, it would not do. His own son was in the room. Still, if he didn't awaken, what Jimmy didn't know wouldn't hurt him. No, he decided, and felt better, as if his decision made Jimmy better, too. He wanted Jimmy to be a serious type, not a Cuban. For all her nastiness, Elena was right. Cubans put too great a value . . .

He answered Armando. "We were very young," Esteban explained. "I hadn't really had my fling yet."

Armando persisted. "Is it true you were running around with other women?"

"Why do you say that?" Esteban asked.

"Tonight I'm curious. I'm going away," Armando said. He had shaken off his moodiness from the moment he put the gun in his pocket. "I heard that Clara once swam out to you at Clearwater Beach where you had been talking to a woman in the water. When she got to you, they say you still hadn't gotten your swimming suit back on."

Esteban was taken aback. He looked at Armando and saw he did not mean to be insulting. Then he looked at Robert and finally turned to Armando again. "You sound like a thirteen-year-old who has just discovered hair in his crotch. You don't want me to tell you about sex, do you?"

They passed Nebraska, and Robert began to laugh aloud.

"No, no, I don't mean that," Armando said. "I have noticed for a long time that people—at least, men—don't really talk honestly to each other. I have decided not to be like that, not with my friends, anyway. I'll tell you what I was doing today when Walliché was being killed. Roberto already knows. I was in a whorehouse, getting laid."

Esteban looked puzzled. "So?"

"I feel better for having told you," Armando said. "These things should be out in the open."

"And am I supposed to feel better?" Esteban asked. "Or is it supposed to give me a thrill?"

Armando insisted. "You don't understand me. I mean, I thought I'd be ashamed when it had to come out that I was at a whorehouse, but now I see things differently. I'm grown up. We all are. I want to face things squarely from now on. That's why I asked you about Clara and yourself."

"I don't agree. These things are not to be talked about. Sex is not a political question." Esteban shrugged his shoulders. "And no matter how you explain it, I don't understand sex with whores." He put a warning hand on Armando. "Don't tell me. I'm not asking for details. It's a very delicate thing, sex. It's a way of being happy. I could not be happy with a woman if what she wants from me is money." He interrupted himself by slapping his knee. "*I have* to feel this way; I don't have any money," he said with a laugh. "But I have other gifts and I like to give *them* away."

"Yes, yes," Armando said, still eager to talk, "I understand."

Again Esteban raised his hand. "But it is not to be discussed. Only fools like Feliz like to talk about their exploits. That's because their exploits never measure up to their expectations, and they try to make more of it by talking about them. And, believe me, they convince nobody but other fools like themselves. Do you know what they call Feliz at the clubs? They call him the Talking Cock! But let us not talk about him. If there's one thing I don't like, it's gossip. It is all very well to talk about me at Clearwater Beach, but you implicate a woman when you do so. You must not bandy a woman's name about, for all women are ladies."

They had gone past Florida Avenue and were now crossing the bridge over the Hillsborough River. Evenly spaced ranch houses had been built on either side of the river. It had once been all palmetto groves, with dirt paths where cars parked at night. There still were pines and palms scattered here and there on either side of the road, particularly where the land flattened out on the way to the airport. Robert had disliked such vistas when he was young, but now he had to admit they had a sad, lonely beauty. Where palm trees hovered on the edge of the water, they made a classic scene. They were right, he thought, to photograph them for picture postcards.

Robert took a deep breath. He was sure they were beyond some danger point, and he could forget about looking out for an ambush. "He is right, Armando," he said. "We all have at some time or other slept with a whore. But that isn't love. It's not even sex. It's some kind of function, like urinating, and if you do it often enough, it's not even as healthy as that. It makes you forget what love is. When you're in love, sex is like a profound conversation. It is the way of saying, I love you. And that, of course, is something that you can say with sincerity and feeling to only one person."

"I believe you," Armando said. "You are both right."

Robert felt suddenly self-conscious; he had been carried away. "Of course, that's what one tries to be like. I make no claims for myself."

Esteban had been listening very carefully. "That is beautifully said, Roberto, and no apologies are in order. I, too, believe in that ideal." He looked out at the palmetto scrubs. "Sometimes I think that love is the most beautiful sentiment in the world—love and freedom."

Remembering how Esteban had talked about Clara, Robert turned and gave him a quick glance. "Do you really?"

"Of course, of course!" Esteban said. "I never deceived my wife. It was the others I fooled."

With a grunt of dismissal, Robert turned the car into the airport driveway. They were there and nothing had happened after all. He parked the car and turned to the others. "We have half an hour," he said, "just enough time."

"I feel as if I'm only beginning to live now," Armando said. "I am resolved that from now on I'm going to do things. I have just been existing for a long time. Since my wife left me, as a matter of fact. I did not make her happy. I could not move her in bed either, hungry as I was for it. She never once moaned except in pain. No woman ever moaned for me. I thought this whore I had been seeing did, but tonight, right in the middle of it, she interrupted herself to put out a cigarette she had left burning. I tell you it's going to be different from now on." He flicked a cigarette away, like a purposeful, virile movie actor he admired. "No one's going to take advantage of me anymore."

"Enough! Enough!" Esteban said. "No more confidences of this type. You'll end up a practicing Catholic, going to confession every week." He smiled and offered him an alternative. "When you're in Cuba, you'll have a chance to meet young men among the rebels who have a purpose in life." He slapped Armando's shoulder playfully. "Join them."

"I'm going to be practical and look out for myself," Armando answered; then, to prove he was mature, added, "I also want to find love."

Esteban looked at him as if he were mad. "Well, it's good-bye then," he said. "I'm staying in the car." He turned to Robert. "I don't think I should be seen in there."

Robert nodded quickly and handed Armando one of the suitcases. Now that it was almost over, Robert was frightened again. He took one suitcase and then shook Armando's hand. "I'm going to pick up your ticket. You stay in the men's room until I come for you. Understand?"

Armando nodded. "Roberto, in case I don't get a chance, thank you . . . You've got a friend in me, remember that." He gave Robert's hand a final shake, squared his shoulders, and felt the comforting swing of the pistol's weight in his pocket.

Robert could only smile in return. He looked over the roofs of the parked cars. There seemed to be no one in the parking area. Ahead was the brightly lit glass entrance to the airport building. No one was there either. He started toward it and Armando followed a few steps behind.

Esteban sat in the car and watched them go. He shook his head at the thought of Armando's future and sadly put him down as a useless person. He leaned his head back on the seat and thought about Clara—a delicious woman. Not very sensible, it was true, but delicious nevertheless.

When Robert returned to the car he found Esteban asleep. "You were asleep?" he asked, his voice a mixture of surprise and admiration. "How can you do it?"

Esteban stretched himself. "It's good to nap. Sometimes you can go on for long periods without sleeping, if you can nap now and then." He took out a cigarette, stretched again, and thought fleetingly of the women with whom he had spent nights of sex, interrupted now and then by a short nap. "Is he off?" he finally remembered to ask. "Is everything all right?"

Robert took out a cigarette, too, and sat behind the wheel. "In a minute," he said. "I won't feel right until the plane takes off." He leaned his head back on the seat and looked up at the control tower.

Esteban joined Robert in watching for the take-off. He did it out of sympathy for Robert. The man was obviously tired. Why, he wondered, had he been angry with Roberto? I am just jealous, Esteban thought, because he comes from a big city like New York, the very center of the world. He sees only the larger world issues, it is true, but he is obviously a radical. It was foolish of him to reproach Roberto, he decided; there was no reason for him to be concerned with what's happening in Cuba.

The whirr of the plane's propellers reached out to them like a cheerful farewell. Robert wondered if it could be heard all over the city, the way the trains of his childhood could be heard at night. The sound became steadier and more intense, until suddenly it changed as the plane was airborne. In a moment, they saw it make its turn over the field.

"He's off," Esteban said. "The idiot."

Robert turned on the ignition and began to back out of the parking space.

"He was an easy target for Elena, but she's going to have trouble with me." When Robert ignored him, he added, "He was very high. He thinks he's a man now, but he's really trying to be like his big sister Elena." He sighed when Robert still didn't answer.

"Poor kid, he worries me," Robert finally said. "He's not a kid; he's twenty-seven. That's the trouble. He doesn't seem to know what he gets into."

"He's a little boy," Esteban confirmed. "That's why he fell into the hands of gangsters—and now this."

"This time he has a gun with him," Robert said. "I wish had taken it from him. What does he need it for?"

Esteban sat up. "He has a gun!"

"Yes, a pistol. He thought he was alone in the room, but I saw him put it in his pocket."

"Why didn't you take it away from him?" Esteban said. "I would have given it to people who could turn it into a real weapon!"

They were back on the road leading into the city. Robert turned his head slightly and looked at Esteban. "Really?"

"Why are you so astonished? You think only gangsters and cops use guns?"

Robert laughed.

"As a matter of fact," Esteban confided, "one of the things I did for months was to go from sympathizer to sympathizer and persuade them to give us any guns or rifles they had. You'd be

101

surprised how many we collected; old ones that went as far back as the First World War, some from boys who had just come out of the Army. Even my father had one I didn't know of. He had bought it when I was a kid, during the eleven-month strike of the cigar makers. In those days they used to bring the crackers from the backwoods to break up the meetings at the Labor Temple, and the crackers came right into the place with rifles. My old man decided if one of those rifles ever went off, he was going to shoot two or three of those KKKs."

"And?"

"He's seventy-two," Esteban answered, "and he has given up hope of shooting down a KKK cracker. Now he hopes his gun got safely to the Sierra Maestra."

"This is a dangerous game you're playing, Esteban."

"Thank God in Ybor City, Americanized as the Latins are getting, people still don't rush to the Americans to turn you in—even if they disagree with you," Esteban argued. "Anyway, we're not collecting old guns anymore. We buy new rifles."

Robert looked at him, surprised again.

"Not from a store," Esteban explained. "There are a lot of Army camps here, in Georgia, Alabama—you know—and the supply sergeants are only too happy to sell. They're corrupt; they act as if they are merchants."

"My God, that's really dangerous!"

Esteban laughed. "Sometimes I think the capitalists will someday sell us socialism, if they can do it at a profit."

"I would be for that," Robert said appreciatively. "I don't believe in violence."

"Come on, let's talk about what is on our minds," Esteban said. "I want you to help us out tomorrow. I'm not going to argue with you; I know you are one of us. Up there in New York, Communists and Socialists and liberals argue a lot of fine points, but when it comes right down to it, you all get together to do the decent thing." He paused and added cajolingly, "Even when it's for a little thing like little Cuba."

They were crossing the bridge on Michigan Avenue, and Robert slowed down. "Just a moment," he said. "I just want to check if it's all right with you if I don't take you home right away. I'd like to pass by Dolores' house first to see if Elena has taken my mother and Mina home, and if they have settled down for the night. It occurs to me we've left a houseful of women by themselves."

"Oh yes, of course," Esteban said. "No hurry."

"Well, then," said Robert, getting back to the argument, "you're wrong. There are all stripes of Communists, Socialists, and liberals. Some of them would think they were being used."

Esteban thought it over. "Then I would class them with your cousin Feliz. They are useless people, and I would not ask them, the way I didn't ask him."

"What a utilitarian you are!" Robert exclaimed.

Esteban did not quite understand. "I have always known that you have very advanced ideas and that in New York you were involved in political activities. A week ago I saw you at the grocery store, but I couldn't stop. It occurred to me then that sometime you could be of help, and tonight when I saw you I remembered, especially since tomorrow has been on my mind all day and I still didn't have a solution."

"Then I am not a useless person?" Robert said patronizingly.

"Oh no, on the contrary," Esteban assured him, "particularly since you have a delivery truck at your disposal."

"What delivery truck?"

"From the grocery store. You make all the deliveries. Doesn't El Rubio let you use it on Sundays if you want?" Esteban stopped to check that point.

Robert was on his guard, but he had to admit that he probably could get it.

"Look, I've figured it all out," Esteban explained. "If you weren't around we'd have to use at least three cars, and there would be that many more chances of being found out. When you consider that all the cars at our disposal have already been on such trips, you can see what a godsend it is to have you and El Rubio's truck. Innocent recruits. I don't mean you are innocent, but if we have been watched, no one will be looking out for you or the grocery truck."

At some point, Robert thought, it will be possible to say no. "I don't want to disappoint you," he said aloud, "but in New York radicals never do much more than sign petitions and distribute leaflets."

"That truck is perfect," Esteban continued. "What is more natural than that a truck should drive up to the pier and deliver groceries to a yacht?"

"All I have ever done," Robert said, "is to talk commercial artists into joining a union."

103

Esteban looked at Robert and smiled very carefully. He didn't want Robert to think he was laughing at him. "We have all been very scared," he said, "at one time or another. I was nine when they had the hunger march in nineteen thirty-one, and they marched to the schools to take out the children. I carried the red flag at the head of the parade with my father, and he almost pissed in his pants!"

"I remember . . . they were crazy!"

"They all thought the revolution was coming any minute. Weren't the veterans marching on Washington?" Esteban answered. "Wouldn't it have been wonderful if the revolution had come then?"

Robert said nothing. He remembered he had been in junior high school, and the marchers had never gotten there. The principal had the high gates closed, and Robert had been stationed, like all the eighth-grade patrols, at a side entrance. Nothing had happened. It had been a disappointing day.

"You don't have to know what's in the truck and you don't have to actually deliver the contents," Esteban said. "How's that for a proposition?"

"What do you mean?" As soon as he had said it, Robert wished he could take it back. He had as good as said yes.

"All you have to do," Esteban explained eagerly, "is get the truck from El Rubio and bring it to your house. Then I'll take it and bring it back within the hour." He looked at Robert to see if he had understood that much.

"Is that all?"

"No," Esteban said. "You get in the truck then and drive it to Sarasota. I'll tell you where. Someone else will take it from you and return it within the hour too."

Esteban spread out his hands and looked to Robert for congratulations. Robert said nothing. He turned off Michigan Avenue and started toward Dolores' block.

"That's the beauty of it; it's so simple," Esteban said.

Robert took his foot off the accelerator. Esteban's talk had made him speed without his meaning to. "It must be almost five," he said in a whisper.

They looked at Dolores' block. "It doesn't look as if anybody's up." Armando's car was in front of the house, but Robert noticed that it was parked just below the palm tree now. "I guess Elena has already taken them home and come back." Three women and one little boy alone in that house tonight. She's brave, he thought. He went past the house slowly.

"Stop on the corner," Esteban said.

Robert looked at him questioningly, but he stopped. They were across the street from Walliché's house.

Esteban didn't explain. "What do you say, then?" He had one hand on the door handle.

"Why are you getting out?" Robert asked. "I'll drive you home."

Esteban waited for his answer. "There are so many arrangements I have to make," he said. "It costs money to keep a man in a fancy hotel in Sarasota pretending he owns a yacht." He stopped. "I have to know if I can count on you."

The note of impatience in Esteban's voice made it possible for Robert to get angry. "What do you expect from me?" he said harshly. "What the hell do you think I'll do? Say yes, yes, count me in, as if this were some kind of game and we were all little boys?"

Esteban could not believe it. He did not mean to do it, but he stared so fixedly at Robert that their eyes finally met. Then Esteban relented. "Listen, I'll make you another offer," he said. "You don't have to drive the truck, just bring it to me. You don't even have to know what I'm using it for."

"But *I do* know," Robert answered. "How can I say I don't know? Besides, I don't believe in your methods."

Esteban threw up his arms. "You believe in Armando going off to Havana with a gun?"

Robert shook his head; Esteban was being foolish.

"Then why did you help him do it? Why did you run the danger of some gangster taking a shot at your car?"

"For the family," Robert said, remembering that Esteban could not know about Elena's offer. "You do things for your family—to be nice."

Esteban looked up and down the street and came up with another argument. "Then do this for *me*—to be nice. I'm family too." He saw Robert smile and added quickly, "Just leave the truck parked on the street with the keys in it. If I'm stopped, you know nothing, you didn't give me the truck."

"All right," Robert said. "Let me discuss it with Shirley."

"What? What? For God's sake, leave the women out of it," Esteban demanded. "I have to know now."

"All right, all right," Robert said. "Where do I leave it?"

"Right on this block," Esteban said. He slapped Robert's shoulder and got out of the car. "By eight in the morning. I knew I could count on you."

"Get back in," Robert said. He was irritated now, but he knew that later he'd be glad that he was doing this for Esteban. "I'll take you home."

"No, leave me here," Esteban said. "You probably won't get any sleep as it is. The truck must be here no later than eight o'clock."

"I know, but let me take you home now."

"Don't insist," Esteban said, shaking his head from side to side. "You know I don't like confessions." Then he explained, "I have a little private business to attend to."

"At this hour?" Robert said. "Okay, I'll take you."

"No, I'm there," Esteban said, and smiled.

Robert was puzzled.

"Clara," Esteban whispered.

Robert let out his breath loudly. "No, not really!" he exclaimed. "You're as bad as Feliz and yet you talk about him."

"Come now," Esteban said, "it's not so terrible."

"It's the Don-Juanism of the Latins," Robert said. "You all suffer from it."

Esteban looked at him with interest. "Really? What do you think is the reason?" he asked sincerely.

"It's the family setup we've been raised with," Robert answered. "It's the matriarchy."

"Matriarchy?" He was ashamed not to know.

"The women have too great an influence," Robert explained. "Look at our families. Our mothers run everything, and the boys grow up waiting to get even. Every woman that comes along becomes a challenge, a chance to win out over the mother."

"You're pulling my leg; you can't be serious." Esteban leaned on the car door, looking in at Robert, and shook his head. "There's a much simpler reason. Every woman is a temptation because they're all so delicious. You know the song that goes, show me an ugly woman and no matter how ugly she may be, I'll show you something delightful about her."

"Forget it; I'm no puritan," Robert said. "But how do you square this with your political ideas?"

Esteban thought it over. "Politics should not stand in the way of a little love."

Robert nodded and put his hand on the gear shift. He just wanted to get home. The hell with Esteban.

With a smile, Esteban stepped back from the car and immediately forgot their discussion. He leaned down and whispered loudly. "Right on this block, eight o'clock in the morning."

Robert pulled away, and Esteban remained on the corner until the noise died away. From a hedge around Walliché's lawn one cricket chirped loudly. He walked back toward Dolores' house along the grass, so that his footsteps would not be heard. He stopped across from the porch and looked at Armando's car, then at the dark house. For a moment the cricket stopped, and he listened to the stillness of the street. He was sorry Clara was not in the front room where they had slept during the first year of their marriage.

When the cricket began again on a startling, high note, he responded to it as to a call and stepped up on the lawn. He skirted the palm tree and went around the side of the house where there were no bedrooms. The azalea bushes had grown higher since the days when he used to water them on early, hot evenings, just after the sun had set. The back porch was a surprise. It wasn't there ten years ago. He followed it quickly and found, to his relief, that it did not extend behind the last bedroom; the window of that room still gave on to the yard. He looked at it from the stoop of the back-porch entrance. There was no one at the window. She had not stayed up for him.

He tiptoed toward it, but before he looked in, he saw that the screen was unlatched. He did not bother to call her. He went back to the porch steps, without tiptoeing, took the large garbage can and returned to the window. He set the upturned can under it. First he took off his shoes and socks, then his shirt, pants, and shorts and lay them on the grass next to the can. Then he got up on the can and steadied himself on it before leaning down to pull the screen back. The cool night air on his bare flesh was a new sensation, exciting and delightful. He climbed into the room, eager and fresh, ready for the act of love, and walked straight to the bed.

Clara was lying on the bed in a long nightgown. She had both hands on her breasts, and she stared at him with wide hypnotized eyes.

"Here I am, my sweet papaya!" He stumbled on one of her slippers and fell toward her, propping himself up at the last moment with one arm on the bed. Frightened by the noise he had made, they were still for a second, listening for some sign that he had been heard. When Esteban moved again, Clara raised a hand to push him off, but she touched the line of black hair that ran into his navel and sighed with pleasure.

She did not help him until she had to pull the nightgown over her head.

He crouched over her until the nightgown was off. Then he let himself down slowly on her. "You have ripened under the sun of beautiful Cuba," he said.

Clara put a hand to his lips to keep him quiet, and everything was done in silence. It was not until Esteban lay beside her on the bed that Clara spoke. He was resting but kept one hand on her breast, moving it back and forth. "I won't go back to Cuba," she said. "I'll stay and we can live here. Now that Armando is gone, there is room for us and Mother won't be alone."

Esteban stopped the play of his hand and lay still, as if asleep. Clara did not notice that he did not respond. She was happy and satisfied. His perspiration on her body made her feel cool, and she shivered happily. With one hand she reached for the sheet and pulled it over them. When she fell asleep Esteban moved out of the bed without disturbing her. He looked down at her and saw one of her breasts was uncovered, and for a moment thought of waking her and taking her again. But it was close to dawn, and he had many things to do. Carefully, he took a corner of the sheet and covered her.

The window screen creaked when he pushed it to slip out of the window, and Esteban found it very awkward to step out onto the garbage can. Once on it, he had to crouch low to let the screen swing back to the window without hitting his head. He was still crouched on the garbage can, like a circus lion on its stand, when he heard Elena's voice. It was harsh and low at the same time, and he whirled at its sound, trying with the same movement to cover himself with his hands.

"Making yourself another one, eh?" She stood on the back-porch stoop pointing a small pistol at him. "Who is going to support this one?"

"Look away," Esteban commanded. No longer bothering to cover himself, he stepped onto the grass. He picked up the shorts with one hand and turned his back to her. "That's what happens to old maids who look under beds."

"Disgraceful," Elena answered, "disgraceful. I could shoot you and say I thought you were a thief."

With his shorts on Esteban turned back to her. He had not noticed until now that she held a pistol. "Go on. Kill me."

"Who's talking of killing? I'll shoot you in the leg, then go do something about it. How would it look in the papers? Naked under your former wife's window?"

He kept his eyes on her and bent down for his pants.

"Stop!" Elena said. "Leave them or I'll shoot."

She was so cool; it was frightening. "What do you want?" For a moment he thought she wanted him in her bed. "I admit I was foolish, but why make this scene?"

"I want Clara and Jimmy to go back with me to Cuba. Don't tell me how he's better off with you. There are no bullets in this thing." She lifted the pistol and pointed it at him. "See." She pulled the trigger, and it made a sharp click. "Say that he can go back with me."

Esteban leaned down and picked up his pants. "All right," he said. "You're right, I don't make a very good father." He heard a gasp behind him and turned to see Clara at the window. "That's right," he said and pulled on his pants.

"Go back to your bed, dear sister," Elena said. "Pretend that you were ravished in your sleep."

Clara stepped back from the window and from the dark room called out, "I hate you both!"

"Ah!" Elena exclaimed, then stopped. She could not account for it but she was going to start crying. "Little Jimmy is mine!" she said, her voice cracking. "Remember that." She turned and went inside, letting the door slam behind her.

Esteban sat on the garbage can and put on his socks and shoes. Once, he looked up at the window and called to Clara, but she did not answer. He finished dressing and returned the garbage can to its place by the stoop. He stood a moment in a trance by the porch entrance, trying to figure out how he had gotten into this fix, before he carefully put the lid on the can, without making a sound.

VIII

THERE were times during the morning when Shirley was sure everyone in Robert's family was mad. Robert, too; he had, of course, told her before he fell asleep what he had promised Esteban; and she had been up since five-thirty to keep the house quiet, so that Robert would sleep through the morning and forget about the whole thing. Clemencia knew nothing about this; she was up to take care of Jaime's breakfast and to be hospitable and helpful. It *was* madness; Shirley didn't know whether she was angry with the old woman because her activity might wake Robert or angry with Jaime that he allowed Clemencia, who was probably exhausted, to wait on him. Both of them, anyway, were an irritation to her.

To be near the phone, Shirley watched them from the living room. It had rung twice already, and although Clemencia assured her that all the arrangements were made—Elena was coming over in a taxi, and she and Jaime were going straight to the airport for the seven-fifteen flight—Shirley did not trust the family not to call again. The funny thing was Clemencia did not mind at all that Shirley had quite bluntly asked Jaime to be quiet because Robert needed to sleep.

Clemencia had nodded to Shirley and led Jaime to the kitchen. "Señor Campos, you must forgive us today," she said to him, and as they drew away Shirley thought the two were going through the motions of a minuet, so much mincing, maddening courtesy was involved. "But please do us the honor to have some breakfast. We cannot let you go without some breakfast, such as it is."

Jaime looked at the table in alarm. There was too much there. "You are too kind," he said. There was orange juice, a bowl of dry cereal, a bottle of milk, a covered dish, rolls, butter, jam, and an empty cup. An American barbarism, he thought. All he wanted was coffee and rolls. "And you must not be so formal with me; my name is Jaime."

Clemencia drew back the chair for him. "You have plenty of time. Elena knows you will have breakfast here." She stepped back

110

and looked proudly at the breakfast she had made for Jaime. She could not serve Jaime the kind of breakfast cigar makers have, coffee and rolls. Jaime was a sophisticated man, after all. "And now, I'll leave you in peace for a moment."

Jaime hesitated before picking up the glass of orange juice. "You are too kind," he repeated, and swallowed it carefully.

Clemencia poured his coffee and left him, to take another look at herself in the bathroom. She had been in such a hurry, she could not remember if she had combed her hair. On the way to the bathroom she looked at Shirley and flashed her a happy smile. Shirley shook her head; that generation, she decided, must be made of iron. The thought made her feel a little kinder toward Clemencia, and she immediately began to think of Robert. She looked up and found that Jaime had turned in his chair and was looking through the doorway at her. She had probably been speaking to herself, and embarrassment made the blood rush to her head.

She got up and walked into the kitchen. "Yes?" she asked.

"I'm such a nuisance," he said, "but I cannot seem to find the sugar."

In a rush she crossed to the cabinets near the window and took out the sugar bowl. Jaime looked at her carefully when she put the bowl on the table, and in pulling her hand away she knocked the top of the bowl off. He put up a hand to stop her from bending for it and picked it off the floor himself.

"I beg your pardon," she said stiffly.

"I am putting all of you to so much trouble." He slowly poured sugar in his coffee cup and looked around the table again. "I wonder if I may ask another favor? Would you heat some milk for the coffee? I have become used to having it that way."

Shirley lighted the stove, poured a little milk in a pot, and kept her back to him while she warmed it. Just before it came to a boil, she removed it from the stove and deliberately served him from the pot. Her mother-in-law would have done so naturally because she would not have known it was indelicate. Shirley did it to show that she did not care for his lordly manner.

To her surprise, he seemed not to notice it. "I cannot tell you how grateful I am for your husband's many acts of kindness," he said. "I don't know how to thank him for having handled everything so well last night. I think you understand my position did not allow me to do what needed to be done. Being an outsider like myself, coming as you do from a metropolis like New York, from the great world, as it were, you can appreciate how events of this kind can engulf one in scandal and undesirable attention from the newspapers. One would think that in a small city like Tampa, one could escape attention, but one cannot count on it. No, I told Elena, it cannot be expected. The smallest disturbance can be the subject of dispatches to every foreign office in the world. Ah, yes indeed."

Shirley stood in the middle of the kitchen, pot in hand, waiting for him to release her.

"It is all the more reason why I am so grateful to your husband," he continued. He picked up the cup and tasted his coffee. "Elena thinks he is the right person to manage our sugar-cane fields. She thinks very highly of your husband, but I told her—and I am happy to tell you, too—that she does not need to extol his good qualities to me. I can see for myself." He stopped and waited for her response.

Shirley heard herself say, "It's very nice of you. Robert will have to make his own decision."

"Ah, yes." He did not believe her. He pulled back from the table a little and crossed his legs, looking as if he had lost all interest in her. She was much too gauche, he thought. He lit a cigarette and pulled the coffee cup toward him. "I beg your pardon." He held up the cigarette. "May I?"

Jaime did not hear Shirley's reply because he turned to Clemencia who came back in with her hair combed. Shirley was left to say effusively, "Yes, of course," to the top of Jaime's head. She felt herself blush.

"Señora Clemencia," Jaime said, in a complete change of manner, "you cooked me too good a breakfast. I have made myself too much at home, but it is your fault, because you have made me feel I've never left Cuba." He remembered he had said the same to Dolores last night. "It was the same last night at Dolores'," he added, in case Clemencia repeated what he had said. These old ladies are probably in each other's pockets all the time, he thought, certain he was the topic of their conversations.

"Not at all, not at all," Clemencia said. "On the contrary. I hurried back because I forgot to serve you milk and sugar with the coffee. Ah, I see Shirley has covered up for me."

"She has been very kind," Jaime said.

Clemencia looked at the pot in Shirley's hand and darted a quick look at Jaime. She turned to the stove and brought him a covered creamer. "Here's some more milk. Let me pour you more coffee." If Dolores and Mina were here, Clemencia thought, they would be surprised to see how much I can talk when put to the test. "I do not know if in Virginia, where you are going, they will serve you proper coffee."

Jaime smiled and let the old woman pour him another cup. "Coffee-making is not one of the best achievements of the North Americans."

Shirley did not bother to look at them. She just walked out of the kitchen and sat down in the living room again. At seven-thirty or eight, if she were lucky, the children would wake up. She'd keep them away from the front of the house. Why did she worry, she wondered. Let Robert do what he wants. The children are my job; let him handle the other problems. They hadn't started out that way, but that's how it had worked out. Too many problems, she thought, too many problems.

Last night Robert had sat on the edge of the bed and sighed. She had wakened immediately and touched his shoulder; she had not been annoyed with him then. "Go to sleep, honey," she said. "You must be exhausted."

Robert shook his head. "I don't know what to do," he said, thinking that he should be up in a couple of hours to take Elena to the airport and then to borrow the truck. Thinking of Esteban irritated him, and his anger showed.

"Don't worry, do what you want," Shirley said. "Let's go back to New York right away if you want."

"Yes, let's go back to New York," he said. "It'll solve nothing, but if that's what you want, let's do it."

"Isn't that what you want to do?" she asked, and was suddenly completely awake. "Oh I forgot. What happened? Did something happen to Armando? Was there any trouble?"

"No, no, nothing's wrong," he said. "There's nothing to worry about." He closed his eyes. "Go back to sleep." He opened his eyes again and said accusingly, "Wake me up early. I have to be up in an hour."

As soon as she sensed his tone, she knew how to soothe him. "I was just sleepy," she said. "You know how dense sleep makes me. Tell me why you have to get up so early."

"Please, I can't talk now. I must go to sleep," he said irritably, but her interest had begun to make him feel better. "I have to do Esteban a favor today and lend him the store truck. It will take no more than an hour, but I have to be up early."

"Oh no, darling!" she said. "You're too tired. You can't ruin your Sunday that way. Tell him you can't."

He turned on his side. "Please," he said.

"Well, if you won't tell him, I will. It's your only day off and you've already been up all night." She sat up in bed and looked down at him. "Besides, what right does he have to ask you favors? You're not friends, or family either."

"No, but he thinks we are comrades in the same political struggle," Robert said, happy to be talking. "And I'm getting up anyway to drive Elena and her husband—how can I say no to him?"

"Oh, you don't have to worry about Elena," Shirley said quickly. "They've made other arrangements."

"*I want* to take them," Robert said. He looked at her in the dark. "They've offered me a job with them in Cuba. I owe it to them."

"Do you want to take it?" she asked in a careful, neutral voice.

He waited a moment. "Would you want to go?"

It dismayed her that he was forcing all these choices on her.

She felt it as a criticism of their life together, but she closed her mind to this and tried to think of it in the way he felt it. "And New York?" she said, still careful. "Don't you want to go back?"

"I've failed there; I'm sick of it," he said. "I'll never paint, you know that. And I don't see why you should put up with it any more. If we go to Cuba, you'll be comfortable for the first time. It's time I thought of you."

"I really can't stand it that you think of me like that!" she said, exploding with her real feelings. "It makes me feel as if I'm the villain in your life."

His surprise was genuine. "Why? It's you I'm thinking of."

It pained her, but she laughed. "And it's you I'm thinking of, and at this rate we'll never go to sleep." She put her hands on his head and gave it a playful squeeze. He turned and laid his head on her thigh. "What started us off?" she asked.

His voice was muffled but she heard him tell her clearly. "Esteban wants me to borrow the grocery truck and drive it to Sarasota with a load of things for the Cuban rebels."

She looked down at him. "Things?"

"Yes," he said. "Things."

Involuntarily, she put her hands on him. "And what did you say to him?"

"I told him I would *lend* him the truck." Her answering laugh made him feel so good that he told her exactly how the conversation with Esteban had gone. "And while you and I worry about this, he is in Clara's bed, screwing."

At first Shirley did not believe him, but he told her what their parting argument had been like. "Why should I take him seriously?" Robert said, aggrieved, half-conscious that he should have agreed to drive the truck for Esteban and his friends. "If that's what he's like, what he is proposing is just another adolescent adventure for him."

"Do you think she will let him?" Shirley asked. "I don't believe it."

"I don't care what he does," he said. "He has no right to get me involved in his pranks."

"No, he has no right," Shirley said half-heartedly. "I don't believe she would let him." She found herself trying to recall how Clara had looked and how she had acted, until she realized that Robert had been talking all the while, worrying about how big a chance he was taking in lending the truck.

The taxi honking brought Shirley to her feet. She opened the front door and waved; she wasn't greeting Elena; she was stopping the noise. As soon as Robert had fallen asleep, she had decided the whole thing was foolish and Robert was going to sleep the morning through. That was the way she put it to herself; he was going to sleep the morning through. She followed Clemencia and Jaime to the taxi, hoping by example to make them keep their voices low.

"I have one last favor to ask you," Elena said, without getting out of the taxi. "Little Jimmy is still not feeling well. Please keep an eye on things there. Clara is not the most competent person in the world."

Shirley watched the taxi drive away as if life would now be simpler for her, but she went back to sitting in front of the phone.

"Shirley!" Clemencia stood in the doorway of the kitchen and beckoned her. "Come have a cup of hot coffee with milk."

There was a bright, friendly look on Clemencia's face, and Shirley got up without thinking. Her mother-in-law never had been this intimate. She took another look at the phone, giving it one last chance to ring.

"You are worrying," Clemencia said, in the kitchen. "What is the matter?"

Shirley saw Clemencia wanted to have a good talk, now that her guests were gone. "Robert had very little sleep last night," she explained. "Esteban may call him this morning, and I just want to catch the phone when it rings, so it won't wake him."

"You don't want him to answer it?" When Shirley didn't answer, she went to the stove and put a light under the milk. "Well, Elena and Jaime should be off any minute. He was very polite, don't you think? I did my best to make him feel at home, for Dolores' sake. But, of course, he is used to much better."

"You gave him no reason to complain about anything." Shirley looked at the table as it had been set for Jaime and took the dishes away.

"You think so? You really think so?" Clemencia poured coffee for the two of them and sat at the table. "I would not want Dolores to think that we were lacking in hospitality to him. She might take it as a discourtesy to her."

So much milk in the coffee made it too sweet for Shirley, but she drank it anyway. "He liked the breakfast you prepared very much. He praised you to me," she said, lying.

"He's very polite, very polite. I suppose working in the Palace develops one's manners. But he did seem pleased. He spoke very well about Robert." Clemencia stopped and looked cautiously at Shirley. "Do you know that he wants to give him a job in Cuba?"

Shirley nodded and looked at Clemencia. She knew the old woman wanted Robert to stay in Tampa and hoped she could count on Shirley to persuade him not to go back to New York. But Cuba was a different matter. Shirley saw only a neutral look on Clemencia's face. Clemencia wanted to know first how Shirley felt. Before Shirley could reply, the phone rang, and she pulled her chair back and ran to it.

It was Esteban. "May I talk to Roberto?" he asked in Spanish.

Shirley understood, but answered in English. "He's asleep."

"Oh!" There was a pause. Then he spoke in English. "You are his wife?"

"Yes."

"This is Esteban Rios. I am very pleased to meet you."

"Thank you." She waited.

"Roberto is asleep?"

"Yes." She put her hand over her heart. It beat so loudly it seemed to be in her throat.

"Hello?" Esteban said.

"He is asleep," she said, loud and clear. She was going to add that she could not wake him, but suddenly she stopped, for her tight, tense throat told her that this matter was not foolishness for either Esteban or Robert, and she could not interfere.

With a loud noise, the door to the bedroom opened, and she saw, with relief, Robert coming out in his underwear, barefoot, his hair disheveled. With one hand he shaded his eyes and with the other he waved to her. "Let me speak to him," he said hoarsely. He cleared his throat loudly while Shirley stared back in alarm, holding the phone guiltily in one hand. "Give me the phone."

Shirley stepped back and stood at Clemencia's side.

"Esteban?" Robert said. "I'm all right." He cleared his throat again. "I just slept late."

"He should not be standing in his bare feet," Clemencia said to Shirley. "It's not good for him."

"Listen, I don't have the truck yet," Robert said. "I still have to go ask El Rubio."

Shirley was so relieved, she giggled. Suddenly, it seemed to her he just looked foolish, standing there in rumpled shorts, his hair uncombed and his feet dirty.

On the phone Esteban was saying, "You have a wonderful wife. If I had met a woman like that, perhaps my life would be different."

Robert waited a second to reply. "I'll go see El Rubio in a few minutes and take the truck there. Is that all right?"

It was as simple as that, Shirley thought. She watched him hang up and stand by the phone, scratching his head.

"I want to take a shower," Robert said. "Where are the kids?"

"Still sleeping," Shirley said, surprised that she could be talking to him so matter-of-factly. "Go ahead and shower. I'll make breakfast."

Clemencia clasped her hands together. "What is going on with Esteban? Why are you borrowing the truck?"

Robert looked at Shirley questioningly. Shirley shook her head. "I have to take a shower, old woman," he said to his mother.

"Not until you tell me."

Clemencia had never spoken to him commandingly in front of Shirley. "I insist."

Shirley decided to tell her. "Mother, he and Esteban . . ."

"Just a moment," Robert said. He smoothed his hair. "God damn it, I'm borrowing the truck for Esteban. He needs it."

Clemencia waited.

"He has to deliver some things to Sarasota," Robert said with finality.

"Very well," Clemencia said. "Don't stand there in your bare feet." She went back to the kitchen. At the door she turned. "And don't walk around without clothes. Get dressed." She beckoned to Shirley. "You have not finished your coffee. Let him go about his business. Why should you worry so much about him?"

"Yes," Shirley said to her, "yes, I'm coming." She smiled at Clemencia, but she held up a hand to ask her to wait. "Robert, are you sure you can get the truck?"

Robert looked at his mother and then at Shirley. "I don't know. I'll have to make up some excuse." He shrugged his shoulders. "I'll think of something," he added, and started for the bedroom.

Clemencia called after him, "Tell him you want to take the whole family to the beach at Clearwater. Like the days when you were a boy."

Robert laughed to himself and did not turn around. Clemencia beckoned to Shirley again. "Come have coffee. Let him think of something, if he is so smart."

Shirley followed her to the kitchen and sat down at the table. She watched Clemencia heat up the coffee. It all seemed so simple.

Clemencia turned to her and smiled. "Well, it looks like Roberto got as much sleep as was coming to him."

"Yes, yes," Shirley said. "He was so tired when he came home last night."

Clemencia sat at the table with her. "Not that I am going to worry about him any more. I know he is not my charge. I realized that this morning. He is in good hands." She looked at Shirley with wet eyes. "I think they like to feel there is always someone worrying about them at home."

"Mother, do you want us to stay in Tampa?" Shirley asked. She asked it briskly, to keep the old woman from getting too sentimental. "Or should Robert take the job in Cuba?"

"That is very nice, that you call me Mother," Clemencia said. "I have been meaning to tell you how nice that is, to have another child call me Mother."

Shirley looked down at her hands. They were silent a moment.

"I will tell you a secret," Clemencia resumed. "I know Robert very well, but I do not understand him. When he was young, it did not occur to me whether I understood him, but now it is different." She took a deep breath. "And then, he has been all these years in New York, leading another life. I cannot say what would be best for him to do because I don't understand him. Maybe it is because he thinks in English. I thought of that the other night. How can I understand him if he thinks in English?"

"Of course you understand him," Shirley protested. "You understand me."

Clemencia smiled. "I must admit I did not understand his father. Everything he did was a surprise to me. When he died, it was a surprise. I did not expect it. I thought he had a bad cold. It was pneumonia." She drank coffee and thought about what she had said. "And now they have penicillin. He need not have died. Who can understand these things?" She laughed to herself and grabbed one of Shirley's hands. "Listen, do not give me away. Don't tell anyone about our conversation. It would sound silly. I am getting so I talk more than Dolores and Mina."

Shirley laughed and got up to clear the table for Robert's breakfast. "I enjoy it. I was an orphan, you know."

Clemencia turned around and tried to look into her face. "How terrible it must have been for you!"

"Yes, it was terrible," Shirley said. "That's why I want my children to have a family. Not just a father and mother, but cousins and aunts and a grandmother."

"Yes, my dear," Clemencia said, "of course, of course."

Robert appeared in the doorway, dressed. "What are you two agreeing about?"

"When your mother says 'my dear,'" Shirley said to him, "she isn't being patronizing." She turned with a smile to Clemencia, but the old woman was at the stove frying eggs for Robert's breakfast. Her manner was reserved again, and she stood apart from Robert and Shirley. Robert ate without talking. He broke his silence once to ask if Elena and Jaime had left for Virginia. Then, when he finished, he asked Shirley to tell Esteban to wait for him, if Esteban called again—just in case there was some delay in getting the truck. Shirley casually followed him out to the porch.

Before Robert had reached the corner, his mother also came out. "I see he is not driving," she said to Shirley. "I guess he expects to get the truck for certain."

Shirley nodded. "Sit down, Mother. Let's not do any housework today."

Clemencia sat on the rocker, Shirley on the swing.

"I am sure El Rubio will say yes," Clemencia said, "even if he knows what it is for."

Shirley startled her with a glance.

"Oh my dear, I know he is up to no good," Clemencia said, waving a hand. "Esteban is always mixed up in political things, and Roberto is his father's son."

"I hope you're not worrying," Shirley said.

"Oh, El Rubio was a friend of my husband," Clemencia said. "And I have not bought groceries from him all these years for nothing. I expect he will say yes."

No, she isn't worrying, Shirley thought to herself. She brought her legs up to the swing and folded them under her skirt. Clemencia leaned back on the rocker and let it rock to and fro. The lady across the street came out on her porch, and she and Clemencia waved to each other. Suddenly, Shirley laughed. Clemencia looked at her, but Shirley only smiled and rocked the swing in time to Clemencia's rocker. They knew there was nothing more to say. They were just waiting.

When the phone rang, Clemencia went inside to answer it. Shirley got up and walked down to the garden to check on the children. She circled the house toward the back yard. If they stayed in Tampa, Shirley decided she would plant borders around the house. She found the children chasing each other around the grapefruit tree in their pajamas, and she led them inside. Getting them dressed and making them breakfast helped the time go by.

She went out into the back yard with them when they had eaten and circled the house again to join Clemencia out front. On the way, she picked a leaf from the lemon tree. It was a deep, waxy green and became shiny from rubbing.

On the porch Shirley found Clemencia standing at the top of the steps, greeting Mina who slowly climbed up to her. Shirley followed, happy to see her. "Aunt Mina!" she said, and kissed her.

"Well, they have left, Elena and Jaime," Mina said. "They waved to me on the way to the airport. I was sitting on the porch when they went by in a taxi. I thought Roberto was going to take them. Is he still sleeping?"

"Their plane must have already taken off," Clemencia said. "Feliz did not drive you over?"

Mina sighed and sat on the swing next to Shirley. "Baseball games, that's where Feliz goes every Sunday. You would think he would outgrow them," she said. "I don't think men go to watch the game. It is just another opportunity to stand around and talk and chew on their cigars. Good riddance!"

Now that Mina had settled down on the porch, Clemencia was not happy with her. She might ask about Robert again and that made her nervous. "But my Julian does not smoke cigars," she said, "and he goes to the games in Miami all the time, so you cannot say that is why he goes to see baseball."

Mina was surprised by the objection. "That is only a manner of speaking. He does not have to smoke cigars . . ." She stopped a moment to think about it, puzzled by the turn the conversation had taken. "If I say you got out on the wrong side of the bed this morning, I do not mean that you leaped over the bedposts or that you got out any particular side!" She laughed at herself. "You know what I mean. I don't have to explain."

Clemencia shook her head. "If you exaggerate, people will not understand."

"Mother, I meant to ask you," Shirley interrupted. "Who was on the telephone just now?"

Clemencia turned to Mina as she answered. "Oh yes, Clara called. Little Jimmy is sick, as Elena said."

"It cannot be very bad," Mina said, "or Elena would never have left. Clara is the mother, but it is Elena who really concerns herself with him."

"Elena asked us to keep an eye on him. She knew he was still sick," Clemencia explained, proud that she could pass on this information to her older sister. "Clara said he has been worse since Elena and Jaime left, but you cannot tell with children. He may just be complaining because they did not take him with them."

"Of course, of course," Mina said. "Poor boy."

"What did Clara want?" Shirley asked.

"Oh yes," Clemencia said. "I am so distracted. Clara wanted advice on which doctor to call."

"Tell her Dr. Rivera at the Centro Español," Mina said.

"I don't like to interfere," Clemencia said. "I told her Dolores knows just as much. Let her ask her mother."

"You know she swears by Dr. Ortiz and El Recurso Clinic," Mina protested. "He may be a good doctor, but that clinic he runs is not up-to-date."

"She only wants someone to come to the house to see him, not a hospital to send him to. After all, the boy only has a stomach ache."

Mina nodded. "Of course, of course. I think Dolores' children are taking after her. They make too much of everything. Poor Dolores. I must not talk this way. God will punish me."

"Anyway, Clara thought Esteban was here and that is another reason why she called," Clemencia continued, ignoring what she felt were Mina's usual exaggerations.

"Why should she think he would be here?" Mina asked.

"Well," Clemencia hesitated, "he and Roberto were thinking of getting together this morning, and that is what they told her when she called Esteban at home."

Mina did not know which question to ask first. "Roberto and Esteban getting together? Why should she be calling Esteban? Do you think it is just an excuse to talk to Esteban?" She felt slighted and out of things. "Why didn't she call me? I have nothing to do. Once I water the plants on the porch I am not needed for anything!"

Mina got up from the swing and started for the steps.

"Aunt Mina," Shirley said, "don't worry. It's very natural she should call Jimmy's father to ask his advice." After she said it, she remembered what Robert had told her about Clara and Esteban last night.

"Please, please," Clemencia said, "don't get excited. They are getting Dr. Ortiz. I could hear Dolores advising Clara to call him, and that is what Clara decided to do."

Mina stopped and leaned against the veranda, smiling. "Of course, of course," she said. "That Clara has lost the brains she was born with, to call you up this way and get you all excited."

"Do you think," Clemencia asked, "it was just a maneuver to try to get Esteban back?"

"Never, never," Mina said, "not with the company she got used to in Cuba. You heard what Dolores said last night. A Cuban of good family is very interested in her."

"Never mind, Esteban is intelligent and well-spoken."

Mina smiled and brought a hand to her chest. "Oh I have always liked Esteban. He is charming and delightful." She rolled her eyes to explain to Shirley how Esteban affected her. "That Clara is a foolish girl. She thinks about herself so much that she cannot be a good judge of men."

Shirley was certain now that Clara had welcomed Esteban to her bed.

"You are right; I do not think Esteban would be interested in her any more," Clemencia said. "Not with his ideas. I would not tell Dolores, but, after all, Clara is not a serious person."

"Yes, yes," Mina said. She sighed and straightened her dress. "I think I will go there, after all. They may need me if little Jimmy is really sick. Elena would appreciate it. She would not trust Clara to take care of him properly. She and Jaime have come to feel he is their own son. A pity they cannot have one of their own."

Clemencia got up. "Why don't you wait for me? Roberto will drive us."

Mina started down the steps. "No, do not disturb him. I have to stop at home first anyway. Then my daughter-in-law can drive me over. She is going to pick up Feliz at the baseball park afterwards."

"Are you sure, Aunt Mina?" Shirley asked. She didn't see Clemencia's warning look; if Mina left now, she wouldn't find out where Robert was.

"Yes, my dear," Mina answered from the bottom of the steps. "Feliz's wife always goes to pick him up in the car. She is his fourth wife and I guess that makes her nervous. She is not going to let him out of her sight for too long. I don't blame her."

"Don't talk nonsense," Clemencia said, hoping the neighbors wouldn't hear them.

Mina did not lower her voice. "At my age, little sister, it is all right if I talk a little nonsense. It is permitted." She stopped and smiled at Shirley. "That is why we should not blame Dolores for anything her children do. Look at my Feliz!"

"Never mind," Clemencia said, suddenly ashamed of herself. "He has been a good son to you."

"Oh they are all good children. Sometimes they are a little foolish, but they are all good children."

Mina turned away and started toward the street. Clemencia crossed her arms over her stomach and shook her head as she watched her sister go. Shirley still held the lemon leaf in her hand and thought of her innocent children playing in the back yard. She could not believe that she would ever come to think of them like that, but her heart felt as if a weight had been placed on it. It was a warning of the thousand things that could happen to her until, like Mina, her heart was forced to admit that her children could be not without fault.

IX

Mina stepped back onto the walk when she saw the delivery truck turn the corner in a great hurry heading for her. It stopped with a screech. Robert sat next to the driver, and Mina threw up her arms at the sight of him. She turned to the women on the porch and called out, "Look, look! Roberto is here. I thought he was inside asleep."

Clemencia and Shirley looked surprised too—not only that Robert should have come back with the truck but that Esteban should be driving it. Robert jumped out and slammed the door behind him without a word to Esteban. Esteban took off as soon as the door slammed, and Mina waved away the exhaust fumes.

"And Esteban too!" she exclaimed, as she watched the truck speed away down the street. "Where is he going? What is he doing in El Rubio's truck?"

Robert looked at Shirley and Clemencia and saw that they had said nothing to his aunt. "I just ran into him," he said to her. "He wanted to borrow the truck." Then he took Mina's arm gallantly. "And where are you going this Sunday morning?" He narrowed his eyes to imply that she must be off on some romantic escapade.

"Listen, my dear," she said, keeping him at her side, "let me tell you about Esteban. You may not know what he is mixed up in these days or the game he is playing . . ."

"Mina!" Clemencia called from the porch. "Don't stand out there talking. Come inside."

"Oh we should have told Esteban!" Shirley exclaimed. "Little Jimmy is sick."

"He knows, he knows," Robert said. He looked at Shirley and raised his eyebrows to let her know that he couldn't say more. "Come," he said to Mina, "come inside."

"Then you do know about him," Mina said. "It is not news to you what I am saying about Esteban! I can tell. You don't have to say another word." She shook off his arm. "I will go inside, since you cannot talk about your activities in the open." She walked

124

ahead and climbed the steps to the porch quickly. Out of breath, she grabbed Clemencia's hands to claim her attention. "Have you been standing by and letting him get involved with that madman?"

Shirley came down the steps and asked Robert, "What has happened?"

He said quietly, "They may have to take Jimmy to the hospital, and Esteban's first going to load the truck and then find out."

"Is Jimmy that sick?"

They walked toward the steps, Robert slightly ahead. "Esteban may have to stay," he said.

Mina turned from Clemencia and began to advise Robert. "You have a wife and two children. Esteban has no responsibilities; he does not provide for his only child; he is not there even when the child is sick. What is he doing with your truck?"

Robert tried to calm her. "I don't know. He asked me to lend it to him and I did. I have no reason not to."

"Ah, you act so innocent," Mina said. "But your mother should know better. Everyone in Ybor City knows they are running guns to the rebels in Cuba, and Esteban is right in the thick of it. What is poor old El Rubio going to do if they catch his truck full of guns? He has worked all his life to build that grocery store. He will be ruined."

"He's not a poor old man," Robert said. "That scar on his bald spot he got from an Arab while fighting for the king in Morocco. He survived that and he'll survive this."

"And you—it will be worse for you," Mina continued. "This is against the law, and if all Ybor City knows about Esteban, the Americans must know, too. This is not the Ybor City of your childhood—Americans and Latins are friends now. They talk to each other."

"Yes, yes," Robert said, "I know all about that."

"Promise me," Mina said. She turned to Clemencia. "Promise your mother that when that irresponsible madman returns the truck, you will not lend it to him again."

"Oh if that's all you want," Robert said lightly, "then I promise."

Mina was surprised. She tried to catch his eye to see for herself, then turned to Shirley and Clemencia. "What? Does he mean it?" She grabbed him by the waist and made him look at her. Robert nodded and smiled, and with a little gasp, Mina threw her arms around him.

"Come, Mina," Clemencia said, wondering why Robert had returned with Esteban. "Don't get so excited. I don't know what you were imagining."

Mina pulled back and smiled at Shirley and Clemencia, her eyes glistening with tears. "He is still the same child he once was," she said to Shirley, "sweet and obliging."

"He was rebellious and hardheaded," Clemencia said.

"Not that I mean you to abandon your ideas," Mina said to Robert. "You know I am as strong a Socialist as you. And when it comes to that, I like Esteban very much. He is a charming man and that Clara is a fool."

"Aunt Mina," Shirley said and looked at Clemencia so she would listen, too, "little Jimmy is quite sick. Esteban is probably on his way to Dolores' house now."

"What has happened? What has happened?"

"Robert says they may have to take him to the hospital."

"To the hospital!" Mina looked at Robert for confirmation. "And I have been acting the fool!"

Clemencia took off her apron. "Come, Mina," she said, "let us go to Dolores' now. If little Jimmy is really sick, she will need help, and that Clara was never a good housekeeper."

"Yes, yes," Mina said. "She will need us." She looked at Robert and Shirley shamefacedly. "The truth is, I am a coward."

Clemencia took her arm. "Come, we are walking," she said, sensing that Robert wanted to stay home with Shirley. "We do not need drivers. First to Mina's house and then Feliz's wife will take us." Mina nodded at every word Clemencia said, and they helped each other down the steps.

At the curb Mina said to Clemencia, "I had been meaning to go to church and say a prayer for poor Armando, so he will have a safe trip to Cuba." She looked at Clemencia and caught her frown. "But we will not go now, of course. I only meant to get there between Masses, say my prayer, and avoid all that hocus-pocus in Latin."

"But Armando is already in Cuba. Elena told us this morning they had already talked to him on the phone."

"Of course, of course." Mina shrugged her shoulders and looked back to wave at Shirley and Robert.

They were seated on the swing watching the old ladies. As soon as they were out of sight, Shirley asked, "If Esteban has to be at the hospital, if he cannot drive the truck . . ."

Robert smiled, hoping she would see the humor in the situation. "Then, I will drive it—as a favor."

She thought he was just trying to act brave. "And what do you do now?"

"Wait."

"Wait?"

He nodded and took out a cigarette. "For Esteban and the truck."

She licked her lips; they were suddenly dry. "He's bringing the truck here? Loaded?"

He turned to her, beginning to catch her fear, and took a puff of his cigarette. "Then he'll tell me where to drive it."

"You don't know?"

"More or less. He'll tell me exactly, if he comes back." He was silent a moment. "It's nothing very much, you know. Nothing to worry about."

Shirley finally looked at him and saw that he was frightened. She tried to say something to keep him from noticing her silence, but nothing came to mind. He reached out and put a hand on her knee. "I guess I was very tired last night, but, really, there's nothing to worry about. I just can't refuse to do Esteban this favor." He smiled at her. "It's only Latin good manners. It wouldn't be nice to say no."

This time she laughed out loud. "Give me a cigarette," she said.

"I think Esteban suspects that I don't believe it's such a great cause, that I'm only doing it out of courtesy," Robert said, and lit the cigarette for her. She remembered what he had said last night; he couldn't fool her. "The Red scare has frightened me," he had said. "They have cut off my balls."

"It doesn't have to be important to be a good cause," Shirley said hesitatingly, because she didn't want to argue.

"So are the polio drive and the cancer drive and all of them," he said. "I mean the Cuban rebels bother no one, except the President a little bit. And he has his Army. No one cares. They're not going to get anywhere, and they don't antagonize anyone. That's why there's nothing to worry about if I drive the truck to Sarasota—or not."

"You know what?" Shirley threw away her cigarette. "I think there must be some justice to their cause, and you do too, I bet."

"I doubt very much if they know what they're about, those Cuban boys," he answered, not catching the determined gesture with which she threw away her cigarette. "Anyway, I couldn't say no. It's just playing games. That's all it is, and it's not nice to say no. Besides, people in Ybor City, like Esteban, think you're Lenin if you lived in New York during the New Deal and knew Communists and distributed leaflets. You can't let them down. You have to help them keep up their illusions."

"You do?" Shirley asked.

Robert took her seriously. "Yes, that's what makes us human beings; we buoy each other up."

Shirley looked out at the sidewalk. "I didn't know you felt this way."

"What way?" He finally recognized the tone of her voice. "You make it sound as if I'm discussing some personal matter."

"I know, just like a woman." She carefully pulled a loose thread from her skirt. "I didn't know you felt so hopeless." She saw him grip the arm of the rocker and knew she had better say something conciliatory or they would have a fight. "I've been thinking, Robert, that you might really consider Elena's offer. Her husband spoke of it this morning."

"He did?" He turned to her, interested.

"He seemed genuine about it," she said, remembering that she had been rude to Jaime. "It might be a good thing. It could be interesting. I've never been out of the country, and you—you could paint."

Robert looked away. "Do you think so?"

"Yes, I think so. I don't think you ought to be so hopeless." She laughed to keep from crying. "Just because we're middle-aged."

"There would be so much to arrange," Robert said, knowing he raised a weak obstacle. "All our things are in New York. We're half settled here . . ."

The phone rang inside, and Shirley got up. He looked at her with a foolish smile. "It can be done," Shirley said, walking to the door. "We can do it." She didn't have to look at him; she knew he was pleased.

As soon as she took the phone off the hook and said hello, a woman's voice began to talk so hysterically in Spanish Shirley could not make it out. Finally, she interrupted in English. "This is not Clemencia. This is Shirley, her daughter-in-law," she said. "Clemencia isn't here."

"What did you say?" the voice asked slowly. "Who is this?"

"This is Shirley, Clemencia's daughter-in-law."

"Oh, oh thank God, it's not a wrong number. This is Clara. I met you last night. I'm Dolores' daughter."

"What's the matter?" Shirley asked. "How is Jimmy?"

"He's sick, very sick. I'm all alone and the doctor is sending the ambulance. Esteban promised to be here and he's not. It's just like him."

Shirley made her voice very calm. "What is wrong with Jimmy?"

"Appendicitis. The doctor wants him at the hospital because he thinks he should operate on him right away, and I'm all alone—"

"Clara, Clara," Shirley interrupted, "Clemencia and Aunt Mina are on the way. They left a few minutes ago for your house when they heard Jimmy was sick."

"Oh thank God!" Clara said. "Thank God!"

"Listen, Clara, listen," Shirley said. "Jimmy's father will be there too. I know for a fact."

"He will?" Clara's voice was unbelieving. "I can't count on him. They are sending the ambulance for little Jimmy because I am all alone—you understand that? I can't trust myself to drive the car and I can't count on Esteban. When he goes, I never know if he'll come back."

"Listen, Clara," Shirley insisted, "I know he will be there. He said so . . . to Robert."

"Let him come, let him, but I don't need him," Clara said. "I sent a telegram to my sister in Virginia. But Esteban should be here now. I wish Elena hadn't left—I must get off the phone. Jimmy's crying."

"All right, as soon as we can, we'll come over too," Shirley said.

"Shirley! Shirley!" Clara said loudly to get her back.

"Yes? I didn't hang up."

"I almost forgot, please forgive me," Clara said. "You understand, I'm very nervous. A man came here to ask about Armando—a detective. I told him he was away on vacation. He wanted to know where Roberto lives. Tell Roberto. You understand, I couldn't refuse to tell him."

"When was this?" Shirley asked, alarmed. "What did he want?"

"A few minutes ago, when the doctor was here. I didn't know what to do with him. Before I knew it, I told him where Roberto lives. Don't let Roberto tell him where Armando went."

"Don't worry; it's all right." Shirley looked out at the front door, eager to get off the phone and warn Robert. "We'll see you as soon as we can. Don't worry." She put the phone back, suddenly angry with Clara, and rushed to the door.

"Robert—" She stopped when she saw the stranger sitting on the swing. She knew immediately it was the detective. She looked quickly to the street and noticed there was a car parked just behind the palm tree, one that hadn't been there before. If Clara hadn't yet seen Esteban, it would still be some time before he would arrive with the loaded truck.

"What's the matter?" Robert asked. He sounded casual, but his eyes darted from her to the street.

Shirley shook her head. She was too frightened to speak.

"This is my wife," Robert said. "Casper Friend."

Casper got up and smiled. "I'm pleased to meet you. You must also know Armando well?"

Fear made her mouth so dry that she could not speak.

"Casper's a detective on the police force," Robert said, looking at Shirley with a foolish smile. "We went to high school together."

Casper chuckled. "Your husband doesn't trust me, ma'am," he said. "He just couldn't wait to tell you I'm on the police force." He laughed when he saw Shirley bite her lip. "Sounds very impressive, police force and all that, but I guess you know Tampa is a pretty pokey place compared to New York. I mean, they got a real police force in New York and pretty tough characters, I hear."

Casper remained standing because Shirley had not seated herself. She didn't quite know what to do. It seemed to her the detective expected her to go back into the house. "I don't think my husband meant anything special," Shirley said, and sat on an old porch chair next to Robert. When Esteban arrived, she decided, she would run to him and make him drive away with her. If need be, *she* could drive the truck to Sarasota.

Casper raised his eyebrows. "Well, I can't pretend I'm here on a friendly visit," he said, and sat down on the swing as if he were on a friendly visit. He laughed at the serious look on their faces. "I mean, I'm friendly and all, but I wouldn't have the pleasure of seeing you again, Bob, after all these many years, and meeting your charming wife"—he nodded and smiled at Shirley—" if I weren't on the police force, like you say."

"Then you must be talking about what happened last night," Shirley said. "Is that why you're here?"

"Well now, you get right to the point, ma'am," Casper said. He smiled and winked at Robert. "And if I didn't trust you, ma'am, I'd ask you where Armando went." He paused just a moment and looked at her so steadily that she did not feel she could look at Robert without giving away Armando's secret. "And whatever you said would prove that old Bob here doesn't trust me."

"It seems Armando isn't home," Robert explained to Shirley. He looked at her with eyes blank with feigned innocence. "Did you know that?"

Shirley looked at her husband, wondering what she was to say. "No, I didn't know."

Casper looked down, shook his head and laughed to himself. "You sure are both one pair of terrible liars." He took out a pack of cigarettes, chuckled, offered them first to Shirley, then to Robert, and chuckled again. "My advice to you is keep on leading a nice quiet life, 'cause you wouldn't make very good crooks. You just too honest to be, Bob. I can see all over you that you're telling a little white lie."

"Come on, now," Robert said. "There's no reason for me to lie."

"Come on now *yourself*, Bob. You can't tell me you were so concerned about that boy last night and today he disappears like a nigger in a mudhole and you don't know anything about it!" Casper struck a match and held it a moment. He looked at them and shook his head. When the match had burned down almost down to his fingers, he lit the cigarette. "Oh, oh I know if I check on it, I'll find out you just didn't drive him home only."

Shirley sat up straight in her chair. "You haven't any right to question us and there's nothing my husband has to answer."

"That's all right, Shirley," Robert said. If they kept quiet, Robert decided, Casper might leave before Esteban returned with the truck.

"Your husband knows, ma'am, that I'm a friend," Casper said quietly. "Last night he was telling Armando the same you're telling me. Get a lawyer and what not. But he knows now I'm Armando's friend. Didn't he come with us and answer all questions truthfully, and didn't we let him go just like I said?"

Casper inclined his face toward Robert and waited with a fixed, questioning expression.

Robert finally cleared his throat and agreed. "Yes, that's true."

"I know you folks know where he went." He leaned back on the swing. "But that's all by the bye. I don't even want to know. If I did, I'd be down here with a warrant and a couple of police officers, and we'd flush that nigger out of his mudhole for sure."

Shirley got up from her chair. "I don't like that expression. Not one bit."

"I beg your pardon," Casper scrambled out of the swing and stood up respectfully. "That's just a manner of speaking. I don't mean anything about Armando. He's a friend of mine. Hell, we've played a lot of poker games together, begging your pardon."

"I would not care if Armando were a Negro," Shirley said, to make sure he understood.

"Forget it," Robert said. "He doesn't mean anything." He stood up too, hoping that Casper would leave now.

"I forgot you were a Northerner," Casper said. He bowed a little. "You got me wrong, though I got nothing against colored people, and neither do most folks down here, even if they do get riled up about integration. I don't get excited about it at all. The way I figure it, it's no use worrying. I think we'd be all the better for it, if in a few hundred years we were all a light chocolate color. There wouldn't be no problems then. We'd all be a nice even color and there won't be no color lines, no segregation. Mark my words, that's the way it'll be in a few hundred years."

They stood a moment in silence. "Looks like we're playing musical chairs," Casper said. "I'd consider it an honor if you sat down, ma'am. I just have one, two things I'd like to say to Bob and then I leave you to enjoy your Sunday."

"Please excuse me," Shirley said. "I have something to attend to."

Casper remained standing until she opened the screen door. She heard him say, "And then Florida won't be full of Yankees all winter long, 'cause they wouldn't need any sun to warm their bones. They'd stay brown all year round."

Casper smacked his leg and cackled loudly, and she felt as if she had been slapped. At the same time it occurred to her that she could call Dolores' house and head off Esteban. "Son of a bitch," she said to herself. She dismissed Casper with a wave of the hand and rushed to the phone. Clara answered. She was too late. Esteban had been there and was now on the way.

Slowly, she went back to the porch door and heard Casper talking. If only he would leave. She realized now how foolish it had been to argue with him. She could have helped by staying quiet as Robert had. She leaned against the wall and looked out at the street. The woman across the street came out on her porch with a broom and started sweeping dust onto the plants bordering the porch. Clemencia would never do that. "It's dust, not soil," she always said. The woman on the porch looked up as if she knew she was being studied. Shirley watched a car come around the corner, and she immediately guessed it was the delivery truck.

She dashed out to the porch so quickly that Casper looked up in surprise.

"Like I said, ma'am, we're all friends here," Casper said, putting up his hands.

Shirley nodded to Casper and watched Esteban bring the truck to a stop behind Casper's car. He leaned over the wheel and looked at their porch. She could not tell if he could see Casper, and she started down the steps to warn him. She saw Esteban straighten up, look at the woman on the porch across the street and nod to her. He got out of the truck, greeted the woman, and went straight to her. Shirley hesitated. She decided she should go back to Robert; it would look suspicious if she went over to the truck.

When Casper looked up at her, Robert quickly studied the truck. The tires looked as if they needed air. It must be heavily loaded. He was grateful that Esteban had not come to their porch when he saw the stranger, but from the moment that Casper arrived, Robert had resigned himself to the situation. He had the peculiar sensation that fate had taken over, that all the possibilities were very clear; yet the only thing he could do was sit and nod at Casper.

Shirley stopped in front of Casper, hoping to block his view of the truck and of Esteban on the porch across the street. "I guess Robert has told you—uh, uh—I'm sorry, I've forgotten your name."

"Casper Friend. Call me Casper or call me Friend." He laughed. "That's a joke, I always say."

Shirley nodded, still refusing to smile. "Mr. Friend, Robert probably told you Armando is his cousin, but we didn't know Wally Chase or anything about him."

"Why, sure," Casper said, "I understand. I told Bob I only came to see Armando this morning to talk things over, nothing official, and the women over at his house couldn't help me so I came over to see Bob. Nothing official, but if it was anybody else but me, they'd think it funny that Armando up and left so quick."

"I see," Shirley said.

When Esteban went into the house across the street, Robert looked at Casper again and nodded, as if he had been following him closely.

"I wanted to focus him in on what we have been thinking at headquarters, Bob," Casper said to him. "We been up all night, looking into every clue, following our noses, and tracking down every lead like hound dogs. And it looks like we came to the end of the trail."

Robert was interested for the first time. "Then you found out who did it?"

"Not exactly, but that's not important," Casper said. "You can always catch the person. It's the broad picture that you've got to see, and then who did it is just one little old piece in the puzzle. Isn't that so?" He didn't stop for an answer, although he spoke so slowly that Shirley thought each sentence would never come to an end. "What we know now is that old Wally was killed on account of a personal feud, not a gang killing like people are bound to think. That's what I told you last night, wasn't it, Bob? Gang killings are a thing of the past. I mean, we got things too much under control for such a thing to happen."

Shirley shot up from her chair. "Excuse me," she said, and gestured to Casper to remain seated. "I have to see my neighbor." She skipped down the steps and ran across the street.

Robert had not expected this from her, and Casper caught the look of surprise on his face. "Just like my wife," Casper said. "You can be talking along, everything easy as pie, and suddenly she jumps up and runs out right in the middle of a sentence. Likely as not, she left the string beans burning on the stove."

"I remember now," Robert said. "She wants a baby-sitter because we're going out this afternoon."

"See what I mean?" To Robert's surprise, Casper got up. "Man-to-man, I just wanted to make sure Armando hasn't got any ideas of his own how to solve this. I know he thought very highly of old Wally and he might go off half-cocked to avenge him and talk to the newspapers. You never know what people will do in a state of shock. Isn't that so?"

Robert got up. "You're right."

"Sure. The best thing is to let sleeping dogs lie and keep them out of the hot sun." He stopped, happy with his figure of speech. "So it's all right if Armando's taking a little vacation and doesn't talk to the newspapers. We don't need him for any inquest; he's got no information they need, and he ain't involved anyway. So when you see him, give him that little message for me, hear?"

"Of course," Robert said, moving toward the steps. "I'd be glad to."

"Just tell him to keep his nose clean like he's been doing all along. Tell him not to worry; we'll get whoever did this to old Wally. It's no gang killing or anything like that at all," Casper said, walking to the steps. "Got any idea what Armando's going to do?"

Robert shook his head.

"I mean, if he's got a job lined up." He looked at Robert closely. "Well, plenty of time for that. Let him take it easy for a while."

"No, I don't know, but I can tell you he's not going to do anything rash," Robert said. "He was just upset last night about what happened, and that anybody should suspect him."

Casper chuckled to himself. "Well, there's nothing to worry about on that account. I told him myself last night; he's in the clear. Man, we know he's a good boy." He lowered his voice and looked around. "Everything he told us checked. He's sure lucky he's dipping his wick with an honest whore." Casper's chuckle rose to a thin, high cackle.

Robert stayed at the top of the steps and watched him walk to his car. The thing to remember about detectives, Robert said to himself, is that they always wear a jacket to hide the gun they carry, just as all cops are big-assed for the same reason. Casper never looked at the truck. He went straight to his car and got into it just as Shirley came out of the house across the street. She walked casually to the curb. When she saw him, she smiled with relief.

Casper took one hand off the wheel and saluted her. "Good-bye now," he called, and pulled away from the curb.

Robert met Shirley halfway. "What happened?"

"He couldn't wait. They're taking little Jimmy to the hospital."

Robert looked at the truck's tires again. "What did Esteban say?" He started toward the truck, and Shirley followed. "When does he want me to go?"

"Right now, as soon as your friend left." She took a piece of paper out of her dress pocket. "Here, he wrote out instructions for you."

Robert sat behind the wheel of the truck and shook his head at Shirley when she tried to look beyond him into the inside of the truck. She looked away and attempted lightheartedness.

"I think our neighbor is going to think Esteban and I are carrying on an illicit affair."

"What?" Robert asked, serious. "Did he . . ."

"Don't be silly!" She put her hand on his shoulder. "Latins aren't the amorous types you think." She was sure he was wrong about Esteban and Clara.

Robert settled himself behind the wheel, leaned out and kissed her on the cheek.

"What will you do if . . ."

He looked at her with a smile. "If what?"

"If you're stopped."

"Nothing. I'll say nothing. I'll let you come and do all the talking."

"I'm sorry," she said. "I had to say something to that Casper. He's a disgusting human being."

"Yes, I guess he is." He held the note from Esteban in front of him, but he didn't open it. "He has very strong hands, I noticed. I looked at them so much I think I can draw them from memory. You couldn't use them in a piéta. In a lynching maybe, but not in a piéta. They are not exactly helping hands."

"What does the note say?" Shirley asked.

"It's not important."

"Never mind, I want to see it," she said. "I want to know where you're going."

He opened the note, and she looked at it over his shoulder. "God damn it," she said, "it's in Spanish!"

Robert translated for her. "Take Route 41 to Sarasota and make a right turn at the bridge when you get into the city and go for two blocks. Park across from the City Hall in front of Pappas' Restaurant. Leave the keys in the truck. When you get out, a man will say to you, *Hello, Diosdado, didn't your father work at the Clock?* And you will say, *Yes, he used to roll cigars.* Go into Pappas' Restaurant and have a big late lunch for about an hour, and when you come out the truck will be back. Try the crawfish. It's delicious. They serve it broiled and give you melted butter to go with it. I recommend it."

"I envy you," Shirley said, and stepped back from the curb.

"Good-bye now," he said, with a false Southern accent.

"Robert . . ." She stopped a moment. Her mouth had become dry again. "If you want to know where I'll be, I'll be at Dolores' house. All right?"

"All right," he said, and drove away in the rattling old truck.

X

SHIRLEY went back to the house without looking after Robert, but when she reached the porch, she checked and saw he had turned at the far corner. A thrill of fear went through her and she had to sit down. Robert had forgotten his cigarettes on the swing. She took one and lighted it. Robert was breaking the law, and she was helping him. But what law? The question immobilized her until the ash of the cigarette reached her fingertips. She got up and put it out. Maybe there was no law . . .

She went inside, made the beds, and took a look at the kitchen. She couldn't stay there; it might be hours before Robert returned, and she couldn't spend that time alone. Elena had asked her to help Clara with Jimmy, and that was a good enough excuse to leave. Robert expected her to be there, too.

She ran next door and arranged to have her neighbor's oldest girl take care of the children. They'd play in the yard and then go to the movies in the afternoon, and after today things would go back to their normal routine.

No, not the normal routine, she told herself while she dressed. Maybe it had been the children who made her abdicate—they gave her enough to do—but it wasn't going to be like that any more. They were going to decide things together, as they had done before the children were born, and she wasn't going to ask Robert what he intended to do and wait quietly for his answer. For one thing, they weren't going to stay here. It was all very well for Robert—he had one foot in the place—but not her. For her it was like trying to live in some primitive, Margaret Mead society. As soon as she thought that, she looked in the mirror and laughed.

It was the first time she had walked to Dolores' house, and she was not certain of the way, but she had two guide posts: Mina's house and the clock tower on the cigar factory. After the solid concrete of New York, the sidewalks were playfully narrow and undecided; she could almost convince herself that they shifted in

137

the loose sand when she stepped on them. On some blocks there was sidewalk in front of one or two houses only, islands in the gray sand; on others there was none at all, and she had to step out into the red brick streets. Even when walking in the street she could hear the sounds of Spanish from the houses, like radios turned loud. Occasionally, children spoke English, sweet and shrill; it was almost upsetting to hear this English, so unlike the English in the neighborhood park in New York where she took her children. Suddenly, she remembered the little park in The Bronx and her neighborhood friends. It was like remembering who she was. How would she tell her friends about Ybor City without making it sound exotic?

When she opened the screen door to Dolores' porch, she heard Mina exclaim inside, "It is here!" Then Mina appeared at the door and told the others in the living room, "No, it is Shirley."

Dolores was sitting on the sofa with Clemencia. "Oh my dear, look how we are troubling you! You should not have come." She held up her arms to embrace Shirley. "What a thoughtful, sweet girl you have, Clemencia!"

Shirley leaned down to kiss her. "I didn't want to be alone in the house." Clemencia's face was close to hers, the alert eyes questioning her about Robert; and Shirley nodded to reassure her.

Clemencia, too, felt like drawing Shirley near and giving her a kiss. Instead, she asked, "Did you leave the children with Sylvia? Good, good. We are happy you came."

"Shirley, would you like a cup of *tilo?*" Mina asked. There were three cups and a teapot on the coffee table. When Shirley shook her head, she commented, "How wonderful to be young. When you get to be our age, your nerves will not be as strong and you will be able to use a cup of *tilo.*"

Shirley sat across from the couch where the three old women huddled together. "Whom were you expecting?" she asked.

"That accursed ambulance," Mina said. "It is not here yet!"

"It hasn't come!" Shirley got up. "Let me drive him to the clinic. I can drive Armando's car."

Dolores put a hand on Mina. "There, you have alarmed the girl." She shook her head sadly. "No, it is not necessary. Dr. Ortiz cannot operate for another hour and a half, and Esteban is here to drive if it does not come soon."

The door of the bedroom opened, and Clara came out, looking around dully for the owner of the new voice she had heard. Her eyes were wide and grave, and she looked pale without make-up, as if she were doing penance. She looked at Shirley a moment and startled the old women by saying to Shirley, "Forgive me, I had forgotten what you looked like since last night."

"It's Shirley, my dear," Dolores said. "Roberto's wife."

Clara nodded. "He seems to have fallen asleep, Mama. The pills have worked, I guess."

Anxiety had so changed Clara's face that Shirley could not look away from her. She was not the person that she and Robert had gossiped about last night, and Shirley was sorry that she had listened to Robert.

"Clara," Shirley said, and got up to go to her, "may I go inside and sit with him for a while?"

"His father is there now." Clara stopped and looked at Shirley in a daze. "He's sleeping quietly."

Mina sighed with relief. "It is so good that they have all these medicines nowadays. When Feliz was a boy and had the same thing, all the doctor told us to do was ice bags, ice bags, ice bags! He was not only in pain, he was freezing!"

"Oh yes," Clemencia said, "it's wonderful nowadays. It doesn't even matter if the appendix bursts, they just give them penicillin and it cures it right away."

Mina gave her a furious glance. "God forbid it! I am sure Dr. Ortiz knows what he is doing."

"He said it was a very simple case," Dolores said. "I have always had great confidence in him. He has just a little, old-fashioned clinic, but he is one of the finest surgeons in Florida. He could have his pick of the hospitals, if he wanted." She stretched out a hand before her. "Did you notice what delicate hands he has and with what gentleness he examined little Jimmy? If you did not know he was a surgeon his hands would give him away."

"I don't think a man should wear a diamond ring on his little finger," Mina said. "It is his business, but it does not look right."

"No, my dear, it is very elegant," Dolores said.

"Doctors should not show off their wealth," Mina explained. "It has been made off the unhappiness of others. It is unfeeling, that is what it is, to wear diamond rings."

Clara looked at the old women and then looked away. She started to say something but forgot it. She looked at Shirley, momentarily envious; then her eyes moved away, and she quickly forgot.

"But Dr. Ortiz has treated so many who did not have a penny," Dolores said. "You know yourself. Old Consuelo always runs to him, and he has yet to ask her for money. The good Lord knows he has an expensive wife and he has put up with her all these years. He is a man with a great heart." She stopped and sipped the *tilo*. When she saw Clara's distracted look, she tried to draw her into the conversation. "You know, Clara, they say he is in love with Felicia Soler. You remember her; she went to school with you. Now she is a nurse at the clinic. So pretty, so tragic. Ah!"

Clara looked up. "I wish they would come," she said. "I'd feel better if they were here."

"They are as good as here," Mina said quickly. Her eyes said to Clara, *Don't alarm your mother, take hold of yourself.* "It is better when these things happen if they are young. They're not so serious then. Adults don't take illnesses as well as children."

Shirley tried again. "Clara, we don't have to wait for them if you don't want to. Between you and me and Esteban, we can take Jimmy in Armando's car."

"Clara doesn't mean the ambulance," Clemencia said. "She means Elena and Jaime. The ambulance—"

"But they're . . ." Shirley interrupted.

"They are flying back," Clemencia explained.

Dolores sighed. "Their vacation is ruined. It is my fault." Her eyes filled with tears. "But I like my children around me when there is trouble. It is my weakness, I know, but I cannot help myself." She took out her handkerchief and wiped her eyes. "Thank you, my dear Shirley, for coming."

"What is done is done," Mina said. "They can fly back as soon as they see he is well. And in three hours his appendix will be a thing of the past." She waved an arm at Clara as if to shake her out of her stupor. "It will, you know, be just like that, and he will be sitting up and wanting to go out and play. You will have your hands full, and thank God for that."

Clemencia nodded in agreement, hoping to erase in their minds her comments on burst appendixes. "Oh yes, he'll be fine."

"It is a curious thing about an appendix," Mina continued, making an effort to keep the room filled with conversation. "It is a little tail on the intestines, would you believe it? I made old Dr. Perez tell me all about it, years ago when Feliz had it. That little tail just gets inflamed and infected, without any warning whatsoever. I am sure Feliz got it from eating too many guavas, slightly green ones at that. There is nothing worse than unripe guavas for the stomach, as you all know. All those thousands of green seeds settle like balls of lead in the intestines, and it takes a really strong purgative like castor oil to blast them out. It is logical; those guava seeds simply settled at the wrong end of his intestines."

Clara had been listening to her steadily. "And everything turned out all right?" she asked.

"Of course, of course," Mina said, happy to have aroused her. "Feliz has always been very strong, very strong. It did not stop him a minute, that operation. Tric-trac, they snipped it off and that was all."

Clara winced.

"Oh there is nothing that can soothe a mother's heart," Dolores said. A pitying smile appeared on her face, and she joined hands with Mina and Clemencia, who sat on either side of her on the couch. "We are all mothers here, and we older ones know that. How terrible it is, my dear girl, to see you go through the same thing."

"Don't worry the girl," Mina said. "You know little Jimmy is going to be all right." But she did not take her hand away from Dolores.

Clemencia felt her sisters were being foolish, and she was too embarrassed to look at Shirley, for whom all this must seem like a comedy. Yet she could not take her hand away from Dolores either.

"No, no, my dear," Dolores said to Mina, pressing her hand. "My Clara understands. I know Jimmy is going to be all right."

Clara looked at her mother and slowly the tears began to roll down her face. She was grateful to the old ladies. They did not know that she had done so many wrong things, that she was being punished for them. If everything were going to be all right, then somehow she was being forgiven.

"But I remember," Dolores continued, "how it was when our children first contracted any illness more serious than a cold. My dear Clara, this big strong Mina was frantic when Feliz got appendicitis."

Dolores looked at Shirley, nodded and smiled and pointed at her. "Yes, all of us mothers know what it is. Oh how sad it is for us." She pulled herself off the couch and gave her gardenia-scented handkerchief to Clara. "There, my darling, blow your nose. You are feeling the anguish of motherhood. No woman is really a woman who has not felt it."

Clara took the handkerchief and wiped away her tears. "I would feel better if Elena had been here to advise me. She knows how to manage things so well." She tried to return the handkerchief, but her mother made her keep it. "Perhaps we should have consulted other doctors. I want to show her that we thought of everything when she comes back."

"My daughter Elena is braver than us all," Dolores said.

"For heaven's sake, by the time she gets back Jimmy will have been through the operation," Mina said. "She will have nothing to worry about. This is no time to worry about Elena's feelings."

Clara did not answer, but Dolores explained. "Elena has no child of her own to worry about, and all her hopes and ambitions are in that boy. Spare no money, Mother, she said to me, get the best doctor for him." Dolores looked around at her family. "Not that she would not do the same for any of us here, but there was a special quality in her voice . . ."

"Ah!" Mina interrupted and looked toward the porch. "At last . . ."

Old Consuelo appeared in the doorway. Again, everyone was disappointed yet relieved that it was not the ambulance. Consuelo wore the same long gingham dress, and she waved a ten-dollar bill in one hand. "Lola, Lola!" She looked around and said, "Another party! But I cannot stay. Here, here." She waved the bill again and began to giggle and cough. "I don't need it, dear girl, I don't need it after all. This morning when I was making my bed I found my pension check inside the pillow slip. Would you believe it? Consuelo, you old fool, I told myself, the Garcia boy brought you the check when the mailman delivered it, and then someone knocked on the door and you hid it in the pillow. And I forgot all about it. That is what happened, but I cannot remember who it was that knocked on the door that day."

Dolores went up to her and in a low voice tried to persuade her to keep the money. "No, no," Consuelo said, letting everyone hear. "I don't need it. I have everything I want. What could I do with it? I would only forget it somewhere and lose it."

"Then sit with us for a while," Dolores said.

"I have to go. I cannot stay." Consuelo looked around, smiling at the others. She did not seem to be sure who Shirley and Clara were. "I would lose it," she said, referring to the money again. "Look how I forgot the check and the person who knocked on the door."

Clemencia and Mina got up to say good-bye to her. When she saw them close, Consuelo exclaimed, "Oh it's you! I never see you anymore. You should have been here last night. Lola had such a big party with all her children . . ." She stopped and looked at Mina and Clemencia closely. "But you were here." She went off in a series of giggles and pulled her shoulders up and down like a little girl. "I am getting old, dear girls, the other day I made dinner and forgot to eat it. You will see, I will forget to climb into my coffin when I die."

The three old women stood in the doorway and watched Consuelo leave, each certain that they would not be that poor or lonely when they were her age. Consuelo shook her head with every step she took, and when she reached the porch steps she turned back. "But I remember all the important things," she said, and then took the steps like a little child, standing with both feet on each step before she ventured the next one.

"Poor old woman," Clara said to Shirley. "I never used to like her; she used to give me the willies and, to be honest, she still does." She looked at Shirley directly, as if to say, *That's the way I feel and I don't care what you think of me.*

"I don't know her, of course," Shirley said, "but I think she is happy and contented."

Clara looked at her as if Shirley were being perverse. She started to say something dismissive, but remembered Jimmy and decided she must try to be good. "You're from New York," Clara said apologetically. "We must all seem very strange to you."

"Oh no!" Shirley said, sounding more emphatic than she had meant to.

Clara looked at her a moment longer. "Esteban is here because Jimmy is sick. Otherwise I wouldn't let him," she said harshly. Then she put a finger to her lips, for Esteban came into the room at the same time that the old ladies returned from the porch.

Esteban looked unlike himself. His eyes were strained with worry and his mouth was set in anger. When Dolores asked if Jimmy had awakened, he only shook his head, not trusting himself to speak, for he respected the old women and in the old days, when he lived in this house, he had been as attentive as a lover to Dolores.

While the old ladies settled themselves on the couch again, Esteban went to Shirley and asked her softly about Robert. Shirley nodded, yes, he had gone off without any trouble from the detective.

Clara watched them, feeling left out and ill-used, wondering what they could have to say to each other. What had made them

143

friends? The sight of Esteban talking to Shirley made her feel that she had lived the wrong life. She got up and started for the bedroom. That's where she belonged, she decided, with her son. She must concentrate on seeing him get well.

Esteban turned quickly and called after her. "Don't go in. It's not necessary. Let him sleep."

Clara turned to face into the room and looked at them blankly, her arms hanging at her sides, not knowing what to do.

"Yes," Mina said. "There is nothing you can do now."

"You all hate me," Clara suddenly screamed. "You all hate me!" She began to cry and she brought an arm up and covered her face, holding herself about the middle with the other.

"My dear, my dear," Dolores said. She tried to get up but fell toward Mina.

When she heard her mother's voice, Clara sobbed louder. "You think I'm a bad mother." She put both hands to her face and wailed. She shook her head from side to side, moving her whole body at the same time, denying whatever they thought. She wanted to talk, but her sobs would not let her.

"For God's sake!" Esteban said angrily. "Control yourself."

Dolores finally managed to get up, and threw her arms around Clara. "You are too sensitive, my dear," she said holding on to her. "We love you. No one has any reason to hate you. What makes you say such things?" She tried to rock Clara in her arms, but Clara was too tall for her. Instead, Dolores stroked her head. "You are upset, my dear, it is too much to bear. We understand with all our hearts, dear child." Clara's sobs began to subside, and Dolores spoke more softly. "We are upset ourselves, for all our brave talk, and we must have said something to make you feel this way. Forgive us, forgive us."

"Yes, yes," Mina and Clemencia called from the sofa. "We are all worried and nervous."

Esteban looked away. He was extremely angry. Just before little Jimmy had fallen asleep, he had told him proudly how he had met El Presidente at Uncle Jaime's *finca*, and Esteban had been withholding what he wanted to say to Clara since then. To Jimmy he had only said, "If El Presidente told you to be courageous, that was good advice." He had remained silent a moment and then added, "I tell you, you will be all right, okay?" And he had smiled and winked at Jimmy, his heart pierced by the realization that someone else was bringing up his son.

In the moment of silence after Dolores succeeded in comforting Clara, they heard the knocking at the front-porch door. Mina rushed out to let them in. "Yes, it is here," she said, and held the door wide open for the two men with the stretcher. The first one to appear in the living room looked at Clara and Dolores, his eyes wide with apprehension. "Where is the patient?" he asked in a level voice. He looked at a piece of paper in his hand. "James Rios?"

"This way," Esteban said, and led them toward the bedroom.

"Wait," Clara said, her voice still thick with tears, "I want to be there when he wakes."

They paused for her, and she went ahead of them.

Dolores turned to the women left in the room and sighed. "And the poor girl worries that we think that she is not a good mother? She is an angel!"

Esteban was the last to enter the bedroom and saw Clara leaning over Jimmy. He moved around the men and got to the bedside. She turned toward him and took her hand away from Jimmy's forehead. "He's moist," she said. "Let me dress him in clean pajamas."

The man at the head of the stretcher shook his head. "No matter. We'll cover him with a blanket. If you want, bring pajamas with you to the hospital." He reached out with one hand and touched her elbow. "Let us take care of this. We know how." He motioned to Clara to move out of the way, and his partner did the same to Esteban.

Clara stood at the head of the bed and Esteban at the foot, and both watched Jimmy in his drugged sleep. They involuntarily made all the same efforts that the men made to roll Jimmy onto the stretcher without the satisfaction of having done anything. Jimmy did not wake; he only moaned as they moved him from the bed. Once on the stretcher, he lay still, and the two men neatly wrapped a blanket around him, keeping the arms down alongside his body. When they pulled the straps over his body, Clara reached out a hand to stop them.

The man looked up at her. "It's only to keep him from falling out, a safety precaution." He buckled the strap and waited for the other to finish with the strap over Jimmy's legs. "We're set, ma'am," the man said. "Who is coming with us?"

"Both of us," Esteban said.

"Only one," the man said.

"Both of us," Esteban insisted.

The man gave in. "It will be cramped. Suit yourself."

Esteban stepped to one side to let them out. Clara came behind them, carrying a bundle of blue-and-white pajamas. The cloth was silk, and the pants of one of them slipped out of her hands. Esteban picked them up, not knowing what they were, and when he felt the cool, luxurious cloth, he asked, "What are you taking these things for?"

Clara took the pajama bottoms from him, but she didn't seem to hear his question. Her eyes were on the stretcher which was being lifted at the head to get it through the door. Jimmy lay still, peacefully asleep, although at the angle they held the stretcher he was almost standing up.

As soon as he asked Clara, Esteban realized that they were pajamas for Jimmy, expensive, delicately made pajamas, such as he had never seen; not one, but several pairs. Only Elena and her husband could have bought them for the boy. He tried hard to think of the last time he had bought something for his son, but he could not remember. He felt bitterly ashamed of himself, and he despised Elena and Jaime because expensive clothes for Jimmy were easy for them to buy. They could buy his own son without depriving themselves of any luxury, just as they had probably bought Clara to get Jimmy.

"Aie, aie," Dolores moaned softly, "grandchild, grandchild." She put a hand on the stretcher and looked down at Jimmy. She held the stretcher fast, not allowing the men to move with it.

"Lady, don't do that," one said.

"Mama," Clara said, "he's sleeping, that's all."

Dolores held one hand over her heart and stared a moment longer. Overcoming her fright, she leaned down and kissed him on the forehead. It was cool with perspiration, but she felt his breath on her cheek. "Dear, dear Virgin," she whispered, "keep him well." Behind her, Mina turned away from the others and crossed herself quickly so that no one would see her. Then she turned back, put a firm hand on Dolores' arm, and took her away from the stretcher.

"Esteban!" Dolores called.

He looked at the old lady, trying not to appear as shamefaced and worried as he felt. When he and Clara separated, it was harder for him to face Dolores, from whose house he was moving, than it was to leave Clara.

"Esteban," she called, as if there had never been any break, "take care of them for me."

"Do not worry, do not worry," Mina said, still holding on to her. "Clara, do not forget, get Esteban to telephone from the clinic. Not that there is any need, but we will feel better."

Esteban went to Dolores and put his arm around her. "I'm sorry I did not cancel the ambulance and take him myself in the car," he said. "All this paraphernalia has made you think it's more serious than it is." He smiled at her, but his voice was on the point of breaking.

Clemencia almost said aloud, *Yes, in the old days the ambulance came only when there was no hope.* But she stopped herself in time. She must stop this talkativeness she was developing. If not, she told herself, she would become as foolish in her old age as Mina and Dolores. She reached out to Shirley and touched her arm. "Did Roberto go off?" she asked, knowing the others would not hear.

Shirley took her hand and said yes.

"If I believed in God," Clemencia burst out, "I would ask Him to take care of him."

Dolores pulled Clemencia to her so that the three old ladies made a tight group. "He will, God will," she said, thinking Clemencia was talking about little Jimmy. "You will see. Little Jimmy will be all right."

"In any case, Dr. Ortiz will help Jimmy," Mina said. "Do not forget to call us, Esteban." Whatever happened, she reminded herself, she must have a nitroglycerin pill ready for Dolores.

The old women followed the stretcher together, and let Esteban and Clara go ahead, one on either side of it. Clara looked back for reassurance as they went down the porch steps, but they only watched the stretcher and did not see her appeal. The talk of God had unnerved Clara, and she began to feel the old fear of God's retribution that had worried her as a child. You asked for God's help only when you were afraid He was about to punish you. If anything happened to Jimmy, it was a punishment for a crime for which she was to blame.

The sunlight blinded Clara momentarily, and she lagged behind the stretcher for a moment. The dark blotches at the edge of her vision turned out to be the neighbors attracted by the arrival of the ambulance. They stood quietly on the sidewalk or on the short lawn, waiting to see who was on the stretcher. In a moment they would be in the house to offer Dolores their help and to find out exactly what had happened. To Clara, they were the people who had seen her grow up into tight dresses, marry and divorce, and marry and divorce again. They were her judges, she felt, and they surely did not like her. She walked ahead, cringing a little, afraid to look at anything but the straps on the stretcher. She believed what the men had said about the straps, but she wanted to undo them, for they looked cruel to her.

The doors of the ambulance opened like those of a hearse. The two men slid Jimmy in while she and Esteban stood by helplessly. Then Esteban helped her climb in, and she sat on a pull-down seat where she could watch over Jimmy. Esteban knelt on the floor next to her, and watched her stroke Jimmy's forehead again.

"Is he all right?" Esteban asked.

At the same time that Esteban spoke, the ambulance started to move away, as smoothly as one of the limousines from El Palacio. Clara looked up and saw her mother with Mina and Clemencia, still standing on the steps. She felt like waving to them, but she knew they were not waving because it was not proper on this occasion. Instead, she nodded and then averted her eyes from the people on the sidewalk.

Esteban felt slighted that she had not answered, and the gesture she made to avoid seeing the neighbors also made her turn away from him. "I understand from Jimmy that he has had the honor of meeting El Presidente," he said under his breath, so that the attendant in the ambulance could not hear. "It's an honor I am going to make sure my son will not enjoy again."

She turned to make a disclaimer and saw on his face everything she had hoped to miss by not looking at the neighbors. She wanted to defend herself, but her chin trembled and she could not speak without sobbing. She looked at Jimmy a moment and wondered how he felt, if he could feel pain in his sleep. Finally, she was able to say to Esteban, "I had nothing to do with it. It was a fiesta at Jaime's *finca* . . . for people from El Palacio."

"Ah—ah!" Esteban said. "How grand it sounds." He looked at her angrily. "How proud you must have been!"

She shook her head. She had been interested in a man from El Palacio, someone having to do with protocol, with arrangements of all sorts that involved the President. He was tall and courteous and handsome, and he was known as the "Pig's Pimp" by his enemies. That afternoon she had made herself charming to him. Whenever he was near, she would find a bench on which to spread wide the white skirt of her silk chiffon afternoon dress. The dress had brilliant yellow polka dots, and she thought it would attract him since it went so well with her smooth brown skin. But he kept slipping away.

"A fiesta for that animal," Esteban said, "while he kills all the young men."

Clara looked down and said low, "Don't wake Jimmy. Besides, it was only an obligation." She had shaken the President's hand and had been thrilled for a moment. He had seemed less ugly than his pictures. Still, it was the other man who interested her. Standing by one of the tables in the back patio, she saw him walking toward the end of the formal garden on the edge of the small wood that divided the gardens from the sugar-cane fields. On an impulse, she picked up a bottle of cold champagne and a glass and started toward him.

To forget what came next, Clara threw her head back and closed her eyes.

Esteban was startled. "What's the matter?" he asked.

"Don't torment me!" she said with a passion that Esteban was unused to from her.

The attendant looked at them with curiosity, and Esteban did not answer, ashamed of himself.

With eyes closed, she recalled how she had gone through the hedge at the end of the formal garden. A noise in the woods on the other side told her he had gone that way. She dropped the glass but held on to the bottle and followed the turning path until she came upon a field hand, a *guajiro*, barefoot, wearing the usual white cotton pants with the shirt tails tied in a knot to hold the worn pants up. In his hand was a whole broiled chicken, and the *guajiro* looked like a startled wild animal.

"The cook said . . ." He extended the hand holding the chicken, and Clara laughed and shook her head. She had to hold on to the slim trunk of a pine tree, but she could not steady herself and slowly slid to the ground, her skirt billowing about her. The *guajiro* took a step toward her to help, and she said, "I'm all right." He stopped, and she looked up at him. In white shoes and a linen suit he would be as elegant as that other man. She held up the bottle and offered it to him. He was reluctant. She waved the bottle again, and he came forward and leaned over to take it from her, an uncertain smile on his face. Perspiration rolled down his neck into his shirt. She pulled back the bottle a little and with her other hand suddenly reached up and touched him. The cotton pants were thin and she easily found him and waited. He did not move, and she felt nothing happen. She laughed and let her hand drop, and the *guajiro* ran as though he had been released from a trap.

And, of course, she was being punished for this. Esteban was right to treat her like an old whore into whose room he could climb whenever he felt the urge. She was ashamed to look at Jimmy, and she put her hands together and began to pray. She could not remember all of "Hail Mary," and when she had gone back to the beginning three times, she tried Our Father and stopped at the words "our daily bread." It was inappropriate and perhaps blasphemous; God might punish her for saying the wrong prayer. There was nothing for it but to look up and tend to her son. She pulled at the blanket a bit and smoothed it down, and then there was nothing else to do for him.

"He's all right, ma'am," the attendant said. "He's resting easy."

Clara nodded. She appreciated his sympathy, but she could not smile or look at him in reply because the only way she knew how to do either with a man was seductively. It confused her and made her feel helpless and nervous. There was no doubt that Jimmy would be better off with Elena. She would know what to do for him at a time like this.

Esteban put a hand on the edge of the stretcher. He cleared his throat softly. "Do not worry, Clara," he said, without anger, "one more block and we'll be there."

She could not turn to him either, but she saw his hand stay quietly beside hers on the stretcher. It was hairy, and the slim fingers seemed in repose, unlike what she had known them to be. She had allowed that hand to violate her last night, when by all that was right she should have been taking care of Jimmy. She should have known he was very sick.

"I'm sorry," he said. "I've neglected my boy. I have no right to be angry."

Clara put her hand on his, and Esteban brought his other hand up and covered hers. "You're cold," he said. He rubbed her hand. "Come now, you must not get sick too."

When he's not angry, Clara thought, he always sounds as if he's making love. "I'm all right," she said, and took her hand away. "I'm sorry too."

Esteban tried to take her hand again, but she did not let him. She resolved that from now on she would act like a lady, and she saw that he immediately respected her. He was not angry; he simply waited for her.

"We're there," the attendant said as the ambulance came to a stop.

Clara put her hand on Jimmy's head and cursed herself for having spent her time thinking of herself instead of him.

XI

IF CLARA had not spent two years in Cuba with Elena and Jaime, she might not have noticed how dingy El Recurso Clinic looked. She had seen it converted from a frame building with stores downstairs and furnished rooms upstairs into a clean, white-painted clinic, but she had not noticed while she lived in Ybor City that it had begun to look again like the worn old wooden structure that it had once been. When Esteban helped her out of the ambulance, she stared a moment at the peeling white paint and the abandoned look of the storefront entrance, and she worried about Elena and Jaime coming here to see Jimmy. The Centro Español and the Centro Asturiano had much better hospitals, real hospitals, as a matter of fact, and she had thoughtlessly brought Jimmy to this place where only the poorest Cubans went. She was ashamed to say anything about this to Esteban as she followed the stretcher through the sidewalk entrance.

A woman came out from behind a desk. "What's this?" she asked. "Who is it?"

The stretcherbearers stopped and looked at Esteban and Clara.

"Dr. Ortiz is expecting him," Esteban said, pointing to Jimmy. "He's to be operated on."

The woman looked at him with recognition. "Hello, hello. Of course." Then she saw Clara. "Hello, hello, how are you? What happened?" She broke off her greetings and called to the men. "Take him in here." She pointed to a door off the reception room, and tried to look dignified and stern. "That's the receiving room."

Esteban and Clara started after the men, but the woman intercepted them. "I was taken by surprise. I wasn't notified." She went to a stairway near the receiving room and yelled up, "Felicia, Felicia!"

Little Jimmy moaned and opened his eyes. "Mama!" he called.

Esteban stood over him. "Yes, Jimmy, here I am," he said.

"I want Mama!" Jimmy called louder. "Mama!" He looked at Esteban as if he were a stranger, and he began to toss and move his arms under the straps. When Clara got to him, he stopped tossing, but he looked at her with frightened eyes. "Where am I? Where? I want to go home, Mama!"

Clara put her hand on his head and answered him in a voice that she tried to make soft and gentle. "We're at the clinic where Dr. Ortiz is going to make you well."

Behind her, the woman stood in the doorway and spoke to a nurse coming down the stairs. "Felicia, they've brought a boy here. Do you know anything about it? I wasn't notified."

Felicia nodded and motioned her out of the way. She walked into the receiving room and said in a calm voice, "Why, of course, we're expecting him." Without looking at anyone, she spoke to Jimmy, "You look like a very nice boy."

Jimmy looked at Clara. "I want to go home," he repeated, but he was less frightened.

"As soon as you get well," Felicia said. She looked at Clara and recognized her. "Hello, I didn't know it was you. I didn't recognize the name. Then this is your son? And this is your husband?"

Neither Clara nor Esteban corrected her.

"Well then," Felicia said to the men, "let's take him upstairs."

Jimmy protested.

"Your mama is coming with you," Felicia said and nodded to Clara. She pulled Clara to one side as they moved out of the room, and she said to her and Esteban, "We'll give him an injection upstairs to put him to sleep. Then you can come down here and wait with your husband. It won't be long. We're all ready for him. Dr. Ortiz is getting ready now."

"Mama!" Jimmy called. "Mama!"

Esteban watched them go up the stairs and wandered into the reception room, feeling useless.

"It's Sunday and we are understaffed," the woman at the desk said. "That's why I wasn't notified. Still, it's not right."

Esteban had forgotten about her. "It was an emergency," he explained.

Mollified, the woman smiled. "Well, the important thing is that he is upstairs and being treated, poor boy." She opened a ledger on the desk and looked for a pen in the drawer. When she found it, she called Esteban. "There are certain formalities."

Esteban had to spell Jimmy's name, his own, Clara's.

She stopped him on Clara's. "That's not her last name any more," she said. "She divorced you."

Esteban looked at her. "Then why do you ask me?"

"There are certain formalities," she said. "You don't recognize me? I'm Mercedes Alfonso. I live across the street from Dolores."

"Oh!" Esteban said.

"I have to ask these questions," Mercedes said. She wrote down Dolores' address opposite their names. Then she asked for a fifty-dollar deposit.

Esteban put his hands in his pockets. He had two dollars rolled up in one of them. "There will be time enough for that," he said. "I have nothing on me now."

"It's just a formality," Mercedes said, smiling as if she had known he could not have fifty dollars. "We don't act like the big hospitals, God knows. They want money before you put a foot inside. Dr. Ortiz has personally told me never to close the door on anyone because of money." She looked behind her and pointed to the wall. "Until the other day when the nail fell down, we kept a framed copy of the Hippocratic Oath right here."

Esteban walked away from her toward the front door. He gestured with one arm and said irritably, "That's no more than he should do." He looked out to the street and thought about how Jimmy had not called for him and how this woman knew that Dr. Ortiz need not worry about the bill, not because of him but because of Elena. "Nowadays people expect to go to heaven because they observe the most ordinary decencies," he called back to her.

"There are certain formalities," she said. She made another notation in the ledger, and then looked up and said to the wall opposite, "Poor boy!"

Esteban turned his back on her and gazed out into the street again. Miserable idiot, he said to himself, what has she got to do with what I am feeling? He leaned an arm against the door frame and spat out into the street. He should not have let the women cut him out; he should have gone upstairs with them. He shifted his position and thought it over. They didn't need him, he had to admit.

The screen door at the cafe across the street opened and slammed. Perrito stood on the sidewalk and squinted at Esteban until he recognized him. When the old man started to cross the street, it was too late for Esteban to move away. Perrito looked like one of those small, hairless dogs that are always barking at you from alleyways.

"Esteban, what are you doing here?" he asked. "Visiting someone?"

Esteban made a noncommittal gesture.

"Who is it?" Perrito continued. "Perhaps it's someone I should at least pay my respects to."

"No," Esteban said, "it's my boy. We just brought him in for an operation."

"Ah, an emergency," Perrito said. He scratched his head and looked beyond Esteban into the reception room. "Dr. Ortiz doesn't operate on Sundays if he can help it."

"Appendicitis," Esteban said. He stopped leaning against the doorway as a hint to Perrito that he might have to leave him momentarily.

"Oh it's nothing, nothing at all, my boy. To modern medicine, appendicitis is no worse than a cold." He stopped and looked at Esteban and saw that his words had not dispelled Esteban's mood. "Well, what do you think of the events in Cuba? What do you say to the latest?"

"What latest?" Esteban straightened, thinking of the load Roberto was driving to Sarasota.

Perrito stared at him a moment, and Esteban saw the old man consider and then reject the possibility that Esteban was one of the nonpolitical younger generation. Joyfully, Perrito put a hand on Esteban's shoulder. "They found another apartment in Havana where they were making bombs in every room!"

That was a sad development. Esteban shook his head, as if this might be a bad omen for their own venture.

"But think of it, man!" Perrito insisted. "Things are not as quiet and under control as they would have us believe. Not at all. They didn't catch anyone, only the evidence, and they are acting as if they had squashed the revolution."

"No, there's no keeping them down," Esteban said, managing a smile for the old man. He was oppressed by the feeling that Jimmy's illness showed him in a bad light; not to others—the hell with that—but to himself. He was unaccustomed to thinking so much about himself.

Perrito watched Esteban's face darken and lose interest in him, and he took his hand off Esteban's shoulder. "Well, I must be moving on." He hitched his pants and waited for Esteban to say something. "Don't worry about the boy. Dr. Ortiz is a master with the knife."

"Thank you," Esteban said. "Thank you."

The old man smiled in return, happy that his words were of value. He straightened his thin body and walked away in the direction of Seventh Avenue. Esteban knew he was on his way to another cafe for another espresso and another game of dominoes. There, he would discuss the revolution with old-fashioned phrases.

A master with the knife, Esteban repeated to himself. That's what Dr. Ortiz would be doing upstairs, wielding a knife. He had not thought about it like that before; they would be cutting his boy open with a knife. He stifled a womanish cry, but walked quickly across the room to the stairs.

Mercedes got up from the desk and went toward him. "You are not allowed up there yet."

He turned on the stairs to see how seriously she meant it. He was short of breath and could think of nothing to say.

"You are not allowed to interrupt the routine," she said. "You will cause a disturbance."

He had paused long enough to realize that he was afraid to go up, and he yelled at her to help propel himself upstairs. "I've known this place since whores did their business in the bedroom at the end of the corridor." The shocked look on Mercedes' face made him turn and start upstairs again.

"Esteban!" Clara held an arm stiffly before her to keep him from bumping into her. With the other she held onto the bannister.

Esteban stared at her for a sign. "What happened?"

Mercedes stood at the bottom of the stairs and looked up at them.

Clara shook her head and began to sway. "They are beginning to operate."

In one leap he was up beside her, so she could lean on him. Her body felt weak and lifeless. "There, my dear, there," he said contritely. "In a minute it will be done."

She moaned in protest and tried to descend on her own, but could not. "Oh no," she said. "Oh no! You did not see the frightened look on his face." She took her hand away from his arm and held it to her cheek. "He is just a little child." She gave Esteban the look of someone who has taken a blow too hard to bear and does not know what to do about it.

Before he put his arm around her waist, Esteban took a long look at Clara. She was different, unalluring and almost unfeminine. Even her smell was different; the perfume of sex had evaporated, and his heart rolled over with aching sympathy. Mercedes was still at the bottom of the steps looking up, her eyes bright with curiosity. But he did not care; he put his arm around Clara's waist and did not make a caress of it, although he wanted to. How else could he comfort her?

Clara's body did not give to his support, but he stayed with her, taking each step haltingly. If only she would let him comfort her! He saw Mercedes at the bottom of the steps and returned her stare angrily. "What do you want?" he asked impatiently. She turned as if she had been slapped and went to her desk.

At the bottom of the stairs, Clara steadied herself. "Mercedes?" she called, and waited for the woman to turn around. "Mercedes, can I go into this room here?"

"The receiving room?" Mercedes said with a stern look on her face, but lost it when she saw Clara's face. "Of course, my dear, right there." She got up and went to her to take her in, but Esteban preceded her. "Help her lie on the bed, man," she said commandingly.

Esteban closed the door on Mercedes and followed Clara to the bed. When she sat down on it, he leaned down, picked up her feet together and lifted them to the bed. Clara stretched out on the bed and rolled on her side, putting both hands, palms facing each other, under her head to make up for the lack of a pillow. "Oh Esteban, Esteban . . ." she complained. "Why haven't you cared about Jimmy?" Her voice was thin and weak, and she did not expect an answer.

He looked around the room and found a dirty white metal chair to sit on. "Why do you say that?" he asked mildly, not wanting to contradict her.

"Why haven't you taken any interest in the boy in all this time? None at all." She sighed and was quiet for a moment. "He needs a father and he doesn't have one, except for Jaime," she continued, and then stopped again.

Esteban shook his head. "You forget that you took him to Cuba and kept him there without my consent. And yet you reproach me."

She closed her eyes and thought it over until Esteban imagined that she had forgotten what he had said. "Oh no, Esteban, that does not make sense," she protested, her voice still thin and wailing. "You did not protest, not once. Why didn't you write and ask him how he was doing or send him money? And Elena and Jaime love him, love him better than you and I, if the truth be told."

"Don't say that," Esteban said. "It's not true. I listen to it only because you are saying it."

Slowly, she propped herself up on one elbow and kept her eyes on him. "It's true; it's true. They love him better and they deserve him more."

Esteban slapped his knee in reply. The sound of it was like an explosive denial. "All right, they love him. Why is that to their credit?" He saw her subsiding to the bed again and held his voice under control. "In any case, they don't deserve him more than we do. Why do you demean yourself so? They're the kind of people who grab everything they want, and after they've got it, everyone thinks they deserve it because they've got it. To hell with that!"

Clara pulled herself up and sat on the edge of the bed. Her dress was wrinkled, and every move she made cost her an effort. "I don't know," she said. "Poor Jimmy."

"Anyway, it's not a question of who deserves him," Esteban said. "He's ours, that's all."

She nodded and looked down at the floor for a long while. "I am sitting here listening to you and agreeing, but as soon as I stop to think it's not the same thing at all. That's my trouble; anyone tells me a story and I believe it and listen and listen. I can't think for myself; that's my trouble. Is that why you left me? Because I'm stupid?"

He smiled at her. "You know what happened between us—we were just too young. Come, my dear sweet girl, why are you being so philosophical?"

"It's true; I'm stupid. Last night you told Elena she could take Jimmy and today you tell me something else, and yet I listen to you. What am I to believe?" She covered her face with her hands and let herself fall back on the bed again. "Oh Esteban, why did you do that last night? I'm so ashamed, so ashamed. God is punishing me. Don't laugh. He is punishing me."

Esteban got up and sat on the edge of the bed and put a hand on her back to comfort her.

"Esteban, please go back to your chair, please," she said, hiding her face from him. "I'm not a good person and why should He not punish me this way? I'm not good, and it's only because I am stupid that I'm bad. That's why."

Leaning over her, he rubbed her back until he paused at her waist and squeezed it. "Oh you are very bad, very bad, I am sure," he said soothingly. "That's why I like you, my pear. That's why I climbed into your room, because you're so bad and so delicious and so good for me. Let your sister be ashamed, not you."

Clara shivered when he squeezed her and gasped. "Please, Esteban, listen to me seriously," she said. She turned and looked up at him and closed her eyes, ashamed to talk while he looked at her. "I need someone to help me to be good. I cannot go on like this. I will get worse and worse." She opened her eyes, determined to be straightforward. "You must not treat me like that. I am Jimmy's mother and you must respect me. You have to help me."

He smiled down at her, and with one hand he helped her turn on the bed. She lay back, and her hair spread out on the sheet. "I will do anything you say. I will bow and call you madam every time I see you. I will be a veritable grandee, if that's what you want. I'll do it." He held one of her arms and nodded at her. "Anything you say. But I would prefer to pay my respects in a truer fashion, in the way I feel. What's wrong with that? . . . But you've told me! All right, all right. Let us formalize this relationship and then maybe I'll be good too."

"You don't love me," she said. "You're a good man but you don't love me."

"Oh you foolish girl, you're a woman, after all. How you like the word! Very well. What do you think it means when I do what I do every time I see you?" he asked, and put a hand on her breast.

She grabbed his hand and pushed it away, but she took it back and held it in hers. "It would be so good for Jimmy to have his father and mother together." The tears began to run down her cheeks. "That's what he wants. I don't know what to tell him when he asks me what I did wrong."

"The little fool," Esteban said and squeezed her hand.

"No, no, he's right," she said. "Tell him you won't do it again, Mommy, he tells me, and he'll come back and live with us."

Esteban smiled, glad to know that Jimmy did think of him, after all. "Come, you must not take what he says to heart," he said. "Kids know how to get what they want."

Clara pulled herself up to him and sobbed on his breast.

"The little bastard!" Esteban said without venom. "You mustn't let him upset you this way." He held her to him and felt so sorry for her that he thought he should make love to her, something he had never premeditated before.

"Oh Esteban, don't say that." She looked up at the ceiling as if she could see into the operating room.

"Yes, yes," Esteban said. He stroked her hair. "My enchantment!"

"How can I tell him that you left me because I was stupid?" She brought her legs over the side of the bed and sat up next to him. "Isn't that why you left me? I wasn't smart enough, I know. But I don't mean to be stupid. I want to be educated, to appreciate things. In Havana I went to see the ballet."

"For God's sake, my dear girl," Esteban protested, "if you keep talking this way, I *will* think you're ignorant."

Clara looked at the floor, as if she found the answer there. "You should have married Elena."

Esteban was so startled that he laughed.

"Or someone smart like her who could keep up with you."

"Believe me, I am not smart and I am certainly not educated," Esteban explained. "The truth is, we were too young. We got married in order to be free to do you-know-what as much as we wanted, and then we just got tired of it, that's all."

Clara did not look at him, but she disagreed. "I did not marry you just for that. I remember that there were more things—everything, as a matter of fact. I wanted to marry you for many more things than just that!"

"What's wrong with just that?" Esteban asked. "I am not marrying you again if there isn't going to be a lot of just that." He put a hand on her knee and squeezed it. "We had such a wonderful time last night."

Clara leaned against him. Her body was relaxed, and he could feel that she was breathing easily. He took his hand away from her knee and brought his arm around her, so that her body rested completely against him. His hand came around her waist and touched her thigh. He could feel the curve of her flesh under his hand and felt no need to excite and delight her. Later, later . . . He had forgotten that wonderful sensation of knowing that a woman's body waited for him at his leisure.

"So what do you say, my ripe pear?" he asked.

"How strange to marry you again," she said in a small voice. "I'm ashamed. I won't know how to tell people."

"Don't tell them," he said. "Let them see for themselves. What does it matter? Besides, they don't care. People have a lot of other things to think about, or they should."

"You are right," she said. "I am stupid." She took a deep breath. "Oh Esteban, I feel so much better. It's such a relief for me to know we are doing the right thing for Jimmy. My prayers have been answered."

He laughed lightly. "You can stop praying then. There's no more need, and I will be much happier. I don't want Jimmy's head filled with religious nonsense."

"Don't say that; don't say it!" She looked up. "Not until he is well. You know I agree with you, but please put up with my stupidities just a little while longer." She smiled, no longer desperate about Jimmy because she and Esteban were wiping out their sins by becoming reconciled, and she squeezed his hand as if to tell him that she appealed as much to him as she did to God.

"Yes, my dear," he whispered in her ear. "Yes, my enchantment!"

For the second time that day she responded to his touch as the touch of male flesh. The hairs on his hand, the thick bones under the skin were mysteries in her hands. The feel of them became precious to her, and she moved her hands over his and squeezed them as if they talked to her. "Ah!" she sighed in reply, "ah!" His hands answered her, one pressed into her thigh, the other held one of her breasts, and her flesh swelled to meet them. "Ah!" she said to them. "Ah, ah, ah!"

Esteban stretched her out on the bed, and leaned over her on one elbow. He stroked her with his free hand and saw her lose her pallor and her nervousness. She looked up at him. "You are the only person I have really wanted," she said.

"I caught you when you fell off the tree," he said. "I should never have let you go."

Her eyes watered. "Oh Esteban, do you mean that?"

"This time I am going to eat you like a mango, carefully, so that I won't lose a drop of juice." He smiled to see her cover her face with one hand. "I'm going to tear off the skin with my teeth and scrape the underside of each strip of its meat. And when I've eaten the fruit, I'm going to keep the pit in my mouth to suck on. I'm going to leave that pit as clean as a bone."

She uncovered her face and giggled.

"What do you say to that?" Playfully he put his hand on her breast and drew it back and forth, tickling the palm of his hand with her nipple.

"You're terrible," she said, and ran a hand up and down his arm.

He got up quickly when they heard the knock on the door. Standing by the metal chair, he called, "Come in."

Mercedes opened the door and took a step inside. She carried a demitasse in one hand, and she stopped when she saw Clara on the bed. "Is she all right?" she asked Esteban. "Here's some coffee."

He nodded, and Clara opened her eyes, as if she had been resting. "Oh Mercedes," she said, "it was very kind of you to let me use this room."

"Yes, it was," Esteban said, apologizing for his part of their run-in. "It was just what she needed."

Clara sat up on the bed, and Mercedes took her the coffee. "Drink it, it will do you good," Mercedes said. "It's a stimulant." She looked at Esteban like a professional. "Very good in these cases."

"You shouldn't have gone to all this trouble," Clara said, and took it from her.

"Not at all," Mercedes said, "not at all." She looked from one to the other, ready to stay and talk. "As soon as they call me from upstairs I will let you know. It should be another half hour or so." The phone rang outside. "Oh I must go," she said, disappointed that she could not stay with them. "I'll let you know as soon as you can see him. You understand, there are regulations."

"Yes, yes, we understand," Clara answered for both of them.

Unfortunately, Mercedes did not close the door when she left, and Clara signaled to Esteban when he started for it. "It wouldn't look right," she said.

Esteban returned to the chair and sat on it. "Busybody," he said. "She doesn't care what we do in this room. She just wants to be in on it. Women like her are happiest working in a busy whorehouse where they can be in charge of all the arrangements." He mimicked her. "Ah, señor, you cannot have the little one today. You are too big for her we have discovered. There are regulations, you know—"

"Esteban!" Clara interrupted. She put the cup down on the saucer with a clatter. "We have to tell Elena today. She will be back and she will surely be making plans."

"So?" He waited. "We'll tell her and she won't have to make plans."

Clara thought it over a moment. "I will tell her. You might antagonize her."

He groaned. "What is she to us? I don't care if I antagonize her. As a matter of fact, I would prefer to antagonize her."

"There! You see what I'm afraid of," Clara said. "You'll fight with them, although they love Jimmy."

"It's no more than they should," he said impatiently. "Why should it be to their credit?"

"It will be to Jimmy's credit," Clara said. "They have no children."

Esteban looked at her a moment to make sure he understood. "What? Who cares? Do you?" He got up from the chair and pointed a finger at her. "If you're thinking of their money, I tell you we don't want it. Don't you realize how they make it?"

Clara's eyes clouded over with thought. "But you know they are not involved in politics. You've heard her say so. They just have to know all the politicians."

"What are we arguing about?" Esteban said. He sat down again. "I don't care what they think or do. Just don't act as if we need their permission to marry."

"I'm afraid," Clara said. "As soon as you take your hands off me, you start to fight."

To her surprise, Esteban laughed and relaxed in his chair, his head thrown back. "You're a woman of wit!"

"Don't make fun of me, Esteban. I'm too upset today," she said. "Elena is my only sister. She has taken care of all of us since she grew up. Even before Papa died. Armando gets into trouble and she gets him away. My older brother goes to Miami and she buys him a home. There's nothing she won't do for the family. Don't you think I have obligations to her?"

"Truthfully, no." He took a deep breath and exhaled it slowly. "But have it your way," he added. "I just hope you're not going to be talking this much after we marry. You used to be quiet as a mouse. Deep thoughts, but quiet as a mouse."

"I was stupid," she said. "I still am. That's my trouble."

"Don't be silly," he said. "About Elena—I'll be with you when you tell her." Clara shook her head, and he added, "All right, it's just as well. I don't think I could control my temper. Just stop talking to me about it."

Mercedes appeared in the doorway with a big smile. They stopped talking and looked at her expectantly. She nodded her head happily.

"Well?" Esteban said.

Mercedes spoke to Clara. "Just as I told you, he's all right. They have finished the operation, and they are taking him to his room. Don't be impatient, you'll be able to see him in a few minutes."

"Oh thank God!" Clara got up to embrace Esteban, but she remembered before she got to him that Mercedes might be shocked. Instead, she only touched his arm. "Esteban, call home and tell Mama. They are all waiting."

"Yes, you must tell Dolores," Mercedes said, like one of the family. "Jimmy is the grandchild she is closest to."

Esteban threw an arm around Clara. "Where is the phone?"

"Here," Mercedes said, watching him embrace Clara, "out here."

Esteban passed by her and, on an impulse, pulled her to him by the waist and squeezed her. Mercedes squealed and pushed him away. Then she looked at Clara as he went into the reception room and explained, "It's his son. You can't blame him for being happy."

Shirley answered the phone at Dolores'.

"It's good news," Esteban said to her. "Jimmy came out of the operation well."

He could hear Shirley call out to the others that Jimmy was well and the old ladies exclaim in reply. "Have you seen him yet?" she asked.

"In a few minutes we'll see him," he said to Shirley. "Well, it seems this is our day for talking on the phone. Tell me again, did everything go well with Roberto?"

"Yes, he went off fine," she said.

"I did not thank you for all you did—"

Shirley interrupted. "How soon will Robert be back?"

"Let me think," Esteban said. "Not for another two hours yet."

Clara put a hand on his shoulder. "What are you talking about?"

On the phone Shirley said, "Here is Dolores. She wants to hear the news from you."

Esteban could hear Dolores breathing as soon as she took the phone. "Clara wanted me to phone you right away," he said, "before we saw him."

"Ah, my dear boy, you are such good children," Dolores said.

"I have never been able to complain about any of my children and not about you either, Esteban, you know that. But you are not coloring your story for this old woman, are you? Is my little Jimmy really all right?"

"Yes, he is," Esteban said very seriously. "I swear to you."

"God bless you!" she said. Without taking the phone away, she called into the room, "Mina, Clemencia, it is true. Little Jimmy is fine."

"Well, that is all now," Esteban said.

"Wait," Dolores said. "How is Clara?"

"Fine," he said. "Do you want to speak to her?"

"Listen, Esteban . . ."

"I am," he said, and laughed because he knew what she was going to say.

"Be good to her," Dolores said shyly, "for the sake of the child."

"I am," he said, "for her sake, for my sake. And even for yours. You know it is you I have always wanted. I shall throw myself at your feet once more and see if you will resist me again."

"Esteban, Esteban, you must not joke," Dolores said. "Oh no, it is true—I had a presentiment last night. You are your old self. Oh my dear, my dear! My Clara is irresistible."

"And I—and I?" he asked laughingly.

Clara touched him again. "What are you talking about?" She blushed because Mercedes was listening.

At Dolores' house, Mina warned Dolores that the food at the clinic was not good. "This is no time for romantic nonsense," she added.

"Esteban, Esteban," Dolores called, afraid he might hang up, "tell Clara I am sending food for little Jimmy."

"Not now. I talk to you of affairs of the heart and you talk to me about food." He waited to hear her laugh. "No, really, wait till we see him and talk to the nurse."

"Tell Felicia Soler that I have a clear chicken broth. Someone can take it over right away," Dolores urged. "And a piece of the chicken boiled. It is very plain. It would be perfect for a convalescent. I have even resisted the temptation of shaking a little salt over it."

"All right, I promise," Esteban said, "I'll ask."

He hung up and turned to Clara. "Well, that made them very happy."

Mercedes nodded and smiled. "There is nothing like good news to make everything fine again," she said, expecting Clara and Esteban would take her into their confidence. But Felicia Soler came down the stairs, and Mercedes felt obliged to sit at her desk and present a formal appearance.

Felicia Soler looked tired. "I see you know," she said. "If you'll come with me, you'll be able to see him. The other nurse has taken him to his room."

They followed her up the steps. "He should be coming out of the ether, so don't expect him to say much. It would be best if you didn't either."

"I just want to see that he's all right," Clara said. "Can I stay with him?"

Felicia nodded sympathetically. She led them down the narrow rooming-house hall. The rooms facing the street were for the patients. "We put him in the corner room," she explained. "It's the largest, but he's sharing it. It has cross-ventilation."

They stopped in the doorway and looked in. Clara knotted her hands when she saw him lying on one of the two beds by the window. It had been cranked up a little, and she could see his pale face turned to one side. He looked frail to her, more peaceful than when he was in pain, but less healthy. "He's so pale," she whispered.

"There's always a loss of blood," Felicia said.

"Is he in pain?" Clara asked.

"Not now," Felicia told her. "Tomorrow he will feel uncomfortable, but we'll give him something. Don't worry." An old man sat up in the other bed and watched them. "She takes very good care of us," he said to Clara and Esteban. "Hello, Felicia."

Felicia nodded. "This is Señor Pelayo," she said to them.

"Esteban Rios, your servant," Esteban said. "I used to see you at the Cuban Club."

"Ah yes, it will be a while before I get back there," he said. He pointed to his legs. "They cut off my left foot. Bad circulation, but I'm all right. It's the first time they have had to use the knife with me and I'm seventy-two."

They looked at him, not knowing what to say.

"Diabetes. Ask Felicia," the old man continued. "It causes poor circulation and they had to cut off the foot. But I'm not letting them cut off anything more." He raised one hand oratorically. "I need all my appendages."

"Very well, Señor Pelayo," Felicia said, to stop his chatter. She crossed to Jimmy's bed and motioned to Clara and Esteban. "I think he's about to wake up."

They entered the room cautiously, and the old man followed them with his talk. "And your boy? Appendicitis, I understand, and only eight. I'm seventy-two, as I told you, and this is the first time they got me in a hospital. I don't plan to stay for long, I can assure you. Dr. Ortiz tapped me on the chest and told me I'm perfect. I have a perfect constitution."

To be polite, Esteban turned to him and said, "I can well believe it."

Jimmy turned his head and opened his eyes a little and then closed them again. His mouth fell open slightly. His arms were on top of the coverlet, one hand resting on his chest, the other stretched alongside his body.

"I was raised in Key West and I was always in the salt water or the sun," Pelayo said. "That's what I attribute my health to. I never smoked cigarettes. From the age of five I smoked cigars with Havana leaf and drank good Cuban coffee. Now I can't have sugar in it. It's a bitter thing, not to have sugar in your coffee. Bitter."

Felicia stood alongside Jimmy's bed and put her hand in his. "Jimmy?" she whispered. "Jimmy?"

Clara stood by her and looked down at him. "Jimmy," she said too. He opened his eyes and looked blankly around. He turned his head sideways and looked into Felicia's face. Slowly, his eyes became frightened. He pulled his hand away from Felicia and tried to speak. Finally he saw Clara and tried to grab her. "Mama!" he cried desperately. "Mama!"

Felicia moved back and let Clara and Esteban get close to the head of the bed. "There now," she said coolly, "everything is all right."

"Here I am, darling," Clara said, her eyes watering.

Jimmy lifted his head. "Where am I?" The tendons in his neck stood out and his eyes were wide with fright. "Mama!"

"Lie back, darling," Clara said. "Don't try to get up." She put one hand behind his head and felt his neck relax, and slowly she let his head fall back on the pillow. "Careful, there," she said.

Clara took her hand away from his head, and it rolled to one side, his eyes half-open. "You rest now," she said. "Your father and I are here." He did not stir, and she waited and looked at Esteban, happy they were together with Jimmy. He was staring fixedly at Jimmy, and she turned back and saw Jimmy had not moved his head. "Jimmy," she said. "Jimmy."

Felicia came back to his side. "He has to rest," she said. She reached out and took Jimmy's pulse. "He has to rest now."

"What's wrong?" Clara asked. She looked at Jimmy and saw that his eyes still had that frightening, half-closed look.

Felicia kept her hand on his pulse. "Just a moment," she said. Then she put Jimmy's arm down. "Go and wait outside." She looked at Esteban beyond Clara's shoulder, counting on him to obey. "Go out in the hall. The doctor has to see him."

"What's wrong?" Clara insisted. "Tell me!"

Esteban put his hand on her arm and began to draw her away. "Nothing. The doctor has to see him now. Come, we'll wait outside."

"Felicia!" The old man called from the other bed. "Why does the boy look so strange?"

No one answered the old man. When Clara allowed Esteban to take her away, Felicia quickly straightened Jimmy's head on the pillow and with a swift motion closed his eyelids, so that he looked quietly asleep.

"Why did you do that?" Pelayo asked. He beat his bed with one hand. "Holy Virgin, it's bad luck! The boy is dead!" His voice was a thin shriek. "He's dead!"

Felicia walked across the room and slapped the old man. Dr. Ortiz appeared in the doorway and nodded at Felicia. He motioned with one hand that she was needed out in the hall, and he went straight to Jimmy's bed.

Clara was waiting in the hall. She was very quiet, and she would not let Esteban near her. When the nurse appeared in the doorway, she saw in the way Felicia hesitated that it was true; Jimmy was dead. Nevertheless, controlling herself, she asked, as if pleading for another chance, "Tell me, is it true?"

Felicia walked to her and opened her arms. Clara let the nurse embrace her and began to shake in her arms. "It's my fault," she said in a strange voice. Her teeth chattered, and in trying to talk she bit her tongue.

Remembering another occasion like this, Felicia held on to her and said, "You must think of yourself. Your other children need you."

"But I have no other," Clara said. "He's all I have!" It struck her for the first time that it was true, she had no one else; and she began to scream uncontrollably.

XII

AFTER Clara stopped screaming, the nurse led her slowly down the hall to Dr. Ortiz's office and seated her in a leather chair. She left her alone a moment to get her a tranquilizer, but when she returned with the pill Clara would not take it. She got up as if she had just awakened and left the office without a word. In the hall she passed Esteban and Dr. Ortiz.

Dr. Ortiz held his gold-rimmed glasses in his hand, a sign that he was impatient, and he was trying to explain the case to Esteban, something he was unused to doing on demand. "Only the postmortems could really tell," he said, turning his head toward Clara to include her, "but it could be adrenal insufficiency; in other words, shock."

Since Clara did not stop but went directly to the stairs leading down, Esteban left Dr. Ortiz in the hall without answering him and followed her. He did not call Clara. He knew she would not stop. He simply followed her, down the stairs, past Mercedes, who tried to stop them with questions about Jimmy, and out into the street. There, he caught up with her because she first turned left toward Seventh Avenue and walked a few steps before she remembered that home was in the other direction.

"Clara, wait here," he said. They were in the shadow of the clinic. "I'll go get a car."

She shook her head and walked on without looking back at him.

"Then let me call for one." It was very hard for him to speak because his throat was tense with the effort not to cry. "Please, my dear. You're upset."

She turned her head slightly toward him. "You don't have to come with me. I know my way," she said. "I only turned back to Seventh Avenue because that was the way I used to go to the movies in the old days." She put a hand to her mouth to stop her sobs.

Ah, good, he thought, she is talking, and he took her arm. They walked alongside each other, their heads down as if avoiding the blinding blaze of the afternoon sun. He kept his hand on her arm with the excuse that he was helping her up and down curbs, and she did not pull it away. Yet there was no other response from her, and slowly Esteban felt his desire to help her recede from his hand, so that he finally dropped it and walked by her side like an attendant.

As soon as he let go of her arm, Clara pulled her elbows in and walked faster. She had felt his disappointment with her, and although she could not feel angry with him any more, it seemed very clear to her that he only wanted to help her in his way, not in the way she needed. It meant that he did not love her. Everything seemed very clear to her. Every step Esteban took told her how he felt, although she did not care. She could foresee how everyone she knew would feel, how her mother would act, and how Elena would take it. As for herself, she knew how she would feel from now on, cold and aged. She had had two husbands and divorced them. She had had a son and he died.

"Oh, oh!" she moaned aloud and looked up, surprised at her own emotion. She saw she was at the corner of her block, and she broke into a run.

"Clara!" Esteban called harshly, as if she needed to be brought to her senses. She kept on running, and he ran to stop her before she got to the house. But his call made her run faster, and when she turned into the walk to the house, she slipped and fell. Esteban saw her get up and fall again. "Clara!" he yelled.

He caught up with her and pulled her up. It took an effort because her body was heavy with grief. She looked dazed and did not notice that her right arm was gray where she had scraped it on the cement walk.

Mina opened the porch door and stood at the top of the steps looking down at them. "What has happened?" she asked, her voice sounding the alarm. "You have hurt yourself, girl!" She searched their faces when they didn't answer. "Mother of God! What has happened?"

"Mama! Mama!" Clara yelled, then pushed Esteban away and ran up the steps. "Mama!"

Mina put out her arm to stop her, but took it away when she saw Clara did not mean to stop until she had found Dolores. She moaned and followed Clara with her eyes. "Oh poor girl, don't tell me!" She stopped Esteban and pulled his arm roughly. "What have you done to her?"

Esteban looked down and shook his head. "Jimmy is dead."

"Jimmy is dead!" Clara screamed at her mother.

Dolores was standing in the middle of the living room, and she was still for just a second when she heard Clara. Then she opened her arms and brought Clara to her. "Oh my darling child, my dearest, my love, my darling child!" Her hands kept stroking Clara's back and smoothing her hair. "Cry, my little daughter, cry. I'm just your mother and this is your family." Clara leaned her head on Dolores' shoulder and breathed loudly. "Oh what a terrible blow to bear! I shall always hold it against God that He did this to you." Dolores stopped talking because Clara, thank God, had begun to cry.

Clemencia got up from her seat and looked quickly at Shirley. "Aiee! I do not believe it." She grabbed Shirley's hand. "What happened? Why did Esteban say everything was all right?"

Mina heard her as she came into the room with Esteban. "Yes, yes, what happened, for the love of God!" She turned to him. "You must not fool old people like us. We have too short a time."

"I was not fooling," Esteban said. He looked at Clara sobbing on Dolores' shoulder and decided to say nothing more. "Please excuse me now." He walked to the dining room, took a bottle from the sideboard, and poured himself a drink.

"There, there," Dolores said soothingly to Clara. Now that Clara was crying she was hoping to calm her. "Don't cry, my dear, do not torment yourself. There is no reason in these things."

Clara lifted her head from Dolores' shoulder and looked around the room at Mina, Clemencia, and Shirley. "The truth is, all of you think I did not take proper care of him," she said. She nodded insistently and gasped for air. "He died before anyone could do anything. He looked at me and said 'Mama' and died. I tell you I saw him die!"

"Girl! Girl!" Clemencia called out to Clara. "I do not believe you did not take care of him. You did everything you could for him. These things cannot be foreseen, and you will never think that you have done enough for your children. That is the way with the people you love. But others will see things as they are, especially us. We know you did your best for him."

"There, my little girl, listen to Clemencia," Dolores said. "You know that she never says what she does not mean." The tears began to run down Dolores' face; she had begun to accept the fact that little Jimmy was really dead. "I blame myself, too. I should have known last night when he complained." She looked around at Clemencia and Mina. "The trouble with this girl is her emotions are too fine. They rule her, as they rule me."

"You are a good girl, Clara," Mina said in a strong voice, as though she had made a decision. "I know you took care of him. So do the rest of us. And that's what counts. Poor boy!" She was dissatisfied with what she had said and stopped a moment and put a hand on Clara's shoulder. "Go on and mourn him, but do not blame yourself."

"I thank God that you were with him, my darling," Dolores said. "I thank God for that—"

"But for nothing else!" Mina said. Her voice shook with defiance. "A child on the threshold of life, and He took him. I do not accept it; I do not accept it!"

Clara had stopped crying, and she looked at Mina and Clemencia dumbly, accepting the fact that they did not blame her. "I want to lie down," she said. Then she noticed that Shirley sat in a corner by herself, quiet and alone, looking steadily at her. "He was so frightened. I think he died because he was so frightened!" She began to cry again.

"No, Clara, no," Esteban called to her. "I talked to the doctor, and there is a medical reason for it."

The old woman looked at him for an explanation.

"Dr. Ortiz says that maybe his adrenal glands were not large enough. They were insufficient."

"What does that mean?" Mina asked.

"It means his constitution could not stand the shock of the operation." To keep from crying, he slapped himself on the chest several times. "He was knocked down by it. His heart could not keep going."

"His little heart!" Dolores exclaimed. "His little heart!"

Clara paled and hung on to her mother. "What do you mean— his heart?" she asked. Her voice was small and frightened. "What happened to his heart?"

Sorry that he had said anything, Esteban spoke softly. "Dr. Ortiz said that his adrenal glands were not sufficiently developed." He looked about him for help. "I don't know what it means, but because of that he could not take the shock of the operation."

"But what has that to do with his heart?" Mina asked.

Clara began to moan and sway, still hanging onto Dolores.

"Shirley, what does that mean?" Mina asked. "Do you know?"

"I don't know exactly," Shirley said. She saw Clara on the verge of fainting and jumped up from her seat. "It's Clara who needs help now, for God's sake. Here, take hold of her."

"Yes, yes," Clemencia said, "let's stop all this talk."

"What will I tell Elena?" Clara asked. "What can I tell her?"

"That he is not hers," Esteban said. Clara had not looked at him even when she had asked him a question, and he saw that she had forgotten the talk they had had at the clinic. "You don't have to explain anything to her."

Dolores was puzzled with what he said. "All she means, Esteban, is that it will be a blow to Elena," she explained. As she talked, Esteban saw Dolores recall the conversation they had had on the phone, and her eyes fill with fear that his promises about Clara would not be fulfilled. "You see, my boy, Elena has been very devoted to little Jimmy, both she and Jaime. We will have to be very gentle in breaking the news to them, out of respect for their love."

Esteban avoided returning Dolores' questioning look. He nodded and looked away. It was too late to explain to the old woman what he thought of Elena and Jaime.

"Do not trust him, Mama," Clara said. "Esteban has no respect for anything." She began to moan and her legs started to double under her. "Help!" Mina and Clemencia tried holding her up, but she slumped to the floor, and they only succeeded in softening her fall.

"Aiee, aiee," Dolores exclaimed. "Help her, darlings, help her!"

"Raise her head," Mina said. "She has only fainted. It was bound to happen."

Esteban put his arms around Clara's crumpled body and pulled her up. Clemencia and Mina took her arms.

"Into the bedroom," Mina said, and they began to move off with her in a clumsy group. "She needs to lie down and get over the shock."

"Shirley, bring a wet towel," Clemencia said.

It took Shirley a long moment to respond. She had just divined what Clara meant by saying that Esteban did not respect anything; it was true then, he had spent the night in her bed. Shirley looked at Clara, trying to find some explanation in her looks. What kind of person was she? And the old ladies? Did they know?

Clemencia called again. "Shirley?"

"Don't hold her head up," Shirley said suddenly, and got up, impatient with them all. "Let it hang down and she'll come to."

They looked at her skeptically. "Are you sure?" Clemencia asked.

"Sit her on the bed first," Shirley said. "Listen to me." She pushed Esteban aside and stood in front of Clara where she half-lay on the bed. "Hold her up in a sitting position."

Mina and Clemencia obeyed.

Shirley took Clara's head and pushed it down to her knees. Immediately, Clara began to moan and her head bobbed up, pushing against Shirley's hand. Shirley held her down a second longer, until Clara began to struggle harder. The woman was a fool, Shirley thought, to allow men to use her that way. Wondering how long she had held Clara's head down, Shirley suddenly took her hand away, and Clara sat up with eyes wide open and looked at Shirley as if she had been taken advantage of.

"There, you're all right now," Shirley said, and ashamed of what she had been thinking of Clara, she took her hands and rubbed them at the wrist gently.

Dolores put a hand on Shirley's head. "Thank you, my darling," she said. "You are efficient, like my Elena."

"I will get the wet towel," Clemencia said, proud of Shirley.

"I want to lie down," Clara said to Shirley. "I didn't mean to . . . "

Shirley leaned forward and kissed Clara on the forehead apologetically. "Good, you rest now," she said. "It'll be good for you." She looked to Mina for help, and between the two of them they helped Clara lie back on the bed.

"Here," Clemencia said, holding out a wet face towel.

Shirley sat on the edge of the bed and wiped Clara's face with the towel and then folded it over her forehead.

"That girl is an angel of mercy," Dolores said to Mina and Clemencia as they watched Shirley.

"Get me another wet towel and a dry one," Shirley said. "She's all right."

"Yes," Clemencia said eagerly, and left the room.

"And two aspirins and water," Shirley said to Mina. Shirley stood up and removed Clara's shoes. Then she unbuckled the belt of her dress. When Clemencia returned, Shirley wiped Clara's face with the fresh towel and dried her. She took the aspirins from Mina and helped Clara sit up on the bed to take them. Clara took the tablets and sipped some water obediently. "Lie back and rest now," Shirley said. "You need to be quiet a while."

Clara nodded, and Shirley backed out of the room, hoping the old ladies would come to her. In helping Clara she had worked out all of her emotions, but the old ladies looked at her admiringly and stayed by Clara's side. They knew that when someone dies you must not leave the bereaved to mourn alone.

In the living room, Shirley found Esteban sitting with his head in his hands. She could not help herself; a sorrowful man brought out all of her softness. "She's calmer now," she said, sitting next to him. "We got her to lie down and rest."

"I am afraid," he said, looking into her face, "that the calmer she gets the less she will like me."

"Like you?" Shirley asked hesitantly. Then he did care for Clara!

"Very well, love me," Esteban explained. He smiled ruefully at the confusion in Shirley's look. "Any woman who has time to think about me doesn't love me. I decided that just now, sitting her and feeling useless. You must understand, I do not like useless people. And that's what I am in this situation, useless."

Shirley shook her head. "That's not true. What would we have done . . ."

He waited patiently for her to finish and smiled very shyly when she only trailed off. "You see," he said, "that's the way you feel too. So what should I be to Clara? Only an ex-husband, not even her last husband. Not a father anymore."

"I am very sorry, very sorry," Shirley said, and found that she had to stop because she had begun to cry, not knowing that she cared so much for these people. "Oh I am very sorry," she repeated.

Esteban took one of her hands. "Latin men are not supposed to cry, you know, and American women are supposed to be very unfeeling. So stop your tears."

Shirley involuntarily smiled and took her hand away. She wiped her tears on the sleeve of her dress. "I'm not much help, am I?" she said.

"You thought I was sitting here mourning, but I was not. I was thinking about this matter of being a useful person." He looked at her to see if she were interested and continued. "I always thought about people being useful in other ways. You and Roberto would know what I mean—useful to your fellow men. Useful in political ways, in a strike, and in a revolution, and I have just discovered that we can be useful in other ways. You women know this."

Where was Robert? Shirley wondered. It was time he were back.

To Esteban, she only looked uncomprehending, and he tried to explain. "I mean, useful as husbands and fathers can be useful. Like a hand to help you across the street, that's the way a man should be. You understand what I mean, all mothers do. It's built right into the word 'mother.' A mother is someone who does something for someone, or she is not a mother. A father is different. He has to make an effort to be useful."

When he stopped, Shirley nodded, hoping that by listening she could be of some use to him. They were quiet, and Shirley waited until it would seem right to ask about Robert. But Esteban looked so crushed that she could not pass over it. "It's natural to feel this way when somebody you love dies," she said. "You can't do anything for them."

I will have to make an effort in the future, Esteban said to himself. I may never be able to look at women in the same way again. He felt a pang of regret at the thought. "I guess you are right," he said, but he did not believe it. No one should feel this way.

"Shouldn't Robert be back?" Shirley asked. "He has been gone a long time."

Esteban hit himself impatiently. "I should be reassuring you," he said. "I should have known you'd be worrying."

Mina and Clemencia came in from the bedroom at that moment, and Shirley warned him with a glance to say no more. Mina did not know that Robert had gone off on Esteban's errand, and Shirley did not want to remind Clemencia either.

Mina went over to Esteban. "Tell me, now that Dolores is not here, did the poor boy go the way you said? Or were you just sparing Dolores?"

Esteban shook his head. "No, it was the way we said."

"Strange, strange," Clemencia said. "At least he didn't suffer."

"It was very sudden," Esteban explained. "But there's a medical reason for it. Dr. Ortiz explained, as I told you."

Mina sat down across from Esteban and looked toward the bedroom before trusting herself to speak. "What do doctors know? The things they do not know yet!" She looked at Clemencia and then at Shirley. "A sneeze! Do they know what a sneeze is? No, they don't. Why does anybody sneeze and what use is it? Ask any doctor. They do not know. Ah, there are so many things they do not know, and until they at least know what a sneeze is, I'm going to keep up my novenas."

"Please," Clemencia said, looking toward the bedroom. "That is not the point. These things happen and it is no use talking about them."

Mina kept her voice down. "Well, what is the point?" She leaned toward her sister. "Don't tell me you, too, are going to start saying there is no God. It is all very well to talk like that in conversation, but it is not proper at a time like this." She stopped because Clemencia looked so troubled. "Are you feeling all right?" she asked, remembering Clemencia was the youngest.

Clemencia looked down at her hands, which she held together on her lap. "I did not mean to hurt your feelings," she said, wishing Robert were back safely from his trip.

"You are right," Mina said, grateful for Clemencia's apology. "There is no point to something like this. Why should little Jimmy die at a time like this? There is no reason for it."

Clemencia did not answer, and they were all silent a moment. Mina sighed and Clemencia felt ashamed that she had not cleared up the confusion she felt her sister Mina had interjected into the situation. She realized she was keeping quiet because she was appealing to God to bring Robert back safely. "But there is less point," she said suddenly, "if it is your God that did it. What kind of a God is that?"

"My God?" Mina said. "Why do you say my God?"

Clemencia looked away and held her lips tight, sorry that she had spoken. "Oh I suppose there is a God," she said, forgetting to speak softly. "But let Him mind His own business. I don't want to bother with Him!"

"You are making too much noise," Mina said, and continued loudly, "and you are not being logical. Yes, it is not logical what you say. I believe you are only repeating something you have heard Roberto say."

"No, no, that is not true." Dolores stood in the doorway of the bedroom and spoke to Mina. "You know Clemencia has a mind of her own. It is a wonderful quality." She looked from Mina to Clemencia and held one hand on the door knob to support herself, smiling pityingly to acknowledge the blow that they had been dealt by Jimmy's death.

"Oh, come sit here," Clemencia said, pointing to the sofa. She got up to help Dolores.

Mina got up too. "Is Clara asleep?"

Dolores shook her head and stopped to catch her breath. "No, but I had to come out to speak to Esteban, to settle about the funeral." She looked around for him and smiled sadly when she saw him in the dining room at the sideboard.

Esteban finished his drink and came to the arched doorway of the living room.

"I'll go inside and stay with Clara," Shirley said in English. She got up and paused before the old ladies to get their assent. "Yes?" she asked in Spanish.

Dolores reached out a hand and patted her face, purposely delaying the moment when she would have to talk about Jimmy's funeral. "She means to stay with my Clara, doesn't she? I can understand a good heart even when it speaks in English."

Shirley took Dolores' hand, and Dolores drew her to her and kissed her. "You are one of us," she said to Shirley, and then let her go to the bedroom.

Leaning on Clemencia and Mina, Dolores took another step toward the sofa and then stopped again. Now that she had helped Clara, she was free to feel the full weight of her loss. "Ah, my dears, I also had to be with you," she said. "You are my sisters; I need your comfort." She took a deep breath and moaned. "I cannot hold it any longer." She bobbed her head up and down, shaking the tears out of her eyes. "The only grandchild who has grown up with me! They have torn my heart out!" With a sudden spurt of energy, she took three fast steps to the sofa and held her arms down to feel where she was lowering her body because the rush of tears did not let her see.

Clemencia and Mina sat on either side of her, and each took one of her hands and patted it. Esteban sat across from her in a straight-back chair and shaded his eyes with one hand. He could not watch Dolores and still hope to avoid crying himself. Her head was thrown back against the high back of the sofa and her bosom shook each time she breathed and tried to keep from sobbing. The sound of her troubled breath throbbed insistently in his ear.

Finally, Dolores turned her head without raising it and looked at Clemencia. "Of course I want to live to a very old age. I shall never be ready to die." She rolled her head to the other side and looked at Mina. "I have never understood those wise old people you find in novels—never—the ones who have lived so much that they are ready to die. All I know is that I want to die before all of you. I could not bear to outlive another one. Not another one, I cannot bury another one."

"Do not say that," Clemencia said. "It is a terrible thing."

"They do not have the right to ask me to bury another!" Dolores insisted. "Let them bury me instead. I am not strong enough to take these blows."

"That is the legacy of the poor," Mina said. "We are spared nothing. They make us live through everything—hard work, the factories, not enough money for both food and clothes, and then the death of our children. It is a full life we lead."

Dolores sat up. "I would like a little less."

Clemencia stopped patting Dolores' hand. She pretended to look down in order to hide her tears. Thank God, she thought, my children are all alive.

"Oh the rich live to see their children die, too," Mina said, "but they have been able to conserve themselves for it. They take it with all their faculties unimpaired. They are so strong they do not even need to cry. If you have never scrubbed out the toilet bowl or cleaned the kitchen floor on your knees . . ." She stopped to slap the tears away from her cheeks. "Then you can take the death of your children philosophically. God has not wiped out your work then."

Dolores had stopped crying and listened distractedly to Mina, nodding at every phrase. "What a good heart you have, my dear," she said.

"I do not; I do not," Mina protested. "My heart is a dehydrated orange, hard and light and long-lasting. That is the way to be."

Dolores and Clemencia paid no attention to her protest.

"Mina is right," Clemencia ventured, when they had been quiet a moment. "The work we do for our children is the kind we do not do for money. It's the only kind they cannot make a profit from."

"Ah yes, we do it out of love," Dolores said, her eyes shining. "It is like art, the work of our souls."

"The two of you are innocents if you think that," Mina said. "It is with our children that they most exploit us. We work and they make a profit, and with the little we get, we give them children from whom to make a larger profit when we are too old to work well. It all comes to them. You would think that at least they would make the children."

"You forget about love," Dolores said. "You cannot make children for all those reasons . . . You can only make them because you love."

"And because some can get away," Clemencia said boldly. "I do believe that some will get away and play them a dirty trick."

"I do not understand the silence of God about this," Mina continued, as if she had not heard the others. "You would think Jesus Christ might have made Him listen, and yet I can excuse Him for having done nothing then, because Jesus was treated so badly on earth. But He should have listened to St. Francis, and He has not. That is why those who want to do something for the poor do not expect His help. Why should Lenin have directed a single prayer to Him, I ask you? It would have put him in the same parish with Primo de Rivera. Why should the Chinese Reds call for help from Francisco Franco's God? It is a disgrace. I no longer pray for anything worth while, just for small, petty things, the kind of vain stupidities that God understands."

"I can assure you of one thing," Esteban said. "No one is going to commend my son to God."

They had forgotten he was in the room and were startled to hear his voice.

"Oh Esteban, do not take us seriously," Mina said. "Do not give it a thought. He is surely in heaven if there is one."

"I mean about his funeral," Esteban said. "I don't want to offend you, Dolores, but I don't want any priest saying prayers. I know you and Mina will say prayers for him. I don't mean that."

"Do not be bitter, my boy," Dolores said. She took her hands away from Mina and Clemencia, folded them in her lap, and leaned toward him. "We have set you a bad example in our talk, but we are old and we are permitted to quarrel with God."

Esteban said nothing. He looked down at his hands and waited.

"You will not offend me," Dolores said softly, "if there is no priest."

"You know that," Mina said.

"We have buried our husbands without priests," Clemencia added.

"Forgive me." Esteban looked up at them. "Listen, Clara will not talk to me. I don't blame her, but I want to arrange about the funeral. How do you want . . ."

"Yes, yes, yes," Dolores said, not knowing what she meant. She took the handkerchief out to keep from thinking of little Jimmy. "I thought Elena would arrange it. She is so efficient, and there is no reason for you to . . ."

"My son Feliz will arrange it all," Mina said. "He will soon be here, and you can talk to him. Let him do it. That is what family is for. Do not torture yourself with these things."

"Let Esteban be," Clemencia said. "Do not give him so much advice."

Dolores got up, and Esteban stood up to meet her. She took his hands. "I understand, Esteban. You do it." She looked to the bedroom, wondering how to offer him money. "You and I will do it. I have some money. I keep it with my poetry . . ."

Esteban shook his head.

"Later, I will give it to you later."

"No, it's not necessary," Esteban said.

Dolores did not let go of his hands. "Why are you angry with me?"

He looked at her and his eyes began to water. "Very well, I will count on it."

Dolores pulled him to her and cried into his chest. "She needs you more than ever now!"

The screen door slammed, and Feliz appeared in the doorway. His eyes were wide with apprehension; he expected to find hysterics and did not know what he was going to do about it.

"Feliz!" Mina called. "His little heart just stopped from the shock of the operation. It happened before anything could be done!"

"Then it is true," Feliz said gravely. "I am very sorry." He walked to Esteban and shook hands.

"Feliz, talk to Esteban," Mina said. "Tell him to let you make all the arrangements for the funeral. He is taking too much on himself. It is not right."

"Certainly," Feliz said. "Please—"

Dolores turned to Esteban. "All I want is to have him here again. I want him to rest here before they take him away for good!"

"It will be done," Esteban promised. "He will be here tonight and then tomorrow afternoon—is that all right?"

Dolores looked to Clemencia and Mina. "So soon?"

"It has to happen sometime, my dear," Clemencia said.

Dolores covered her face with her handkerchief and nodded.

"In that case, there is a great deal to be done," Mina said.

"People will be coming. We must send for food. Do you have enough spirits?"

Feliz cleared his throat. "I'll notify all the people who'll want to come to the funeral. I'll get people with cars. Have you thought of someone for the funeral oration?"

Dolores shook her head.

"I recommend Aquiles Montiel," Feliz said. "He is sensible, not oratorical."

"But go with Esteban first," Mina said to Feliz. Then she looked around. "Where is Roberto?" she asked.

"He was not with me," Feliz said. "I was at the baseball game."

"Clemencia, where is he?" Mina asked. "You ought to know."

Clemencia shook her head. "Let us not talk about that now. There are other things to do."

"Ah, ah!" Mina said. She turned to Esteban. "What have you gotten him mixed up in? He has a family to take care of, and you get him to do your dangerous work for you!"

"What? What?" Dolores asked. "What are you talking about?"

Mina pointed a finger at Esteban. "He is engaged in sending contraband to the rebels in Cuba, and I suspect he has roped in Roberto to do it too."

Dolores gasped. "Esteban!"

"You do harm by talking this way," Esteban said.

Mina turned away from him to Clemencia. "You are his mother, what did you do to stop him?"

Feliz cleared his throat and reached out and touched Mina. "Mother, you are meddling." He took his hand quickly away, afraid Mina might slap it.

"When will you learn to protect your children!" Mina continued to Clemencia. "Feliz listens to me, believe me."

"I am his mother," Clemencia said, "and I do not object."

"You are a fool!" She turned to find Esteban and saw he was gone. "He's gone!" She looked at the others. They were quiet, each wondering if there were going to be more sad events that day.

"Do not tell Elena when she arrives," Dolores said, to end the talk.

Mina did not listen. "Well, that Esteban is a man, anyway. He knows what he is about, God bless him," she said.

"Come, there is a lot to do," Clemencia said. "I am going into the kitchen and see what I can find to cook."

182

Dolores took her arm. "You will need me."

"No," Clemencia said, and led her to the sofa. "I know where things are. What I cannot find I'll send Shirley for."

Dolores lowered herself into the sofa. "I have been blessed with you and Mina." She closed her eyes to meditate for a moment.

"Feliz," Mina said, "you can go to Seventh Avenue for pastries. When you get back, we will tell you all the people to be notified."

Feliz drew her to the door with him. "Look, Mother," he said, "you are acting very foolishly, and what you say reflects on me. You have put me in a bad light with your outbursts."

She looked up at him and saw his big eyes bulging with offended pride. "Don't mind, son," she said apologetically. "You know I love you more than anyone."

"Then mend your ways," he said, and left before she could answer.

Mina sat down with Dolores and put Feliz out of her mind. She called Clemencia to come join them, for they had all lived a long time and there were a lot of people whom they would have to remember to notify to come to the wake and the funeral. Perhaps, with all three of them to make the list, some names might still be forgotten.

XIII

CLEMENCIA came out of the kitchen wiping her hands on an apron of Dolores' that she had found hanging behind the porch door. "I have taken the little steaks out of the freezer," she said. "I do not suppose Elena and Jaime will have eaten when they arrive."

"No, no," Dolores said. "They may be here soon. They little know the terrible news that awaits them." She covered her face with her hands. "I am a coward. I wish it were not up to me to tell them."

"In any case, they will be hungry," Mina said, "and the rest of us must eat, too."

Clemencia sat down on the edge of the chair. "I think I can find enough things to make. I have black beans soaking at home . . ."

"Consuelo," Dolores said, taking her hands away from her face, "We must send for her. Someone must go for her . . . She would never forgive us, poor soul."

"What can she do?" Mina asked. "Why not at least wait until tomorrow? Then she cannot say that she was forgotten, and she would not be in the way tonight."

Dolores thought it over. "It would not be good for her to be up all night at her age."

"Oh but she would be in her element," Mina said. "There is no denying that."

"Don't talk that way about her," Clemencia said. "Feliz's wife can go get her." She turned to the kitchen and went to the phone.

"Yes, please get her," Dolores said. She looked at Mina with an anguished smile. "I should not be ashamed of Consuelo because she is colored. You know she is part of us all."

Mina agreed. "Remember when my own Claudio, may-he-rest-in-peace, died. Her mind had already begun to wander, and she kept praising Clemencia for taking it so well, forgetting whose husband Claudio was. But I should not laugh, poor woman. She stayed at the house when we all went to the cemetery for the bur-

184

ial, and when we returned, she had not only tidied the house but had a complete meal ready for us. Of course, it was indigestible."

Clemencia returned and spoke in a false, light-hearted tone, hoping to distract Dolores. "I remember Consuelo brought that Varon woman that day, the one who lost her skirt on the steps of the Clock during the ten-months strike. That woman always had a lot of push. I guess she thought that under cover of Consuelo and our grief we would all forget that she had broken the strike in nineteen twenty-one. My bunch maker was on the picket line the day they pulled the skirt off her as she went into the factory. She just picked it up when it finally fell to her ankles and walked in with it over her arm."

But Dolores had stopped listening, and the tears were running down her face unheeded.

"Now, now," Mina said to her. She took Dolores' handkerchief from her and wiped her tears. "You must not start up again. Think of your heart. You will infect us all with your tears, and we will not be able to do the things that need to be done."

"Forgive me," Dolores said. "I was really thinking of Armando. He should be here now, and as soon as I thought we should call him back, I knew I could not." She stopped to take her sisters' hands. "Oh the lies we mothers tell ourselves! I knew in my heart that Armando had done something so bad that he could not come back to Tampa. At least, not now, when he should be with his family. There, I am lying to myself again. Armando probably will never be able to come back."

"What are you saying!" Mina protested. "It was his chance to take that job—"

Dolores raised a hand and let it fall to her lap. "No, no, do not tell me stories. Let it be, I shall live with it."

"He has not done anything bad," Clemencia said weakly.

"And my other boys . . . they are so far away too," Dolores said. "Cheo in Chicago and Mario at the other end of Florida, in Miami."

"We can call Mario," Clemencia said. "Maybe my Alice and her husband can come too. All they have to do is get in a car and they will be here before morning."

"Yes, yes," Mina said, "I want to see them all. Ah, if only they could bring their children too."

"Do you think it is possible?" Dolores looked at her sister.

Mina nodded vehemently, and Clemencia's eyes looked back at her happily. "And your Alice too?" Dolores said to Clemencia. "I want to thank her for taking care of Mario and his wife when they were sick with the virus."

"It is settled," Mina said. "We will call them and they will come."

"Please do it, Mina," Dolores said. "There are only a few telephone numbers here in Tampa that I know how to call. And to dial them I have to put on my glasses."

"Clemencia will do it," Mina said. "She will speak to her Alice first and Alice can go over to Mario's."

Clemencia shook her head. "It is only since Roberto came here that I have a telephone in the house, and there has been no occasion to call long distance. You get the number for me, Mina, and as soon as it starts ringing, I will talk to Alice."

"No, no," Mina said, "I don't like to tangle with those American operators. Feliz always gets the number for me."

Dolores looked puzzled. "You mean you have to talk to someone to get the number—of course, of course, I forgot."

They were quiet a moment. Mina was the first to smile. "What useless old women we are!" she said.

Dolores sighed. "What would we do without our children?"

Clemencia got up. "I will not have it that way. I am going to try. I know Alice's number." She started for the kitchen, where the new white phone hung on the wall.

"I'll come and help," Mina said, and got up. "The zero is the operator. Just dial the zero and wait and an American girl will answer. Then you will have to have your wits about you."

Dolores pulled herself up from the sofa. "Let me be with you," she said. "I want to talk to them, too."

They did not get to the kitchen because they stopped to confer again in the dining room, and then Robert arrived. He was surprised to find them having a lively conversation. The neighbors had told him about little Jimmy's death when he stopped at home, and he had rushed here. When they turned and looked at him, he saw from their faces how upset they were.

Clemencia broke away from them. "You are back!" she said, and ran to him. She threw her arms around him. "You are back!" she said a second time. When she felt his arm reassuringly around her, she became shy and did not know what to do to get out of his embrace.

Robert looked over his mother's head at Dolores and Mina. They made no move to go to him while he held Clemencia, but waited like respectful children. "I stopped at home," he explained, "and the neighbors told me what happened."

"Oh, Roberto, each new person I see is like a stab in the heart," Dolores said, throwing her arms up to be embraced. "It is a terrible reminder. I remember now what it is to mourn. It is meeting people with whom you must go over it again and again." She held his face with both her hands when he leaned down to kiss her, and made him look directly into her eyes. "Not you, my dear. You suffer like the rest of us; you come to me with a full heart."

Robert nodded. "It is a terrible thing. Terrible. How is Clara?"

Dolores gestured toward the bedroom. "Your Shirley is . . ."

Robert followed her glance and saw Shirley standing in the doorway. "I knew it was your voice," she said calmly, and went to him. But when she put her hand on his arm and looked up at him, she began to cry.

"The children are all right," Robert said. "I stopped by the house."

She nodded without looking up and butted her head into his chest. She was ashamed to answer in any other way, for she had been wanting to see the children all afternoon, to make sure nothing had happened to them. It was selfish to have been feeling like that, she knew, but she could not help it. "And you are all right," she said finally, grateful for that and for his knowing what she had been feeling about their children.

"You do not deserve her," Mina said loudly to Robert. "Look whom you have been endangering with your games. What were you doing all afternoon? Your mother does not talk, but I know. Playing the rebel! With two children and this girl here, do you want to lose everything you have built?"

"Oh my dear aunt!" Robert looked at her and slowly a smile took command of his face. "Despite everything, I feel very good. Maybe it's like a game, but I'm happy that I played this game before I got too old."

"You are too old," Mina said. "You should know better."

Dolores turned to Clemencia and asked her privately, "What is Mina talking about?" She had already forgotten.

"Pay no attention," Clemencia said. "Mina makes up things to quarrel about."

Robert shook his head at Mina. "I thought I knew better." He kept an arm around Shirley and smiled at his aunt. "Don't pretend you disagree with me. I can see you're already inflating it into a heroic deed."

"Well, aren't you going to kiss me?" Mina said, and crossed her arms. "It seems to me I always have to ask."

Shirley looked from one to the other. They all seemed to have forgotten about little Jimmy. She began to suspect that they were tougher than she thought, but Robert leaned against her and squeezed her waist, making her forget what she was thinking. He whispered to her, "You don't act as if you were worried about me." She looked up, astonished that he should think that, and saw that he was smiling at her.

Mina struck Clemencia playfully. "I have just realized that Shirley could have called Miami for us! There is no cure for what ails us. We are getting senile."

"Oh yes, yes," Clemencia said, and turned to Robert. "I want you to call your sister in Miami."

Dolores took his arm. "She will go see Mario and give him the news. We want them to come here for—for tomorrow. Say you agree it is not foolish of us old women to want to see our children at this time."

Shirley fell a step behind and let the old ladies surround Robert as they walked to the kitchen to phone. She heard him say to Dolores that he did not think it was foolish, and although he spoke soberly and his voice was tempered by the sorrowfulness of the news, she marveled at how happy he was.

"Oh my dear Roberto, this is a terrible day," Dolores said to him in the kitchen. "You have your own dear children. You understand."

Robert breathed deeply. "I have been thinking of them since I heard the news. Jimmy's death has shown me how precious they are and"—he squeezed her arm as he said it—"and how lucky I am that they are all right."

"You should not say that," his mother said.

Dolores stopped her. "Oh no, Clemencia, he is right. It is the most natural feeling in the world. It shows he is the best of fathers. To feel lucky is the perfect way of expressing it. We are lucky to have been given the gift of little children."

"Yes," Mina agreed, but sounded as if she were arguing, "they are wonderful when they are little."

They stopped in front of the phone that hung on the wall. Dolores looked at it and held her hands together as if pleading with it. "There it is," she said. It rang loudly, and she instinctively reached for it and took it off the hook without bringing it to her ear. "Who can it be? Oh, oh!" She looked at the others. "It must be Elena!"

Mina took the phone from her and spoke into it. "No, no," she said. "This is Mina. Yes, we are all here. We have been expecting you to call."

Dolores turned to Robert. "It is Elena. She and Jaime flew right back when they found out about the operation."

"Wait, wait," Mina said into the phone, "Roberto will go pick you up." She shook her head and then remembered Elena could not see her. "No, my dear, you cannot go to the hospital. It is no use. He did not take the operation well." She stopped to control her voice. "It was very bad, very bad. I have to tell you he did not survive."

"Elena! Elena!" Dolores called. She took the phone from Mina and began to cry and talk into the phone. "Elena, my darling, come home. We need you here. Yes, yes, my dear, he is gone; he is gone!" Her tears did not let her continue, and she gave the phone up to Mina.

"All right, Elena, we will wait for you," Mina said. "No, do not worry. Everyone is all right."

Mina put the phone back on the hook. "She was calling from the airport. They wanted to go straight to the hospital. I had to tell her."

Dolores sat down at the kitchen table. "I fear she will take it very badly."

They were quiet. Mina sat down at the table, too, and said nothing.

"Aunt Mina?" Robert said.

Mina shook her head. "She thought it would be better if they took a taxi and came straight here."

Shirley and Robert retreated to the doorway and waited. Clemencia went to the stove and looked into the oven and then went back to the table and sat with Mina and Dolores. Dolores broke the silence. "I am afraid of what this will do to Elena. She never had children, and they were counting on Jimmy as if he were their own. He had private tutors in English and Spanish. They hired a man to teach him to ride . . ."

Shirley and Robert stood aside and Clara came into the kitchen. "I don't want to be alone," she said. She looked at Robert and did not hide her tired-looking eyes. Her long black hair was combed, but she wore no make-up and she had changed into a housedress. "That was Elena who called on the phone, wasn't it?"

Mina nodded. "They are coming from the airport."

"I must ask her forgiveness," Clara said. Her voice was quiet and tired. "She has been very good to me. And so has Jaime." She looked around the kitchen for a place to sit. "I think I would like some Cuban coffee with brandy in it."

Clemencia got up. "Sit down here, Clara. I must get on with the cooking." She went to the stove and looked into the coffee pot. "There is coffee left. I will heat it."

Dolores gave her hand to Clara when she sat down at the table. "Are you sure you do not want to lie down, my darling?"

"Elena would not like that," Clara said, "and I'm not sick, after all. There's nothing wrong with me. I just need a stimulant."

Mina got up from the table. "I will start making the calls," she said. "There are a lot of people we have to tell. Feliz's wife will tell her own family." She took the phone off the hook. "So will Esteban. Then, let us begin with Miami. Here, Roberto."

Robert got the long-distance operator, and when he heard the phone ringing at the other end, he held the receiver toward his mother. She interrupted her cooking and wiped her hands on her apron before she took it. Mina began to take dishes out of the cupboard, and Dolores turned in her chair to listen to Clemencia. Robert took Shirley's arm and led her back to the living room, where they listened a moment to the activities in the kitchen.

Shirley drew Robert to her and kissed him. "I was so worried about you, and everything that happened made me even more nervous." She grabbed his hands. "Tell me what it was like."

"It was just like Esteban's note. Nothing extraordinary happened. I might as well have been delivering a load of groceries." He looked around to see if they were still alone. "Except inside me. I felt all the time as though I were more wide awake than I had ever been in my life. Time went by like lightning, and yet everything I looked at revealed its line and structure and volume to me on sight, the way I wish I could make an object I draw tell me its secrets. Only I didn't have to stare and stare and think and think. It was extraordinary. I felt like Superman."

Shirley leaned her head on his chest. "And you are; you are."

"I guess it was a kind of mirage of the senses." He looked at her happily. "What was not a mirage was the most wonderful thing of all, the man who was the contact in Sarasota. It was someone I had known when I was a boy. His father was a shoe repairman, and whenever I went to his shop near the cigar factory, he would be there helping his father, polishing shoes at a machine with a brush that turned at high speed. How I used to envy him! We were the same age, but we were never friends. Then, when we were in junior high school, his mother and the other organizers of the hunger march were arrested and sent to jail for a year. I remember the talk at home and how my father and mother collected food for them, and the last time I saw him in school I tried to be friendly but he looked away and took no notice. Then his father closed the shop and I didn't know what happened. Until today. He looked at me and said the words and it seemed to me that he knew every thought I had and I did not mind. On the contrary. He did not look away either, but looked at me and let me read all his thoughts. I thought about it on the way back. I have never really known what friendship is."

"How I envy you," Shirley said. Then she shook her head. "No, I know what you mean. I have never really felt until today what having a family means, although I don't understand everything about them." She looked toward the kitchen. "For example, what are they doing? It sounds as if they're preparing a feast."

Feliz came in the front door as Shirley turned to Robert for an answer. He was carrying several boxes of pastries and nodded to them without stopping to talk. They watched him hand the boxes to Mina in the doorway of the kitchen and wait to get more instructions from her.

On his way out Feliz told them he was going to their home to pick up the beans that were soaking on the stove, and offered to take a message to the neighbors about their children. "Let me go instead," Robert said. "I have the car outside."

"No, it's no trouble," Feliz said. "The truth is Elena and Jaime are expected here any moment, and I would rather avoid all the tears and crying. It's an awkward situation for a man."

Robert smiled and nodded, and Feliz hurried away, but when he got to the porch steps he turned back, stuck his head through the door, and said to Robert, "I hope you took no offense at what I said." He did not wait for an answer.

"They *are* preparing for a feast," Robert explained to Shirley after Feliz had left. "They're preparing for a wake. All the family will be here tonight. So will all the families of in-laws. And friends. And all the neighbors on the block. That's the way it was when my father died. In this room the coffin will sit open, and Dolores and Clara and all the women close to the family will sit near by and receive the visitors. Even in this room it will only be relatively quiet, for there will be a lot of tears shed and a lot of condolences exchanged. Those who are not really sorrowful will put on mournful faces, and that is right, for they will be helping the family feel natural about their own grief."

"Doesn't it just make it worse?" Shirley asked. "It seems terrible to me."

"I should think so, but I haven't been to a wake since my father died, so I don't really know," Robert said after a pause. "Still, I don't know how one can feel worse about the death of a child. On the way over I remembered the last time that Paul was sick with his ear infection. He was sitting on my lap in that knocked-out way he gets when he has high fever, and I was holding him in such a way that my right hand was over his heart. That little heart pounded and pounded against my hand, so that his pulse was going through me, and I had the terrible sensation that if I took my hand away his heart would stop beating."

Shirley looked at him with tears in her eyes. "I know; it's unbearable to think of it."

"I think I know why it was such a wonderful experience to turn over the loaded truck to that fellow in Sarasota," Robert said. "It's just that I knew who I was and what I stood for, and there was someone else who saw it and recognized it. It must be wonderful to live like that always, with a strong sense of what you are and what you stand for." He got up from the sofa. "You must stop me. I have been wound up like an old Victrola, and I can't stop talking and recollecting and talking some more. Where's Esteban?"

Shirley got up too. "He's out making arrangements for the funeral. I feel so sorry for him. He's a wonderful person, isn't he?"

"He must be. I was very angry with him last night . . ." They started for the kitchen.

She held him back a moment. "I'm very sentimental, aren't I?"

"Yes, you are," he said, "but I like that."

When they reached the kitchen the women turned and looked at them, expecting to see Elena and Jaime. Clemencia was testing a large pot of rice; Mina turned away from the phone; and Dolores and Clara looked up from the table, their faces tense with waiting. Shirley went to Clemencia to ask how she could help, but Robert looked back because he had heard the front door open. It was Elena and Jaime. "They're here," he said to the others.

"Elena, Elena!" Dolores immediately called. "I am here, darling; come here!"

Clara got up and looked around as if she wanted to run away. She began to moan and wring her hands.

Robert stood aside to let Elena into the kitchen. She had stopped at the door looking from one to the other for Dolores. She was very pale and wore a tight-fitting black sheath; over her right breast was pinned a ruby brooch in the form of a red rooster. It glittered as she rushed to Dolores, whose outstretched arms caught her around the hips. The old lady sobbed like a child, and Elena, half-crouching, held her right hand on her mother's head, so that the bright ruby ring on her second finger shone like a drop of blood on Dolores' gray hair. Elena looked at Clemencia, who stood at the stove with a large spoon in her hand, and seemed not to recognize her.

"Jaime, Jaime!" Clara moaned. She walked to Elena's husband, who came into the kitchen holding his hat in one hand. "Our little boy is dead!"

Jaime put out his free hand to her, and Clara caught it in both of hers. She stopped and looked around at Shirley and Robert, not knowing what else to say or do. Jaime handed his hat to Robert without a word, and he drew Clara to him. "We want you to come with us to Cuba and bring him," he said. "He belongs on the grounds of the *finca* where he was so happy."

Clara nodded and repeated, "Where he was so happy!"

He turned slightly, so that she could not lay her head on his shoulder again and directed her attention to Elena. "Elena and I decided that in the taxi; isn't that so, Elena?"

Elena did not hear him. She was gently removing her mother's hands from around her hips, keeping the old trembling hands in her own as she sat in the chair facing Dolores. "It's good that you can cry," Elena said. She looked at her mother's wet face. "I can't. Isn't that strange? I simply cannot cry. If he had broken an arm perhaps I could cry. It's funny, isn't it?"

She looked around the kitchen at the others, wishing they would leave her alone with her mother, but they did not know that this was what she wished. They only thought she was stunned by the news. She held both Dolores' hands until her mother stopped crying and then she withdrew one of her hands and held it out to her sister. "Clara, come sit here," Elena said, and pointed to a chair. "I am sorry to have left you to take all this alone."

Clara looked at her sister's hand and wondered if she meant her to take it. It was forgiveness, that's what Elena must mean by the gesture, and she reached out gratefully for Elena's hand only to find that she was too late. Elena had turned back to Dolores. Clara walked obediently to the chair and sat down, and Elena waited a moment longer to give the others a chance to leave. But they didn't. Only Clemencia knew that Elena did not want to speak in front of them, but she stayed stubbornly at the stove and began to prepare the steaks.

"Tell me what happened," Elena said finally. "It is such a simple operation; why didn't he survive it?"

"He did, my dear, he did!" Dolores said. "It was later."

"Didn't I tell you?" Mina asked. "It was after the operation—from shock."

Dolores took out her handkerchief. "His little heart could not stand it. It just stopped beating. There was nothing anyone could do."

"And he had a good surgeon?" Elena asked.

"The best, my dear; he had excellent care," Dolores said. "It was one of those rare occurrences that cannot be foreseen. Esteban can tell you."

"Esteban?" Elena looked up at the others to check if he were there. Her eyes finally fell on Clara, but what she saw seemed to satisfy her. "I wish I could cry. There's nothing that wasn't done, but I wish I had been here. There's no expense Jaime and I wouldn't go to . . ."

"Do not blame yourself," Dolores said. "We have done enough of that. Dr. Ortiz himself assured Esteban—"

Elena looked away from her mother. "Dr. Ortiz! What did he have to do with Jimmy?"

Dolores and Clara looked so alarmed that Mina answered. "He operated on Jimmy. What is wrong with that?"

"Dr. Ortiz!" Elena closed her eyes and her body became taut. "But you said he had the best care!"

Dolores reached out to reassure her. "Dr. Ortiz is the finest surgeon in Tampa. He has a modest little clinic, but he himself is a master surgeon."

"Oh my God, Mama!" Elena looked at Dolores closely. "Don't tell me he was at that—that place!" She looked at her sister and then at her mother again. "Oh my God, there are one or two good hospitals here, and if those wouldn't do, we could have flown him anywhere in the world. Don't you know we have the money, plenty of it? Jaime, tell her you would have spent any amount. What do you think we made money for?"

"My dear, don't excite yourself," Jaime said. "It's done, and we must forget about it. Nothing may have helped anyway."

"I do not believe that." Elena got up and paced in front of Dolores and Clara. "I am not a doctor, but I know that people exert themselves for money, and Jimmy would have had the kind of attention that would have saved him. Clara! You have lived with us, haven't you learned anything?"

"Forgive me, Elena, please forgive me." Clara doubled up in her chair and laid her head on her knees. "You're right, I learn everything too late."

"It's the mentality of the slums! You're in the grip of it," Elena said. "How can I cry? How can I cry? He was our little boy, and I should cry when he dies, but I can only feel angry and scream that you sent him to a butcher shop. By rights, he should have been mine. I would have known what to do for him!"

"Elena, Elena," Dolores said. "We all of us loved him, my darling."

With her hands on her hips Elena bent slightly forward and answered her mother. "I am sick of this talk of love. He could have used something more than love. He could have used the care that money can buy. Once and for all, I want you to get it into your heads that I have money, that you don't have to live in this stupid, small-town slum. If we didn't have to come here to visit you, little Jimmy would not have been in a place where—what's the use?" She straightened up as though giving up the argument, and watched Clemencia who, unlike the others, acted as if she had not listened to Elena and was now stirring the large pot of soup.

Jaime tried to catch Elena's attention, but when he failed to do so with his eyes, he spoke to her. "My dear, you must take hold of yourself. You don't mean what you say." He turned to Dolores. "Señora, we are all very upset."

Elena raised a hand to stop him; his smooth tone irritated her for the first time. "Do you realize that every month I put away enough money to buy a thousand operations?" she continued to her sister and mother. "I take it in bundles to Miami and deposit it in the bank so that we can someday enjoy it, not so that you can stay here in this slum trap! And what am I going to take back on this trip for all my pains? His dead body!"

Dolores looked up. "Take back?" She thought better of it and tried to catch Elena's hand. "You are right, my darling. I know you do everything for us, but I am an old woman; I belong here."

"I'm not listening to you any more. You are coming to Cuba for the funeral," Elena said. "And you're staying there with us."

Dolores looked away, acting as if she had not heard. She leaned an elbow on the kitchen table and covered her eyes with her hand. In the embarrassed silence that followed, the others heard the front door slam, and then, to avoid looking at each other, listened to the footsteps approaching the kitchen. It was Feliz. He was carrying a covered pot with both hands and, under one arm, a package wrapped in butcher paper.

He was surprised to find everyone in the kitchen strangely quiet and staring at him. Then he saw Elena. "You were able to get a plane back right away, eh?" he said. "That must be a comfort to you. A few years ago it would have been impossible. The funeral would have had to have been postponed."

Elena nodded and stared at the things he was carrying.

"Oh yes," Feliz said, reminded by her stare. "Clemencia, here are the beans. And, Mother, I stopped at home and brought this meat." He placed the things on the stove and turned proudly to the room. "Roberto, maybe you can help me bring a few things from the car. I persuaded the bartender at the Centro Español to let me have a few bottles. It's Sunday and all the liquor stores are closed, but if you know people you can always manage to get things done. That's what I learned in the construction business. I also got a few boxes of cigars."

"What are all those things for?" Elena asked. She sounded polite, but Dolores knew Elena was cold with anger, and she looked at Mina and hoped she could stop Feliz from answering.

"The wake, of course," Feliz said, and suspecting that Elena disapproved of liquor at a wake, he explained, "Not that I think liquor should be served freely as at a wedding, not at all. But you have to have it, and I can set up a table on the back porch—do not fear. I shall take care of things. At a time like this you must not concern yourself with details. That's what the family is for."

"That's very kind of you, but there is not going to be any wake," Elena said.

Angry at Elena, Mina struck out at her son. "You brought the beans in the water, you fool. You could have poured the water out."

Elena turned her back on Feliz and faced Clara and Dolores. "Mama, did you really plan to have a wake?"

Dolores looked up. "Yes, my dear, of course I did," she said, and burst into tears.

"I didn't know anything about it, Elena," Clara said. "No one consulted me."

"You were going to set up his coffin in the living room and let hundreds of people come and gape at it and count the floral wreaths?" Elena continued. "And the house would be full of people all night long, eating and drinking and celebrating the fact that Jimmy died at the hands of some stupid doctor! What barbarity! What low-class savagery!"

Dolores moaned and covered her face with her hands.

"There is not going to be any wake," Elena continued. "You are going to spend the time packing and getting ready to leave tomorrow. We shall all fly back to Cuba and bury him where he belongs."

Elena turned to leave the kitchen, but the door was blocked. Old Consuelo had arrived, and she moved slowly and tremblingly toward Dolores, so that Elena had to stand by and watch. "Lola! Lola!" she called out to Dolores, with arms outstretched. "I would have come sooner but they had to search for me everywhere and only now found me. Think of it! I had been planning to stay the night with Dominguita Garcia whose husband had an attack of pleurisy, and I might have missed being here altogether."

Consuelo tried to lean down to kiss Dolores, but it looked as if she might topple, so Dolores took her hands and gently guided her to the chair where Elena had sat. "I belong with you here," Consuelo said, looking around happily. "The ties of family are the strongest there are, aren't they?" She did not notice that the silence continued. Instead, she began to nod to herself. "He was such a good boy, Dolores; he was such a good boy. Do you remember? He and my son Reymundo used to play together and I loved him like my own."

Clara began to laugh and then stopped. Elena turned her back on her mother and looked down a moment, considering what to do.

Mina broke away from Shirley and Robert and, in a mild voice that cost her an effort, spoke to Consuelo. "You have it wrong, my dear. It is not Dolores' son; it is her grandchild, Clara's little boy."

Consuelo looked at her with a half-smile. "It's all the same. When you get to be as old as I am, you are always mourning. I only feel at home at a wake."

"There's not going to be a wake!" Elena said loudly. "No wake."

Dolores put out an arm as if to hold her daughter off, but she also pleaded with her, "Elena . . . Elena, do not hide your good heart from us."

Clemencia put a spoon down on the stove with a loud noise; this reflected her feelings so well that it gave her courage to speak. "Wake or no wake, you are all going to have to eat dinner, and I cannot serve it if you do not get out of the kitchen."

"Yes, yes," Dolores said, and got up, "you must all eat. You will feel better after you eat, Elena, and you too, Jaime."

"Thank you for bringing things down to practical matters, Clemencia," Elena said approvingly. "No more talk. I'm sure if you were my mother none of these foolish problems would arise."

Jaime cleared his throat and looked around the room. "Before we go inside I think it would be appropriate to tell all of you that it is very comforting to Elena and me that you are here to spend some part of the evening together with us. I am sure I speak for Elena in telling you that none of her objections extend to you who are her family . . ." he stopped to bow slightly . . . "and consequently mine as well."

Consuelo managed to stand up by herself and began to follow the group as it left the kitchen. "No wake?" she said to their backs. "No wake? How can that be?"

No one turned to answer Consuelo, but Clemencia looked at Shirley who stayed in the kitchen to help her and said, "My poor sister is a prisoner of her children!"

"It's terrible," Elena said to Robert, greeting him for the first time, "but I can't cry." They were in the dining room, and she stopped to let the others go ahead to the living room. "She is getting old and foolish and I shouldn't lose my temper, I know you, at least, understand that they couldn't be allowed to go through with such a barbarous thing as a wake."

"If it makes them happy . . ." Robert began.

"It would finish my mother," Elena said. "Her heart couldn't take it." She looked up at Robert and frowned when she saw he did not agree. "I hate this town," she said, and went into the living room.

Dolores sat on the sofa between Mina and Consuelo, but she kept her eyes on the front door, hoping the coffin would arrive and that Elena would accept the fact of a wake. She twitched nervously and put her hands over her breasts when she realized what a terrible thing she was hoping for.

Elena saw her gesture. "Mama, it's all settled," she said. "It's for your good. I'm going to call the clinic now and make all the arrangements. I'll call the airport too. There should be a morning plane."

"Oh my dear, I know you are only thinking of me. I know." She spread her arms and talked to her family. "Do not misunderstand my daughter. You see, it is her good heart that makes her sound harsh." She looked at Elena as if she had agreed to the wake. "If it is only that, my darling, then you need not worry—"

"Mama!" Elena stopped her angrily. "It's settled!" Elena caught the shocked look on Mina's face, and it made her stop and change her tone. "If you're worried that he'll not have a proper funeral you'll see how it will be in Cuba. All our friends will come; the entire Palace will be at his funeral."

Dolores tried once more. "But Esteban must be consulted—"

"Esteban?" Elena looked at Clara and turned again to her mother. "What has he got to do with it?"

Jaime coughed. "We cannot very well leave him out of it."

"Very well," Elena said. "If he wants to come, then we'll pay his passage, but he shall have to find a place to stay. I will not put him up."

Dolores leaned back and sighed, and to Elena it seemed she was resigned. "It's for the best," Elena said, pausing a moment before she went to the phone.

Dolores nodded, as if accepting the fact. "You can do me a favor, my dear," she said quietly to Mina. "In the middle drawer of my dresser is my black veil wrapped in tissue paper. Get it for me. I need it to pay my grandchild a visit. I have not worn it since my Serafín died, and I must have it to mourn my little Jimmy." With one arm, she tried to pull herself up out of the sofa. "Help me up; I am a fat, useless old woman. I must go and spend the night with him wherever he is going to be!"

Elena stood in front of her, looking down fiercely.

"Help me!" Dolores said, but neither Consuelo nor Mina could get out of the sofa either. Dolores began to sob, and Mina threw her arms around her, and together they cried.

"Cry, cry," old Consuelo said. "That is what a wake is for."

Clara got up, pale and frightened, and went to Elena. "Elena, maybe—"

Elena raised a hand as if she were going to hit her sister. "No! This is another of your messes that I'm going to clean up." She turned and left for the phone, expecting that this would stop the commotion. It did. By the time she reached the kitchen the crying had died down, and she was sure she would have no more trouble.

In the kitchen she nodded curtly to Shirley and Clemencia, as if to acquaintances she was passing on the street, with whom she was too busy to talk. They looked away, acknowledging that they had been dismissed and that things would take the course that Elena had dictated. Elena took the phone off the hook and dialed information to get the number of the clinic. In the moment before the operator answered, it occurred to her that soon she would be through with Tampa and the poverty of her childhood. When she took her mother and Clara with her tomorrow morning, that would be the last she would ever see of it. Thank God, she thought, and at last felt angry tears well up in her eyes. Thank God.

XIV

CLEMENCIA and Shirley watched Elena as she heard the news that Esteban had already begun arrangements for the funeral. Her tears stopped flowing, and with a brusque gesture she wiped them away while she continued to talk to the clinic. "Thank you, I understand," she said in a tone to end the conversation. "I understand his father has given you orders."

Elena put the phone back on the hook, paused to look at the floor while she considered what to do, and then turned to Shirley and Clemencia. "Why didn't you tell me that Esteban had taken matters into his own hands?" she asked. "All my talk has been just a waste of time, and now I have to start all over again. I've got to find out what he's been doing and change it."

They didn't know what to answer, and Elena gave them no time. She turned, going determinedly to the living room.

Clemencia turned off all the burners on the stove. "Come, Shirley, let us see what happens," she said, motioning her to the living room. "It's no use getting the food ready until we know where we are. I'm afraid the rice is ruined. It will be just one big lump."

They found that Elena had again paused, because Esteban had just returned. He was still near the door as Clara turned to Elena and exclaimed, "Oh, oh Elena! Esteban went and made other arrangements!"

Everyone turned to Elena as she approached. "It's all right, I know," she said, and nodded to Esteban.

He looked worn and unwilling to fight anyone. Elena held out a hand to him, and he shook it quickly and turned to Robert. Robert smiled involuntarily and then said, "It went off without any trouble."

Elena waited until Esteban turned again and intercepted him before he greeted anyone else. "Actually, what you did works out well for us," she said. "Tell me the name of the funeral parlor. I'll call them and tell them they are not to bring him here but to the plane tomorrow."

Esteban looked at her. "What? What plane?"

"He can stay at the funeral parlor," she explained. "And you can see him there tonight. We have decided that he is to be buried in Cuba. Clara and my mother will leave tomorrow with us."

Esteban turned to Clara without answering Elena. Clara looked away with intense concentration, making believe she had not heard the exchange between her sister and Esteban. "Clara?" Esteban asked quietly. Clara did not answer. "Clara!"

Clara turned suddenly and looked beyond him. "I've made up my mind."

"What about?" Esteban asked.

"About what Elena said."

Esteban took a step toward her and asked very softly, excluding the whole room from his question, "Why, my dear, why do you want to do that?"

She looked down and her face became flushed under his gaze.

Esteban bent a knee and tried to look into her face. "Don't punish me, Clara. Why did you decide to do this?"

"Don't ask me!" Clara wrung her hands, looked up, and, seeing his face close to hers, jumped out of her chair. "I decided, I decided! I don't have to tell you. I'm his mother, aren't I?"

Esteban followed her as she turned away. "Please, Clara, I don't want to be a bother to you. I want to do whatever you say."

Clara moved back to her chair and held on to it in desperation. "You never bothered yourself about him before. Why do you care now?" She took a deep breath and shivered. "You don't have any right to say anything—and I don't either!" She turned to her sister and said angrily, "Elena, don't let him torment me!"

Jaime extended an arm and succeeded in getting Esteban's attention. "Señor, believe me when I say how I sympathize with you. This has been a terrible loss to us, too, and for that reason you must forgive anything we say that aggravates your wound. Particularly forgive anything the child's mother says." He paused to gauge Esteban's response. "It is our job to help her through this period."

Esteban nodded impatiently and tried to turn away.

Jaime mistook the gesture for embarrassment and put a hand on Esteban's arm to detain him and hold his attention. "She will be happier in Cuba with us and her mother. They will no longer live in Tampa, and it is therefore pointless to bury the boy here. You agree?"

Esteban looked down and did not answer.

"There is the fact—a sentimental one, I grant you," Jaime continued, "that the boy's last two years in Cuba were very happy ones. It seems right that he should go back with us. One cannot ever entirely discard sentiment in these matters; still, I have put it as dispassionately as possible to show you that my sister-in-law's decision is the only possible one."

Esteban waited for Jaime to remove his hand from his sleeve.

"Of course, if you wish to come to Cuba for the funeral," Jaime concluded, "we shall be glad to advance you the passage money."

"Yes," Elena said, summing up for Jaime, "Clara spoke the way she did because she's upset. If you will tell me which funeral parlor you made arrangements with I'll call them up now. I don't think we should delay any longer."

Esteban turned his back on them and faced Dolores where she sat on the sofa with Mina and Consuelo. "And you, Dolores?" he asked. "Are you going away?"

Dolores put up her hands as if he had struck her. "I must; I must," she said, and covered her face.

"What did you say?" old Consuelo asked. "First there is going to be no wake and now you are going away!" She tried to pull one of Dolores' hands away from her face. "But you cannot go away until I die. It is not right; you are my only relative. It is true I am not a blood relation, Dolores, but you are my only relative when everything is said and done; and you must be at my wake. I have counted on it; it is my one consolation."

The old woman pumped her head up and down like a petulant child and began to cry. "If my Reymundo were alive I would still expect you to be there. But as it is, you must; you must." She leaned over and grabbed Mina's arm. "You tell her she must be there to stand at the foot of my grave."

Dolores hugged old Consuelo, hiding her face in Consuelo's bony shoulder.

"My God!" Elena exclaimed. "This is absurd!"

"Clara!" Esteban called. "I am waiting for you to say something."

Clara saw the look on his face and got up to leave the room.

"Clara, tell them what we decided this afternoon," Esteban demanded.

Clara looked first at her sister Elena. "What?" she asked. "I don't know what you're talking about." She stopped where she was, preparing herself for a new humiliation and pleading silently.

203

Elena stepped in front of Esteban. "Leave her alone," she said to him.

"Clara, tell her," Esteban insisted.

Elena leaned forward and spoke quietly into Esteban's face. "Leave her alone or I will talk about last night."

Esteban looked at Elena with hatred, and then turned to her mother. "Dolores, tell Elena what I told you on the phone. There is no need for you to go to Cuba."

"They love each other, my dear," Dolores said. "They were reconciled and they are going to live here with me once again."

"Once again!" Elena yelled.

"No, no," Clara called desperately. "He doesn't love me. What a disgrace! Why am I so unfortunate?"

Elena put up her hands like an announcer calling for silence. Her face was flushed with determination.

"You are not going to call the tune in my life," Esteban said before she could speak. "Just as your crowd cannot do much longer in Cuba."

Elena clenched her hands. "What do you hope to gain?"

"I'm not going to let you browbeat your mother and sister." Elena laughed sarcastically. "They don't want your support. And they don't need it. Just as Cuba doesn't need patriots of your type."

Robert called out to Esteban, hoping to stop the quarrel. "Esteban, it's not important. Let things be."

"Yes, yes, man." Feliz added. "Think of the women."

Elena smiled approvingly at Robert. "Thank you, Roberto, you're a man with sense."

"I am not on your side, Elena," Robert said, his voice loud and contentious. "I think you are only taking revenge on your home town and don't care that you are making us all unhappy—especially your mother."

Mina got up from the sofa. "Thank God you have said it!" she said to Robert. "Elena, you want a good spanking. You are trying to disown us all, but under your fine clothes you still perform the same natural functions as when you wore diapers."

"Not at all, not at all," Elena said. "I don't want to forget what I came from. It makes me appreciate all the more what I have now to remember the provincial mudhole I came from. The difference between you—all of you!—and me is that you love this mudhole, whereas I hate it!"

"See here," Feliz said, "you are mistaken. Tampa is a progressive city."

"You people like to be stuck here, always the underdogs to the Americans, and you talk nonsense like those rebels in Cuba because you can't do anything better, because you're all like him"— she pointed at Esteban—"revolutionaries of the cafes! Well, I'm taking my family out of here and I'm taking my little boy, killed by this backwardness and stupidity. I've given you a chance, Roberto. I would think you'd know better than to be an underdog, like those fools who think that by playing games in the woods they can topple the legitimate government of Cuba!"

Robert blushed, ashamed that he had actually considered Elena's offer once and had thus deserved this public rebuke. "You are wrong, Elena," he said. "Those young rebels may be fools, but they are in the right, like the cigar makers were fools to go on strikes that they never won. Believe me, when I first left Tampa I hated it as much as you do, but there was something to hate where I went, too. The thing is I've learned not to hate myself the way the Americans here want us to hate ourselves."

"Psychology! Psychology!" Elena said. "If that's the best you can come up with, they're right to despise you."

"All right, all right," Robert said. "All I mean is, if you're going to live in Cuba you ought to hate what those foolish rebels hate."

"They hate the foreigners who have taken their lands and the politicians who have taken their liberties!" Esteban held out an arm and pointed a finger at Elena, as if he were addressing a gathering. "They will throw you out. You, who hate your home town, are a foreigner there and a good friend of their politicians. You're an imperialist. You have no country."

"You cheap orator," Elena said. "Money buys any country. It can buy even you."

Esteban paused only a second. "Money only buys whores!"

Elena raised a hand then clenched it to keep herself from slapping him. "You whoring son of a whore!"

Jaime moved quickly and stood between Elena and Esteban. "Take it back," he said, and held his hand up, the palm stiffly open.

"Blood suckers," Esteban said. "We will kill you all!"

Jaime brought his hand down swiftly and slapped Esteban across the face. "Take it back," he said, and raised his hand again.

"No! No!" Mina yelled. "Holy Virgin! Stop them!"

Robert grabbed Jaime's arm and put his other hand up to hold off Esteban, but Esteban did not move. He stood in front of Jaime, and the tears ran down his face. "What do you expect me to do now, you fool? Fight a duel?" To everyone's surprise Esteban turned away from him and threw his arms out to Clara.

Clara whispered. "Don't come near me!"

"I will tell you the truth, Clara," Esteban said. "I do not love you even if I would have you. But it does not matter. Someone will love you because you are a sweet, delightful woman. But not where you are going, not there; no one will love you there. Don't go!"

Clara leaned against the wall and made a move to go into the bedroom, but her knees gave and she slowly sat down on the floor. "Elena, Elena," she called, "help me, I will die of shame. Help me . . ."

"Help her," Dolores said, trying to scream but succeeding only in sounding strangely conversational. "My darling girl cannot bear it."

Mina saw Dolores grab her left breast. "Clemencia," she called, "get the nitroglycerin!"

Dolores waved a hand to stop Clemencia. "No, let me die." She leaned back, and Consuelo raised a bony hand to Dolores' forehead and began to stroke it.

"Get the pills," Mina again urged her sister and left for the kitchen to get a glass of water for Dolores. She said a prayer as she went. On the way back to the living room she stopped in the doorway of the kitchen, struck by the odd poses in which she saw the others. How funny people look, she thought; they are members of the animal world, after all. Their polelike legs, their dangling arms, their middles so absurdly held and so thick, all topped by that unexpected irregular globe called a head—these cannot be the attributes of God's children. "And you," she said to Feliz who was pouring himself a drink in the dining room, "you are like a cockroach always looking for water!"

She went past his astonished eyes, holding the glass of water in front of her as a shield and looking toward the bedroom for Clemencia to return with the nitroglycerin pill. Elena was kneeling down trying to help Clara stand, and Shirley joined her, looking back over her shoulder all the while at Robert, who still held Jaime's arm.

Esteban pleaded with Clara from a distance. "Don't go. They are not the lords and masters they think they are. They have been bought and sold like a share on the stock exchange."

"Let go of my arm," Jaime said to Robert. "This tableau has lasted long enough."

Embarrassed, Robert removed his hand and apologized.

"I gather you, too, sympathize with this man here and his notions of what is transpiring in my country," Jaime said, straightening the sleeves of his jacket. "I do not think you would be happy there, if that is the case."

Robert shook his head. "No, I've already decided that. I'm not accepting your job. As you say, I would not be happy there."

Esteban heard their exchange and turned around to face them. "You do well, Roberto," he said. "But the time will come—and soon—when you will be happy in Cuba."

Jaime refused to return Esteban's angry stare and spoke only to Robert. "What you and your friend do not seem to know is that those heroes of yours up in the Sierra Maestra"—he stopped when he saw Robert's surprised look—"oh, I admit they exist, I'm a realist—those young men are, in the main, educated youths of good middle-class families simply having a fling before they settle down."

"Let him not get in the way of this fling," Esteban said. "It can be fatal for the middle-aged."

Jaime would not acknowledge, even by the tone of his voice, that he heard Esteban. "And if by chance they should come to power—and it is possible; after all, history is just a series of accidents—it would be unlikely that they would create a paradise for low-class revolutionaries."

"You forget one thing," Robert said quickly, to forestall Esteban. "I am not going to Cuba, so it's yourself you must worry about."

Esteban took Robert's arm and pulled him away from Jaime and said loudly, "A middle-class bullet is as deadly as a low-class one."

Clemencia came out of the bedroom door with the vial of nitroglycerine pills in one hand, and stopped only long enough to speak to Robert and Esteban. "For shame!" she said. "Help the women. Can't you see they cannot deal with Clara?" She didn't stop to see if they obeyed her, for Mina was waiting at Dolores' side with the glass of water.

The men did obey her and rushed to help, but as soon as she saw Esteban, Elena dropped Clara's arm. "Tell me the name of the funeral parlor," she said. "You have caused enough trouble."

"No," Esteban said. "I didn't call you back from your fancy vacation."

"Do not fight, please," Clara said. "Leave me alone if you're going to fight."

Elena straightened up. "All right, I'll leave you alone."

"No, no, Elena!" Clara held out her arms. "What have I done?"

Shirley found herself pleading too. "Please, please," she said, and saw the surprised look on Robert's face. "You're all one family. Don't fight with each other."

"I make you a gift of them," Elena said to Shirley. "You can have them."

"Elena, wait," Clara said. With half-closed eyes she turned to Esteban. "Please respect me; I'm his mother, after all. Do it the way we have asked. Tell Elena where to call. I cannot stand the shame. Let me go away in peace. Maybe you are right, but what does it matter?" She opened her eyes fully and looked at him. "It's the last thing I will ask of you."

"Very well," Esteban said, and without looking at Elena added, "He's at the Ybor Funeral Home."

Elena turned without a word to Esteban and went to Jaime, who stood friendless in the middle of the room. Esteban watched Elena pause a moment to speak to her husband. From the casual way in which she put a hand on her hip, he saw that this was the outcome she felt was due her. "They always win because they are hard-hearted," he said to Robert. "Someday we shall learn to be ruthless too."

With only Shirley to help her, Clara was able now to get up. "Thank you," she said to Esteban, and again to Shirley when she got to a seat.

"It's all over," Esteban said to Robert. "I must be going."

"Where?" Robert wished he could turn Esteban into the lively man who had irritated him so much last night. "Can I take you home?"

"I'm not going home. I must tell some others that your job this morning was successful." He looked at Robert gratefully. "I have not even thanked you."

"It is I who should thank you," Robert answered. "It made me feel—I can go back to New York feeling as young as when I first left Tampa."

Esteban looked at him with unquestioning eyes. "Really?"

"Yes," Robert said, although he knew Esteban could see for himself.

Mina broke the momentary stillness in the room. "Elena!" she called, getting everyone's attention. "Clara! Your mother will not take the pill!"

Clemencia knelt before Dolores, the vial of medicine in one hand and the pill on the outstretched palm of the other. "Take it, my dear sister," she said, "for my sake."

"How long can I go on taking pills?" Dolores' voice was low and hoarse, and she gasped for breath. "Sit here on the sofa with me, my dears, and do not talk to me of pills. Stay with me."

"Mama!" Elena called from the dining room, not certain whether she should turn back or go ahead and call the funeral home immediately.

Old Consuelo talked to the room at large. "She must not die before me. It cannot be. Do not let her!" Her shoulders shook, and she tried to steady herself by grabbing her knees with both hands. "It is not proper at a wake. It is our duty to live."

Elena pushed aside Feliz who stood petrified between the dining room and the living room. "Enough, enough," she said, "this is nonsense!" She took the vial from Clemencia. "You must take the medicine."

Dolores put a hand to her breast. "Do not suffer so, my darling," she said, and paused to catch her breath. "I do not need it."

Mina held the glass of water with both hands to keep from spilling it. "Do not listen to her. She must have it. I can tell from her coloring."

"Mama, stop dramatizing." Elena first fumbled with the vial and then with shaking hands took the pill Clemencia offered. "I am not an indulgent old fool. You will take this pill if I have to pry your mouth open by force."

Mina gave the glass to Clemencia and put a warning hand on Elena's arm. "If you speak to your mother like that again you will have me to deal with, and I swear I shall tear your tongue out. You will learn what low-class people can do."

"I cannot go to Cuba with you, my dears," Dolores said to Elena and Clara. "I cannot leave my Serafin. You understand, I have to be

209

buried with your father." She shook her head for emphasis and tried to continue but could not.

"Mama, Mama!" Clara got up from her chair. She was wringing her hands and staring at her mother's face. She put out her hands and cried, but could not speak. "Please," she finally said.

Dolores looked at her a long time, and she opened her mouth twice before she could manage to speak. Her eyes were rigid with fear. "I am an old woman," she said. "You do not need me."

"A doctor! You're all mad!" Shirley yelled. "Get a doctor!"

"Wait! Wait!" Esteban stood in the doorway to the porch and waved his arms to get attention. "Let me talk." When everyone had turned to him, he spoke evenly to Dolores. "Listen to me, old woman, the hearse is outside. Do you want to see your grandson?"

Dolores looked at him with unbelieving eyes.

"Do you want them to bring him inside so that he can spend the night with you—and his family and friends?"

First Dolores nodded and then in an unrecognizable voice cried, "Yes, yes, yes," until her sobs stopped her voice.

"Then?" Esteban looked at Clara for permission.

Clara turned to Elena and pleaded, "For Mama's sake."

Elena nodded quickly.

"First you must take the pill," Mina said, "or I shall lose my mind."

While everyone watched, Dolores reached for the pill in Clemencia's hand. She lifted it to her mouth, took the glass of water, and straightened up to drink, letting her tears run into the glass.

Robert was the first to break the silence. "I'll go out and speak to them," he said to Esteban.

"Thank you," Esteban said, brushing past Elena, and without her permission going to the dining room to pour himself a drink.

Mina and Clemencia got up and helped Dolores to stand. "Ah," Dolores sighed, all her rebellion ended.

Mina said, "You are going to your room for a little while until they get things ready in here." She put an arm around Dolores. "We will go with you."

"Yes, yes," old Consuelo said, "leave it to me." She looked at Shirley. "You are Clemencia's new daughter-in-law? Well, that makes you as good as my niece." She squinted at Shirley. "I once had hair as fair as yours."

Clara looked up at Elena from her seat. "It's better this way."

210

Elena shook her head and walked away from Clara. She put a hand on Jaime's arm. "Well, now you know exactly what I have escaped from. At least I have saved Armando and Clara." She thought of Jimmy and held on harder to Jaime. "Tomorrow we'll be out of here, thank God!"

Feliz overheard her and turned indignantly to Shirley. "I can tell you, this has certainly been a revelation to me," he said. "I thought Elena was a woman of discretion, and here she has classed us all with a visionary like Esteban!" He heard his mother call and immediately said, "Yes?"

"Feliz, go get your wife," Mina called from the door of the bedroom. "She will be needed here."

When Mina turned back to her, Dolores said to her sisters, "I have acted very badly, haven't I? Tell me the truth."

Clemencia shook her head. "Who is to say?"

"I am to say!" Mina answered. "I have never had such a scare in my life."

"What was I to do?" Dolores asked. "I cannot leave the two of you and my only home. And terrible as it is to live through, little Jimmy has to spend this night with us." She leaned against the door of the bedroom, still very short of breath. "My children are so passionate they are not easily swayed." She led Mina and Clemencia to her bed, and the three of them sat on the edge of it. "It all comes from Serafin. He was such an idealist, such a great Cuban patriot, so full of strong feelings . . ."

"And very little practical sense," Mina said.

Clemencia answered, "You say that because your Claudio was a foreman and had the good fortune to be liked by the owners of the factory."

"A good thing too," Mina countered, "or who would have hired your husband with all the union activity he was always involved in? You wouldn't have to be working today if your Bernardo had been a more practical man."

Clemencia suddenly began to cry.

"What is the matter?" Mina asked. "I hope you have not been paying attention to what I say."

Clemencia shook her head. "No, no. I just hope I never made him think that. He had a hard enough life."

"Oh, no, no," Dolores said. "He was a man who was greatly loved."

"If the truth be told," Mina conceded, "my Claudio, I often felt, regretted that no one admired him for his ideas."

"Let us not dig up old regrets," Dolores said. "There are too many of them, and we shall end up fighting for the biggest share." She took their hands and held them tightly. "Let us remind ourselves of all the wonderful things in life, for in a moment we shall have to go inside and look into his face."